Semi-Faithful:
More Coffee with John Heartbreak

Semi-Faithful:
More Coffee
with
John Heartbreak

Dan Krotz

Cahaba Press
Eureka Springs
Birmingham

Semi-Faithful: More Coffee with John Heartbreak

Copyright © 2014 by Dan Krotz

Cover Design by Sharon Laborde and Penguin Graphics II, Eureka Springs.
St. Fiacre image: Notre Dame, Bar-le-Duc, France, 19th Century.

Published by:
Cahaba Press
483 County Road 231
Eureka Springs, AR 72631
www.cahabapress.com

ISBN-13: 978-0692224915
ISBN-10: 0692224912

Printed in the United States of America

To John Else, who has been my good friend
and the creator of many opportunities, for me,
and for countless others.

Acknowledgements:

I especially thank Sharon Laborde for the countless hours she has spent editing and formatting this book. I am a formless and heedless user of words, yet Sharon was undaunted and cheerful throughout the process. I thank Eddie Keever for his appearance here, and for being a good example of grace under pressure. You are a noble man, Edward. I thank Larry Laverentz for being the best traveling companion anyone could ask for, and for also appearing in this book. Dr. Sharon Sloan, many thanks for being not just in the book, but for being the book. You are, indeed, a Warrior Queen. Finally, I thank my wife Susan, who while fabulous by any definition, has accepted my assurances that she is not the model for the Fabulous Mrs. Heartbreak.

Chapter 1

This book is full of problems and none of them get solved. Even though I'm writing the book I can't solve them because the book is full of real people and God only knows (truly) what goes on in the minds of real people. It is possible that you might solve one, or even more of the problems, but I won't know about it because you are not one of the real people in the book. Of course, if your name is Colleen Shogren or Eddie Keever or someone else I know, or who John Heartbreak knows, then you might be in the book. You could solve a problem or two. That would be good.

The first problem is the book itself. It is full of misspellings and bad grammar and it contains no sex (to speak of), no violence, and no strong (bad) language. It is full of parenthetical phrases (just like the two—now three—in this paragraph). And I use commas like John Steinbeck did, about every four words, whether a comma is needed or not. Which I just done, dint I?

The first problem is often a big problem for a lot of readers (that would be you just now) because they want the books they read to go through an editorial process that takes out all the bad stuff. And editors tell writers that the first sentence of a book must HOOK the reader immediately and COMPEL them to read on. Maybe that's because editors think you have the attention span of a fish, but more likely, it just means that you want what you're going to read to be exciting or interesting. If you're still here well, so sorry. I mean, "This book is full of problems and none of them get solved," isn't much of a first sentence. I know that's not exciting. But

1

what you see is what you get. Hang in there, okay? You really can solve some problems just by ignoring them.

Anyway, there are seven problems in this book. We've covered the first one (up there) and will ignore it from now on. That leaves six problems we won't solve. We'll fill about 270 pages and use around 75,000 words not to solve anything. Let's look at Problem Two:

A dull man is writing this book. Try not to be too hard on me. You may also be a dull person and the world has been putting up with you for a long time. You can afford some forgiveness: I mean, think about yourself. Geez.

Not only is a dull man writing this book, he is writing about an even duller man. That man's name is John Heartbreak. John is a retired bookseller and now spends his time gardening and doing whatever his wife, The Fabulous Mrs. Heartbreak, tells him to do. Mrs. Heartbreak is anything but dull (she is Fabulous—get it?) and is often a dramatic and complicated person. But both John and I are afraid of Mrs. Heartbreak and neither of us is willing to risk offending her, especially in print.

Prior to his career as a bookseller John worked for various agencies of the Federal Government. He was always there to help you. John's work required him to travel all over the world. He was on, as Jimmy Buffet sang, the last plane to leave Saigon and the last slow boat to China. John could never adequately explain what exactly it was he did. His few muddled explanations caused Mrs. Heartbreak, her sisters, and Mrs. Heartbreak's Old Deist Quaker mother (Mrs. Betty Kaiser) to believe that John was a spy. Their judgment was satisfied, at least in their expansive minds, by the fact that John never went to Paris or Stockholm or to any civilized place. Instead, he would go to Kosovo, or Malawi, or Laos—dubious backwaters for sure, although the girls in Laos are really pretty.

I wish, and eventually you will wish, that John had been a spy. Sadly, he had only been a minor functionary who did unimportant things and never ever went to neat places like Paris or Stockholm. John had never been important enough to warrant a decent meal and a decent hotel. Not once. So John is what you see: a slow moving shuffling old man with a prostate the size of Idaho.

Late in life John had followed Mrs. Heartbreak to this town—Berryville, Arkansas—where he sold books at Heartbreak's Pretty Good Books and Really Dreadful Coffee (RDC); and now he is a gardener. People in the neighborhood know him, if they know him at all, as his church's Yard Boy and the person who carries Mrs. Heartbreak's parcels. As you can imagine, and as a fact that I live with every day, John is obviously thin literary gruel. That nearly insurmountable barrier to excitement, combined with his physical entrapment in a nondescript town in a clinically dysfunctional state, presents hardships for both of us.

Mortimer Adler says in his book *How to Read a Book* "Since reading of any sort is an activity, all reading must to some degree be active." He goes on to say (for way to long) that the more active you are when you're reading the better it is. I assume he means it's better for you, although I know it is way better for me because you might recommend that a friend buy the book if it has caused you to get active. How are you doing so far? I mean, active wise?

Maybe it helps if I tell you that John spends most of his time communicating with dead people. That's exciting, isn't it? These dead guys are mostly writers— you know, a bunch of other johns like John Cheever and John Updike and John Marquand—but John believes they are still alive because their books are still alive. Yes, I know it makes no sense. We have a guy here, old John Heartbreak, who is observed in nearly constant conversation with no one we can see. But John does not care; he just keeps jabbering on.

Mrs. Heartbreak is driven to distraction by John's constant mumbling, but she has learned to live with it. She explains John's behavior by telling people—who ask "who in the world" (to whom?) is John speaking?—that John is practicing to become a ventriloquist, or that he is going over his lines for a role in the new Billy Bob Thornton film which is being made in nearby Eureka Springs.

Most Berryvillians view these activities—ventriloquism and movie making—suspiciously, much as they view reading as a suspicious activity whether you're reading actively or passively, no matter what Mortimer Adler might think. Consequently, when Berryvillians think of John (not that they ever do), they think of him as a suspicious character, a serial reader who might think or say anything. You probably should know that if you are observed reading this book in downtown Berryville (or any book) you too will be viewed as a suspicious character. After all, there are fewer bookstores in the whole state of Arkansas than there were in downtown Sarajevo after it was bombed. So watch your step.

I may not have mentioned that John is also deaf. He can read lips pretty well and he nods affably no matter what you say. Here's a joke about a dumb guy who may or may not be deaf:

A bus driver greets each entering passenger with the phrase "Tickle your ass with a feather?" Naturally the passengers are startled. "What?" they shout. The bus

4

driver than says, "Particularly nasty weather!" "Oh," the passenger replies sheepishly. "Yes, it is." Then they trot off to the back of the bus, shaking their heads.

A front seat passenger has observed the antics (activity!) of the bus driver and is impressed. "Say,' he says. "Can I try it?"

"Okay," says the bus driver. "You can have the next one." So:

A prospective passenger gets on the bus at the next bus stop. The front seat passenger smiles and says, "Tickle your ass with a feather?"

"What!" shouts the passenger? "What did you say?"

"Think it will snow?"

As you can plainly see by now, John is a problem. His dullness, the ordinariness of his career, the inadequacy of the town he lives in, his fear of his wife, the fact of his deafness, his age (old) and the fact that his prostate resembles a Western state of considerable size, adds up to maybe a pamphlet you pick up at a Christian Science reading room. But an entire novel? We're in a pickle, aren't we?

A final compounding conundrum that Mary Baker Eddie would almost certainly appreciate, and perhaps you too will appreciate as well, is that John is aware that he is a character in this book. From time to time he will speak directly to me (and to you) and argue about the direction that the book is taking. He will point out examples of poor writing and bad grammar or the implausibility of certain activities (activity!) that I'll have him engage. In some instances John may hijack the book and take it away from me (he did exactly that in the first book I wrote about him) (Oh yes, there is a "first" book about John) (which I hope you will buy at Amazon.com) and who knows what fresh hell that will mean. All in all, though, hijacking is the smallest problem that an author (me!) who is unable to distinguish between dead people and the living, real people and imagined characters, and readers like you—who may be there or not there at all—should expect.

You can skip the next paragraph.

John's ontology—whether he is or isn't—is, as you've probably guessed by now, a main idea in the book. It's not really a strange idea when you think about it. Take Eddie Keever, for example. Eddie is a real guy—I'm listening to him on the radio right now even though the music he plays causes instant brain infarct—who I know fairly well. I also know Eddie's life story because he told it to me, so: I know Eddie, and I know Eddie's life story according to Eddie (sort of like I know *The Life of Brian*); but I also know Eddie in my memory of Eddie, and I know Eddie's life story according to Me. I also know (imagine) Eddie's future life story according to Me because I have a future story that may entwine with his; I know this is possible and probable because I have a memory of the past—and a thought about now which was once in the future and is now in the past. This sounds like gibberish but it isn't. It simply (simply) accounts for time and how we interact (activity!) with it. The conclusion is that Eddie is real even as he is a character in a fictional work simultaneously with John Heartbreak, who is as we know, a fictional character in a work of fiction, yet is as real to ME as Eddie is real to me. And who, if you stick with it, will be real to you. Both of them.

You can start reading again in the next paragraph:

As you can see, Problem Two can be summarized by saying that I—and you, for that matter since you have read along so far—don't have much to work with, character-wise and town-wise. Problem One, which is summarized as The Poor Quality of My Work, has been ignored, although, perhaps, you have decided to tough it out with me and are still reading. Problems Three through Problem Seven will be dealt with in the next chapter.

Lucky you.

Chapter 2

The town of Berryville was founded by Henderson Blackburn Berry in 1850. John and Mrs. Heartbreak had arrived in Berryville approximately one hundred forty years after the initial crime. In the years between founding and the arrival of *La Famille* Heartbreak, Berryville had been burned down by Yankees, been burned down by Confederates, been blown away in cyclones and tornados and, in between these natural and unnatural disasters, had otherwise sallied into the 21st Century a bit shopworn but not necessarily worse for wear.

If a single story is emblematic of Berryville's civic functionality it is about the time a Yankee arrived during the Civil War and burned it down. One of the few remaining buildings after the fire was a boarding house owned by a woman known locally as "Mother" Hubbard who, besides offering beds and beans to railroad men, was a Mason and proudly displayed a Masonic badge in a front porch window. In a rare act of *noblesse oblige* the Head Yankee, also a Mason of course, tipped his hat to Ms Hubbard and spared her home.

PS and by the way, I assure you that's the last French language you'll see in this book. Be aware, though, that John will slip into Japanese, Latin, and Old Norse once in a while. He can't help it, and I have no control over what he puts into his largely vacant mind. Why he thinks in the language he thinks in is a mystery. Just assume that these forays into foreignness have nothing to do with us, or the book. Skip them is my advice. But back to Mother Hubbard:

Why the Mother Hubbard-Yankee story is emblematic of Berryville is that it is about a person in power who decides the fate of another person who is, at least momentarily, without power. This example is really a World example as much as it is a Berryville example, but the World is big, and Berryville is small, so it is usually possible in Berryville to not only know precisely who "violated" (a Victorian word for you, and what a good word!) whom, but to actually observe it happening. These violations were so obvious and frequent that John often walked about town in a stupefied state, not only at the public nature of the violations—Wow! In broad daylight!—but also by the unreflective and guiltless energy that the violator brought to his work.

Yet, what perplexed John most was how willingly and unreflectively the violated themselves lined up to get whacked. "Yes! Yes! Do it again!" they seemed to plea. "Please, oh please, destroy every chance, every passing chariot of luck, and every political, social, economic, spiritual, religious, psychological, self-inspired, visionary, imagined, organized, disorganized, meditated, premeditated, and glorious or inglorious scheme that might improve my lot in life."

John's guess as to why the majority of Arkansans (And most Southerners, frankly) allowed themselves to be treated so shabbily was their hopefulness that Local Big Shots would notice the Mason badges they wore, and give them a pass. Okay: so much for Mother Hubbard.

John, a lifelong political neophyte, knew enough politics to be aghast by the local Democratic Party's transparent corruption, and to be annoyed by the local Republican opposition. These Republicans pretended to be honest Conservatives, but they were really and mostly knot heads who wanted to eliminate taxes of every kind except for maybe sales taxes—which should only be paid by folks who gutted chickens for a living. They were generally in favor of war, as long as it could be contracted out to Halliburton with borrowed money, and fought by folks who would otherwise be gutting chickens. Yes, his County's Democrats would steal a hot stove, but at least they didn't demand the right as the LOYAL opposition did, to use say, plutonium in the hot stove, or to insist that such using plutonium was a GOD GIVEN RIGHT and that you must certainly be a SOCIALIST if you suggested otherwise. Of course, there was a local Green Party, mostly centered in Eureka Springs, but it reminded John of a mostly youthful activity that caused blindness and eternal DAMNATION.

If a political party in Minnesota—John's home state—behaved as badly as either of his state's political parties, or governed as ineffectively, that Party's leaders would have been immediately sent off to the State Pen, or driven over the border into Wisconsin where most cheese heads would tolerate hanky-panky longer than the average Minnesotan. Maybe a term or two longer. But even in Wisconsin, where most voters were deaf, dumb, and blind Lutherans drunk on 3.2 beer, two terms would be long enough for them to get the picture.

If you haven't gotten the picture by now, Berryville the Place is Problem Three. This is the place I have to write about, and the place where the unfolding story of John Heartbreak is, well, unfolded. As you can see, Berryville is not a gruesomely dramatic literary backdrop like Solzhenitsyn's gulag, nor as winsome a place as F. Scott Fitzgerald's French Riviera. True, Faulkner made up pretty good stories about a similar place in Mississippi, but Faulkner was drunk all the time, and John and I are teetotalers and therefore lack most of the essential aids for complete honesty. Berryville is, literature-wise, tough sledding, or would be if it had any decent snow. Let's just call what we're doing here a slow, uphill waltz.

Naturally you ask, "Why doesn't Dumbo move back to that Valhalla of Virtue, Minnesota?" I can only, John can only, refer you back to Mrs. Heartbreak, who has a differing view of the Great State of Minnesota. A fair portion of that view has something to do with the weather. She may also mention that the Minnesota State Flag pictured an early yeoman farmer plugging an Indian with a blunderbuss until more sensitive minds interceded in about 1982. (Today, the farmer and Indian are seen exchanging a friendly wave.) In any case, here we are, and as any physicist will tell you, Mediocrity Theory Rules! Mediocrity Theory will be discussed at length (more luck for you!) as we get further along in the book.

Berryville is not without virtue. For example, John and Mrs. Heartbreak are delighted, contented, happy members of the First Christian Church Berryville which, as far as John can tell, is the only "First" Christian Church in town and the only Disciples of Christ Church east of the Kings River and west of Green Forest, Arkansas. It is in this church that Mrs. Heartbreak found the Meaning of Life and where John falls into deliriums of befuddlement over Protestant humorlessness, their celebration of obvious Scoundrels, and their tendency to hurl obscure phrases from the Bible to JUSTIFY any dang thing they want to do. All of which is trumped by the awe he feels for the exceptional kindness of his fellow members, for the example of their lives, and for the love they share freely with him, and with Mrs. Heartbreak.

So, what's the problem, you ask?

Problem Four is the Problem of God, or more correctly, Does God Have a Problem Because There are 35 Different Churches in Berryville, a Town of 5,000 Souls? Of Which 7 are Baptist and 2 are First Baptist Churches? You bet, and John will worry about it and cause you to worry about it too.

Problem Five is Japanese Beetles, and why rhubarb won't decently grow in the Ozarks. Problem Five differs from the other Six Problems because genuine, albeit doomed, engagement of the Problem will be attempted, not only by John—operating in his gardener role under the supervision of the First Christian Church—but by Fiacre, a Saint in the Roman Catholic Church and the Patron Saint of Gardeners. Fiacre's presence in the book leads to Problem Six, which is the Problem of Time and Space.

That we are addressing the Problem of Time and Space, which naturally involves travel through time and space, may lead you to think that the essential nature of this book is one of Science Fiction. Don't be misled! John believes, and I believe, and most physicists believe and know, that time travel is just, well, a matter of time and money. John and I, and all philosophers (and many physicists) also believe that matters of time and space are centrally aligned with questions (and matters) about mind and body. Consequently (subsequently?), there is time travel in this book, reallocations of space (Space!), and much ado about the ensuing to and fro.

Within the context of Problem Six is a confounding variable that may or may not be a Problem. Therefore, let's call it "Sub-set: Problem 6X" which is the problem of a Catholic Saint hanging out in Protestant Garden in a Protestant town. As all Yankees know, and as all Southerners pretend not to know, Catholics are viewed with deep suspicion in the South, except in New Orleans which has, as Walker Percy noted, "more hookers and Catholic nuns than any other city in the world." Throughout the history of the South, and certainly in the bulk of Southern literature (which is mostly fine), there is little in the Southern mind that distinguishes any difference between hookers and nuns. Subsequently (consequently?), the fact that Fiacre is a Time Traveler may play second fiddle to the fact that a Catholic is hanging around the church yard.

Our last Problem, Problem Seven, is the Problem of You Coming Up with $MONEY + Shipping and Handling to buy this book once it is published. I thank you in advance for your custom and will now get on with the show.

Chapter 3

"I want to go to Withered Plum, Missouri," Sharon Sloan, the Artist and Scholar Formerly Known as Sharon Sloan (ASFKA) said. "I want to go there and do the Grand Fandango on Little Billy Cudrup's head. He owes me $6,000,000."

Sharon was referring to the Televangelist Billy Cudrup, who has settled in Withered Plum, Missouri (1 foot north of Withered Plum, Arkansas) after completing five years in the Federal Pen for doing what comes naturally to Televangelists. After his release from the Big House, Billy had started a new (another!) Retirement Village called Endtimes in Withered Plum. He was being helped by a new wife (another!) named Angel who had replaced the old wife, Donna Raye. Note: Only the location of the Retirement Village has been changed: otherwise, nothing has been changed to protect the innocent because no one is innocent.

"I seriously doubt that Reverend Cudrup owes you $6,000.000," replied John Heartbreak. "As far as I know you've never had $6,000,000 to lose, or lend."

"Six million is the amount of money he owes the IRS," Sharon answered. "For back taxes, penalties, and fines. As a citizen in good standing the IRS merely represents my interests. They surely want me to have at least a portion of it. But it is taking them an awful long time to get it, and I'm tired of waiting."
John nodded.

"Your role in the matter is to be my wheel man," Sharon explained. "I need an experienced driver who can keep his mouth shut and play a small but vital role as I execute the Grand Fandango. You'll be driving Mrs. Heartbreak's white Chevy van."

John nodded.

"First, though, we'll need to do a little Recon. I thought we would drive up to Withered Plum this morning and scope things out. Get the lay of Angel, the new lay, and figure out where Little Billy is keeping my cash."

John nodded.

"But we'll need to be inconspicuous," Sharon continued. "So you'll have to carry a bible and look pious. But prosperous enough to be worth noticing."

John looked alarmed. "The only bible I have is a *Jerusalem Bible*," John said. "It's a Catholic bible and a sure give-away of a suspicious cultural background. I may not look as inconspicuous as you might hope. And I'm not sure I can pull off the whole "prosperous" thing."

"You're a bookseller, for crying out loud. Can't you get your hands on the right bible?"

"I'm a retired bookseller," John haughtily replied. "I can't be expected to have carloads and versions of every old bible ever printed just laying around.

"Besides," he continued, "I've had my *Jerusalem Bible* for thirty-five years and it's too hard to keep up with every passing Protestant whim. It's a good enough bible for me.

"…I do have a *Book of Common Prayer*, though…" John's voice trailed off. He began to feel anxious. He considered himself a problem solver, an "ask what you can do for your country" kind of person. He was fairly sure that he was getting in over his head, a frequent and always uncomfortable state of being.

Sharon (ASFKA) snorted (a common and utterly overused device employed by hacks to connote exasperation). "You can't carry a *Book of Common Prayer*. It's a sure sign that you graduated from an accredited secondary school. And they'll think you're an Episcopalian. That's worse than being taken for a Catholic. They'll think you have a drink now and then and enjoy life once in a while."

"I could carry a copy of *The Arkansas Democrat Gazette*," John offered, hopefully. "It's the second worst newspaper in the world and ought to arouse no suspicion."

"What do you think?"

It was Sharon's turn to nod, but she did so sagely, which is differentiated from John's nodding which is merely evidentiary of confusion or of a daffy sort of agreement because he hasn't really heard what you've said but pretends that he has.

You will find that snorting and nodding are frequent acts by the characters in this book. Yes, I have the wit to ferret out other descriptors but really, why waste time when such expeditious shortcuts such as snorting and nodding are so readily available? I am not Zane Grey and this not the *Riders of the Purple Sage*. Almost everyone in this book is a late middle aged person or an old person, too old really to safely tolerate much bosom heaving or beating. And the few young people who appear, would be embarrassed if I strung adjectives and adverbs all over them, or hung them out to dry in public festooned with metaphors and arty phrases. And so:

Sharon (ASFKA) nodded. "I think *The Democrat Gazette* works. It is a reactionary rag, friendly to Big Business, and has a history of tolerating TV Religion. Leave the paper open to the editorial page," she suggested. "That'll make everyone comfortable. Especially the letters to the editors."

"Would you like a cup of coffee?" John asked.

Offering coffee was always a prelude to John's making a request, or offering an ameliorative suggestion. Mrs. Heartbreak referred to these coffee ceremonies as "another bizarre flight of John's fancy" which, not to put too fine a point on it, was manifestly beholding the mote in another's eye while considering not the bizarre, often fantastical beam in her own albeit beautiful eye.

"No," Sharon said; but understanding the drill, opened her hands, palms up. "And…" she encouraged…

"Well," John started. "What do you have against Reverend Cudrup? He is only one in a long line of American businessmen whose product just happens to be Christ. He varies little in practice or theory from any of those other TV birds except that he got caught with his hand in some gal's panties. Had he kept it strictly in the till, no one would have cared. But Americans love reality TV and the Billy and Donna Show was absolutely tops in every sense of the word, except that it lacked a Big finale.

"It is ENTIRELY possible," John continued, "that everything that has happened to Billy and Donna, including Donna's death on national TV and Billy's term in the Big House, was PLANNED out in ADVANCE. Have you thought about the POSSIBILITY that if you and I go to Withered Plum and you "Grand Fandango on Little Billy Cudrup's head," that we will become just another PART OF THE SHOW? Is that what you want? A role on a reality TV show?"

"John, I think you're crazy."

"How am I crazy? You're in this book, aren't you? How do you know that Billy and Donna's writers haven't written us into their story? I mean, think about it:

"ENTER SHARON SLOAN, THE ARTIST AND SCHOLAR FORMERLY KNOWN AS SHARON SLOAN: "Okay Billy, Baby. Hand over my $6,000,000!"

BILLY: "I don't have it! The President is giving it to Negroes and Mexicans as part of a vast leftwing conspiracy to make Islam our National Religion. Praise Jesus!"

SHARON SLOAN (ASFKA): "I'm not buying it, Billy! I want my dough, and I want it NOW!"

BILLY: Please be reasonable, Honey. Be kind to me. Once, I was lost, but now I'm found. That I've been found in Withered Plum, Missouri, pisses me off a little, but who knows how the Lord works? For the Lord's ways are mysterious. Anyhoo, I was wrong! I was a BAD man! But I've been rusticated in the Lord and saved by His Holy Name. Can I interest you in a Time Share? How about a See the Light flashlight! They're only available for a Love Offering of $25.00 or more. But I want you to have one, on me, Praise the Lord!

SHARON SLOAN (ASFKA): Stick it, Shorty! I'm not afraid of Mexicans. I've been saved to my own satisfaction. And I know you're a sleazy crook!"

BILLY: (Theatrical sigh) "Okay boys (two men step out from behind a mural ot the 18th hole at Augusta National). "We've got another non-believer here. Probably a Muslim sympathizer. And I smell Mexican food on her breath! You know what to do with her."

ONE OF THE TWO MEN: "Stop struggling, you dang dame! It's END TIMES for you for sure!"

SHARON SLOAN (ASFKA): (Screaming, struggling.) "John! John!"

CUT TO: A white van is seen from the rear, rapidly leaving the Endtimes compound.

ANNOUNCER: "Next week, find out what happens to Sharon Sloan! Is she an agent of the IRS? A Democrat Party Operative! Or, summarily: NOT ONE OF US!

Sharon shook her head, evincing an attitude of sorrow. "It's hard being you, isn't it?"

"Not really," John replied. "I admit that I find the world a bit more complex in its operation than most people, but I am aware of and grateful for the many blessings in my life. I'm simply not in favor of Grand Fandangos and other such whimsy. Besides," he concluded, "I think we should give Reverend Cudrup a pass. The risk of winding up in a featured role on the Billy and Donna-Angel Show are too great."

"We don't have a choice, John," Sharon said firmly.

"Why? We're not Presbyterians."

"You should know better," she said. "Let me refer you to Chapter Two, Problem Four, specifically:

"Problem Four is the Problem of God, or more correctly, 'Does God Have a Problem Because There are 35 Different Churches in Berryville, a Town of 4,000 Souls? Of which 7 are Baptist and 2 are First?' You bet, and John will worry about it and cause you to worry about it too."

"I think that's a pretty clear directive to go to Withered Plum and Fandango to beat the band."

John sighed. It was bad enough being in this book. But on the Billy and Donna-Angel Show too? It was definitely time to seek counsel.

Chapter 4

There was much about Dr. Sloan's plan to Grand Fandango Billy Cudrup, including John's designation as "the wheel man," whatever that was, that filled him with anxiety. What, for example, did Grand Fandangoing involve?

To the extent that John knew about these things, a Fandango was a provocative Spanish dance performed by a man and a woman who simultaneously played castanets. Did Sharon mean that she and John would perform such a dance on Reverend Cudrup's head? That made no sense in as much as John was already assigned the "wheel man" role, and it was widely known that he had difficulty doing two things at once. He simply wouldn't be available as a dancer.

Therefore, and assuming that Sharon was one of the dancers, who was the other? It is possible that she had lined up a 3rd conspirator, but who could it be? John ran through a list of candidates—Dr. John Else, Dr. Cathy Roller, Dr. Fred Mayer, Dr. Gladys Vaughn (John assumed that Dr. Sloan preferred having a peer-partner as opposed to an ordinary layman)—but it was possible that she had someone else in mind. Perhaps, for example, she was thinking of calling on Berryville's Mayor, Tim McKinney. But this struck John as highly doubtful since McKinney, although kindly disposed to Hispanic people and therefore and perhaps was cognizant of what a fandango entailed, was also not really known to go too far outside Berryville—and certainly not all the way to Withered Plum, Missouri.

And why pick on Billy anyway? Christ as a PRODUCT was surely no more dishonorable a business than selling weapons of mass destruction, books written by Jackie Collins or Susan Sontag, or the Popeil Pocket Fisherman. I mean, Cudrup wasn't exactly Bernie Madolf, for crying out loud.

What was it that Cudrup was doing that was so bad? He had been a charlatan, been brought to the bar, served time, repented and disavowed the prosperity theology that had permitted him and Donna to own gold plated toilet seats and a rhino, and was now serving the balance of his sentence in Withered Plum. Have you been to Withered Plum?

And perhaps Billy was part of a 5th Great Awakening, an Awakening that used technology instead of tents to revive the religious zeal of the great wash of unchurched humanity that predominates in Post Modern America. True, while Catholics—almost entirely Catholic women—opened hospitals, orphanages, soup kitchens and settlement houses across America during the previous three (perhaps four) Great Awakenings (while their Protestant brethren held rival meetings, rolled in sawdust, spoke in tongues, joined, divided, dunked, did not dunk, sang, did not sing, whooped and hollered, sat in silence, and were slain or not slain in the Spirit), it was entirely possible that Billy was on the level and just doing what comes natural to every Televangelist: selling Time Shares in the Name of Christ. What's so bad about that?

John, admittedly, believed that genuine repentance was characterized by a long, long, silence on the part of the guilty, preferably while performing menial labor on behalf of poor folk. Yet, it was possible that Cudrup had reformed even if he had not followed the path of an honest nutcase like Charles Colson (who John admired quite a lot). Perhaps his well-traveled path was not a material fact in judging the quality of his repentance.

And while John wouldn't buy real estate from Cudrup, he was willing to grade him on the redemption curve and give him a pass.

And there was the whole first wife Donna Raye thing to consider. Did you ever see her, or hear her, or observe her, as she'd take a knife out of her make-up bag and stab Reason through the heart? Maybe Billy had already paid the price, had earned our forgiveness even before he erred.

Beyond the philosophical, theological, ethical, moral, and metaphysical questions of the matter, was the logistical nightmare of getting permission from Mrs. Heartbreak to take her Chevy van across state lines to Grand Fandango upon Reverend Cudrup's person. John would have to make up a story (yes, all right, a LIE) about what he and Dr. Sloan were up to. Obviously, they would have to use Sharon's car, or Yodi's (the Artist formally known as the normal person, Cathryn Yoder's) car.

John headed inside and walked upstairs to his retirement office. It was filled with dead guys organized alphabetically and by subject matter. In the middle of them was an old dining room table where he kept his laptop. He fired it up and went to Gmail.

"Dear John (wrote Dr. John Else),

"In Chapter Two, I was dumbfounded—but you realize how easily that happens to me—by your elevation of the political parties of Minnesota to a position of superiority over those in Wisconsin and Berryville. While I realize that the wrestler Jesse Ventura ran as an independent (not one of the two political parties), he did not win the governorship of Minnesota simply on the votes of independents. He also received a substantial number of votes from members of the two political parties. And while it is true that both Minnesota and Wisconsin have had some great governors--and has sent some outstanding statesmen to the U.S. Congress and Senate--it is only Minnesota that elected a professional wrestler as its governor! While Arkansas may have had governors with questionable ethics, I have no knowledge of it ever having elected a professional wrestler to such an esteemed position. Am I correct?

"In short, is a Minnesotan in any position to question the soundness of politicians from Arkansas or Wisconsin?

"I think not!" as the Passenger Locomotive says in Watty Piper's "The Little Engine that Could."
"Sincerely, John."

John sighed. Leave it to his old friend, Dr. John Else, to pin point the one time in Minnesota history where its citizens had lost its collective mind. Else was a Sociologist, of course, so mischief of this sort was to be expected. John was tempted to write back with an analogy involving lemmings—once in a Norwegian blue moon all the lemmings in Norway collectively hurl themselves over a cliff and into the sea. Behavior of this unexpected consequence is rare among lemmings; but it does happen; and it happens, sadly, to voters once in a while—but John resisted the analogy and simply wrote back, asking, "Do you have an interest in going to Withered Plum, Missouri?"

John went to Facebook. Mrs. Kathy Gilmore, a retired educator from Oklahoma living in Eureka Springs—that hotbed of indecency and the final resting place of the Great American Fascist Gerald L. K. Smith—had written:

"I bought a pair of high heeled shoes today. They were on sale at Dillards for 70% off the original price. It was a silly thing to do, but I couldn't resist. I think that I will take them out of the closet on a regular basis just to look at them and imagine how stylish I'd look if I could actually wear them."

John thought about commenting. If high heels were really successful there wasn't the slightest need to actually walk in them. But he did not. (Let's pause for a moment and admire his discretion.)

As you probably know by now, John hasn't even begun to solve Problem Four. What did you expect? I said he wouldn't solve anything, right there, in the first sentence in the First Chapter. Of course, that won't stop him trying.

Chapter 5

How shall we think about time? How shall we think about moving in time? No doubt Dr. Sharon Sloan, the Artist and Scholar Formerly Known as Sharon Sloan, is gathering stones of impatience to hurl at John for this odd aside about time, and for his mulish resistance regarding the Cudrup-Grand Fandango Affair. You may feel impatient yourself; after all, is time spent (spent!) wool gathering over a religious huckster worth spending? Been there. Done that. You might think.

Grand Fandangoing aside, we know that time is different for different people. Impatience causes time to expand; mulish resistance seems conjoined with some people's sense that there is plenty of time. Instead of rushing off to Withered Plum with castanets to expeditiously dance the Fandango, a mulish person will stop for tea, and eventually, after much buttering of scones and slurping of Earl Grey, inquire "How many people can dance the Fandango on the head of a Televangelist? Two? Three? Googleplex? I mean, what are we getting ourselves into? Do we have the manpower?"

Obviously, time is relative. No, not just in the objective way that Einstein meant, but subjectively considered, time can be of any length, and even no length at all if it stands still (long enough) (ho ho) (which is tough to believe... if you think about it).

Time in a dental chair (space!) seems longer than time in coitus (the US average is 12 minutes), which occurs in an entirely different kind of space—unless you're of a kinky bent and then, what the heck, you might as well bring on the laughing gas and alter time and space in a completely different way.

We are sure that we can travel forward in time because we have done a bit of it in our space craft and air travel. But there is some resistance to the idea that we can go back in time—say, if we departed today's Berryville, Arkansas and went back to 1961 and visited the young Donna Raye LaWally in her hometown, International Falls, Minnesota, when she was 17 years old, and thinking about attending the Wowser Bible College in Benton Harbor, Michigan. There, she would meet the young Billy Cudrup.

Much of the moral resistance to time travel has to do with what is called the Grandfather Principle. Imagine if you will, that you traveled back to the time when your grandfather was a mere boy—and you killed him. Would you go poof into thin air, right there? Because your father would have no father, and so you...well, you get my drift.

So we—assume you and Sharon—time travelled back to International Falls in 1958. You see young Donna Raye LaWally rush out of the high school at the end of the day. She is excited; perhaps she has been asked out by this year's (1958!) Football Hero. But she also feels an undercurrent of anxiety; the Hero (let's call him Frankie DeValue) is known as a bit of a scoundrel: Frankie is after only one thing!

Before we go forward with our story we need to provide a bit of clarifying verisimilitude:

You have probably noted that both Donna Raye and Frankie are of French descent. There are a few French people in Minnesota, but they are over-emotional, hot blooded, and filled with self-regard and mostly live in rented mobile homes. They are not natural Minnesotans, who are nearly to a person stoic, hardworking, and self-loathing Socialists of Scandinavian descent responsible for setting high state and national standards for public education, government, and home maintenance.

The reason Donna Raye LaWally and Frankie DeValue, people of French descent, are both in International Falls, Minnesota in 1958, is the result of a geo-political accident made two centuries earlier when Great Britain and French Canada began laying out what they thought was the definitive boundary dividing the future US from the future Canada.

François Du Creux, the cartographer representing France's interests, was drawing a more or less straight line at latitude 49 degrees north when his daughter Sophia's cat jumped on his drawing table and startled him, causing his drawing pen to slip and also jump, just as he came to what is now known as the Lake of the Woods.

"*Mon Dieu!*" Du Creux cussed (in French—because he couldn't speak English or Norwegian like a decent future American). "Now I'll have to start over!"

But: he was hung-over—in the French manner—and tired. And his employer, the King of France, was off diddling—in the French manner—and hadn't gotten around to sending Du Creux that month's check.

"Heck," he said, deciding to ignore the tiny northward blip. "Who'll know?"

Well, now you know. And what you also now know is that Donna Raye is really a Canadian and only accidently a Minnesotan and is therefore and definitively not Minnesota's fault.

So: even though you are probably in Arkansas right now and don't give a rat's patootie about Minnesota history or how I might revise it, please remember that this part of our story is really about Donna Raye

Cudrup, the ultimate provocateur of Large Amounts of Country Western Hair and Televangelism, two matters of critical importance to many Arkansans or, if you prefer, Arkansawyers. Be patient: all will be revealed.

So there you are (here you are), with your time traveling pal Sharon Sloan ASFKA, in International Falls, Minnesota, in 1958. You observe young Donna Raye LaWally rushing out of school; you enter her mind's eye and further observe that she is filled with anticipation and dread at the prospect of becoming Frankie DeValue's object de lust. You imagine yourself in Donna Raye's shoes (which were, interestingly enough, Geisha shoes, made by Ports and resembling a tangle of Japanese udon noodles) and are wondering, "What shall we do?"

Assume you invite Donna Raye to have a soda down at the drugstore. Donna will certainly agree, though she doesn't know the two of you, because she'll be flattered that a couple of out of town slicksters—believe me, even an Arkansan or Arkansawyer is slick in International Falls—have invited her anywhere at all. And she will listen to you with an open heart because, all snooty boy wisenheimer attitudes aside, Donna Raye has a big heart and it is mostly a good heart, if a little simple.

It is possible that you will tell Donna Raye to go out tonight with Frankie DeValue and to give herself up to him heart, soul, and biblically. Tonight is important, by the way, because you know with the prescience of all time travelers that Donna Raye is ovulating; if she and Frankie do the deed they will bake a little bun in Donna Raye's little oven. Then, Frankie and Donna will marry, rent a mobile home, and live happily (enough) ever after. True, they'll vote for Jesse Ventura 38 years later when he runs for Governor of Minnesota. But they're French, so what do you expect?

In the time it takes to drink a cherry coke (it took the same amount of time in 1958 as it does now), you and Sharon can dissuade Donna Raye from going to Benton Harbor and enrolling in the Wowser Bible College. She will not meet Billy Cudrup, and she and he will not produce and star in the Billy and Donna Show and she will not have to imagine Billy getting into Some Gal's panties, or see him go to prison. She won't marry Rodger F.. in 1994, or die on television on June 6th, 2009.

It is possible then, that Billy would find another girl at Wowser Bible College as short as Donna Raye, but one a bit sterner and less acquisitive, who would insist that Billy answer the call of a bricks and mortar Assemblies of God congregation in say, Youngstown, Ohio. There, he could speak in tongues, take a stand with his Church against the War in Vietnam, and travel annually with his stern wife and their five children on vacation to Hot Springs, Arkansas where the modern Assembly was assembled. No prison for that Billy, and no reason for Sharon and John to travel to Withered Plum in Mrs. Heartbreak's white Chevy van.

On the other hand and in complete compliance with the Grandfather Principle, you and Sharon might elect to do nothing, and simply enjoy your coca colas with Donna Raye while she regales you with the story of how she got her lovely Port shoes.

You will pardon my perhaps excessively long explication of the Grandfather Principle, yet it is as common as rain for man in general and writers in particular to wallow in the moral problems of a thing, whether or not such a thing is possible at all [*See* the Church of Latter Day Saints]. Physicists are a bit less likely to moralize, and prefer to stick with the facts of a thing even while struggling to find an explanation simple enough for dumbbells like you and me to understand that proves or disproves the matter in hand.

"Well," Stephen Hawking might say, "If time travel was possible we would surely see Space Tourists. They would be coming to Now from the Future to inform us of what lies ahead. That we don't see Space Tourists seems evidence that Time Travel is not in the realm of our current possibilities."

Sure.

Suppose for a moment that a guy walks up to you and says, "Howdy! I'm a Space Tourist visiting the Ozarks for the first time in, oh gosh, 1100 years. Oh my god, where did all that dead chicken smell come from?"

If you find yourself agreeing that the guy is a Space Tourist, please keep it to yourself. Otherwise, the people you tell about meeting the Tourist will assume: *a*) that you've been smoking a fatty and are one toke over the line, or *b*) that you require expensive professional help and lifelong prescriptions for an assortment of psychotropic pharmaceuticals.

If you explain the credibility issue to Hawking, again for example, he'll get it immediately. He knows that if he met you on the street and you yelled out, "Hey, Stevie! I just met the Most Amazing Space Babe!" he'd assume, *a*) or *b*) pronto. Then he'd sigh and, realizing that the easy on the layman brain objection won't wash, will begin to explain wormholes, cosmic strings, black holes, and "special" relatively. And that's before he gets to the math. So:

In order to avoid my copying out whole chapters from E.U. Condon's and Hugh Odishaw's *Handbook of Physics, 2nd ed.* McGraw-Hill Book Company, 1967, to prove a point which you won't understand even then—not even you, Dr. Sloan—let's just agree that Time Travel is possible, and get on with it. It's science, okay?

Having settled the question of Time Travel we are now allowed to think back to the end of Chapter 3, which concluded thusly: "John sighed. It was bad enough being in this book. But on the Billy and Donna-Angel Show too? It was definitely time to seek counsel."

The person from whom John will seek counsel is a time traveler. Keep turning pages.

Chapter 6

And having turned a page we find poor John Heartbreak in a grand quandary. Sharon Sloan has telephoned him twice since her early morning announcement and has text messaged him as well—also twice: "Did U get Van?" and "Hurry Up!"

John has not gotten the van. Mrs. Heartbreak is using it to deliver a load of newly minted primitive American furniture to Stan and Jeff at Vintage Cargo in Eureka Springs. She will be of no mind to "hurry up" anything simply to humor the misadventure now under discussion. John can hear her:

"You want to take my van to Withered Plum so that Sharon can Grand Fandango on Little Billy Cudrup's Head? Why certainly. By all means. And while you're at it, why don't you shave your head, go Hare Krishna, and start panhandling at the airport? Here's a dime; let me start you off on your new career."

No, John has not gotten the van.

Since Mrs. Heartbreak is not expected back for at least two hours, John goes out behind her studio—Mrs. Heartbreak is a folk artist and decorates the aforementioned primitives—and pulls a rake off the back wall. John, as you might expect, organizes his gardening tools in roughly the same manner that he organizes books: neatly, in rows, alphabetically so that "rake" is to the left of "spade." Try and avoid lodging the phrase "anal retentive" in your mind. I mean, it will stick there all day long. Do you really want that kicking around in your head?

So...John ferries the rake out of his backyard, and goes through the high wooden gate leading to his front yard. He turns right on Pritchard Street and heads over to the Community Garden at his church. He is traveling south and passes by the home of Edward Keever located across the street, and he passes by Juan Guzman's tidy grey house and by Kelly's tidy white house, also across the street. Mary Margaret's lovely white Craftsman is to his left and adjacent to his and Mrs. Heartbreak's small shambling Southern Colonial. He has arrived at the corner of Pritchard Street—his street—and East Church Street. Ten or fifteen of Mary Margaret's cats observe his progress from the safety of her front stoop.

Directly in front of John is the expansive brick back of the First Baptist Church. Once upon a time it was the grand Baptist Church in Berryville, but the attending Grand Baptists fell to squabbling, sundered, and left it to form new Baptist enterprises, five or six of them, I guess.

One of its former members ended up all alone on a deserted island. When he was rescued several years later he gave his rescuers a tour of the island. "Here's the house I built," he said. "As you can see, I haven't been wasting my time.

"And here's my barn," he continued. "And this," he said proudly, "Well, this is my church. As you can see, I have been faithful, even in my loneliness."

"My goodness, you have been productive!" exclaimed one of his rescuers. "And what's that building back there?" he asked, pointing.

"Oh," the man said, shaking his head sadly. "That's the first church I went to, but I had to leave. You wouldn't *believe* what was going on there." (Ho ho.)

John turns right on East Church Street and walks west along the latitude of Mary Margaret's yard. It's a pretty yard filled with varieties of shrubs and trees typical to the Mid-South, but they are drooping a bit because Berryville has been hot, and without rain for more than a month.

John and I both know that both you and Sharon are growing impatient with the slowness of our pace, both through these side streets of Berryville, and through the pages of this book. There are good reasons for taking it slow.

Human beings, especially the American variety, have the attention spans of two year olds. John's friend Kurt Vonnegut—who John talks to often these days since Vonnegut is dead now—wrote a whole book, *Galapagos,* about our brains getting smaller and smaller because our machines got smarter and smarter. This is a book. It isn't TV. Try and keep your finger off the remote for a while longer. The book will get you there, and itself, by and by.

But where is there?

There is Berryville, Arkansas. More specifically, "there" is a neighborhood and a couple of streets where the whole book takes place. Except for our trip to Withered Plum—by and by—you have been everywhere the book will go: a back yard; a front yard, Pritchard Street; Church Street; and pretty soon, a church garden on Church Street. That's it. That's as good as it gets.

Where ever you go...there you are.

It has taken a long time for John to design such a small world. He has been to all the other places, seen the pyramids, soaked his feet in the Danube, been tipsy in Turkey, been robbed in the Caribbean, eaten mice in Laos and crickets in Cambodia and has waited in an airport in every state in the United States.

Where ever he went, there he was.

Now he is in Berryville, Arkansas, walking past Shaffer Street on East Church toward the First Christian Church Berryville where he worked in the church's garden. He is going to work in it now while he waits for Mrs. Heartbreak to return from Eureka Springs.

The First Christian Church Berryville was founded in 1871. It has about fifty members as I write; some of those fifty have been members for more than seventy years. The Heartbreaks have been members for ten; John had chosen to investigate the church for four reasons:

First, he wanted to find a group who might be trustworthy stewards of Mrs. Heartbreak in her old age. Such age—old—was of course years off (decades!) but John is certainly on his last legs and he wanted to get the problem of a decrepit Mrs. Heartbreak onto someone else's plate a bit in advance of her (and his) definitive time travel event.

The First Christians kept a tidy church yard, for second. The church itself was of traditional New England construction that any ordinary mainline Christian will find familiar and comforting. This was an important matter to John since most modern churches are constructed like pole barns and have fiber glass steeples if they have a steeple at all. And while it is true that God can be found anywhere, we can hope (can't we?) that His finders are willing to invest at least as much in His churches as they seem willing to invest in the temples wherein resides their money. Yet, look around any small town in America: you will note that the Grand Architecture and the Fine Materials and the Tidy Lawns are attributes of the banks in that town.

Jimmy Baker is, by the way, the person most responsible for the excellent state of the First Christian Church's lawn affairs and set the example that John now tries to follow. When Jimmy gets to heaven both John and I hope that Jesus won't expect him to keep mowing grass, but will instead assign such chores to folks who habitually neglect the maintenance of their personal property here on earth. Will you be mowing grass in heaven?

That good lawn hygiene was a factor in the hierarchy of the theological decision matrix John used to test First Christian Church's appropriateness as an old age home for Mrs. Heartbreak will strike no one who knows John as strange. Cleanliness is next to Godliness, according to John, and a church (or the member of such a church) that looks like hell is certainly on the way there. You will hear (much) more about lawn maintenance in upcoming chapters. Try and contain yourself. I know it's exciting and perhaps a bit over the top literature-wise, but at least there is no sex in this book.

The third reason is because an old friend of John's, John Else, was a former Disciples of Christ pastor—the members of the First Christian Church are Disciples of Christ—and, before he obtained a PhD in Sociology, was an altogether normal person, and even after his adventures in graduate education is an entirely moral and ethical person who's example always challenged John to think and behave better himself. Dr. Else was a voter registration worker in the Deep South during the 1960s during the period when Civil Rights advocates were hostilely treated, and sometimes jailed and murdered. In John's eyes John Else is a hero and, if a church was good enough for John Else, it is certainly good enough for John Heartbreak.

A fourth and main reason is that Communion is offered every Sunday during services. This is important to John. Communion is part of his religious tradition, and remains at the center of each celebration for him. True, he has come to enjoy a few of the hymns— excluding of course the 65% that sound like Barber Shop Quartet exercises, the 9% that drugstore cowboys might sing while accompanied by peddle gee tars, and the 4% originated by that early wing nut, Martin Luther—but music aside, Communion is a comfort and solace to him.

Those are the reasons why John chose the First Christian Church Berryville as the spiritual home for the care and feeding of the Fabulous Mrs. Heartbreak. The reasons they have stayed are marvelous, and many.

Admittedly, this has been a loosely constructed, discursive walk from 108 Pritchard Street to the Community Garden located beyond the church, and behind a fence festooned with the amazingly vibrant hyacinth vines planted last spring by Mrs. Hudspeth. Behind the hyacinth vines stands a man that John does not know.

I guess it's our time traveler.

Chapter 7

John was about to greet the stranger in the Church Garden—an odd looking duck—when his pocket jumped and rattled. Undoubtedly, the noise in his pants was Sharon Sloan ASFKA, wishing to hurl imprecations at him for his tardiness. He thought about pressing the "buzz off" switch but knew that Dr. Sloan would eventually punish him for his avoidance. He pulled the phone from his pocket and primed to flip…was assailed by……a minor brain infarct that incapacitated him momentarily—these usually lasted less than two seconds and were, truth be told, rather pleasant—and when he slipped back into the present moment found himself nose to nose with one of Mrs. Hudspeth's hyacinth beans.

The seed pods of the hyacinth vine are a striking electric purple and were as populous on the vines strung along the Church Garden fence as Chinese are in Beijing (who are not purple, or electric (generally) but who are as prolific). John loved these vines because their fecundity and voluptuousness made him think about girlfriends he wished he had had when he was younger. They also reminded him of when he was a boy-soldier and ate them in a dish called *dau van*. He reached out to pluck a seed pod off the vine when his phone attacked again.

"Dr. Sloan," John spoke, "How good of you to call."

"Cut the crap, Heartbreak," Sharon curtly responded. "If we don't get a move-on we'll miss the beginning of the show." She was referring to 'The Billy Cudrup Show' which began at 10:30 and ran until noon, or a bit after. "I've called you at least a five times."

"I've been unable to locate my castanets," John said, a bit defensively. "They are nowhere to be found."

"What are you talking about?"

"I can hardly dance the Fandango without benefit of castanets, can I?"

Sharon sighed.

"As you well know, John, and as everyone reading this book knows, 'dancing the Grand Fandango' is merely an allegory or extended metaphor for an as yet indeterminate action still in a pre-design or strategic phase. And for which there is not, as of the moment, a clearly defined *zeitgeist* or structural direction.

"Besides," she concluded, "you are only the wheelman. Castanets are, within the frameworks of your lowly job description unnecessary, and probably a hindrance in the performance of your duties."

"Good to know," John said evenly. "There is also the problem of the van."

"If you have read Chapters one and two," Sharon replied, "you will remember that we have several problems to solve, paramount among them is Problem Four which is The Problem of God. If we don't get cracking up to Withered Plum and ride into Endtimes PDQ, you—and the Authorial I—will resolve nothing and your readers (and God!) will judge you both to be ineffective and of no more consequence than the usual semi-skilled intellectual and Village Time Waster."

"That seems a bit harsh."

"It is the nature of successful literature to demand a beginning, a middle, and an end, each component part driven by vital and interesting and well-integrated characters. So far the book has listed Seven Problems— Eight Problems if you count "Sub-set: Problem 6X" which is the P[p]roblem of a Catholic Saint hanging out in Protestant Garden in a Protestant town—and it [the book] has described you, a main character in the book, as a confused, shallow, deaf, and unattractive late middle-aged man whose best years are behind him.

"I mean, for God's sakes, John," Sharon finished lamely, "You've got hair growing out of your ears. You're not exactly d'Artagnan, or Jason Bourne."

Well!

John put his lips close to the phone and began to swish and suck spit in and out of the spaces between his teeth.

"I'm afraid we've got a bad connection," he said. Swish. Suck. "I'm losing you!"

"Quit stalling, Heartbreak! Get the van!"

"Oh, my. I can't hear a thing."

"Heartbreak!"

John flipped the phone closed and stuck it back into his pocket. It began to rattle and squawk, but he ignored it and turned his attention to the man in the garden. The man was bent over a Better Boy tomato vine and was looking at the attached tomatoes in a more than casual way. After some deliberation he plucked one off the vine and began munching on it.

"Your behavior is certainly rude," John called over the fence. "I don't believe I invited you to eat our produce."

John ambled along the hyacinth scented fence to the gate, swung it open and entered the garden. The figure before him was short and dressed in sandals and tattered Bermuda shorts. He was wearing a T-Shirt that said *'Jesus is coming. Look busy.'*

"Sir, I took this for a Christian garden and you for a Christian," the man said. "If I am mistaken I will gladly pay you Tuesday for a Tomato Today."

"It is, and I am," retorted John. "I also enjoy the occasional social formality of making nice, along the lines of 'Ask and you shall receive' and so on. But yes," John continued, "this garden is partly for poor folks and if you're poor we're glad to have you eat out of it. We don't expect anyone to beg."

"Excellent! Then you won't mind if I have a pepper or two!"

The shabbily dressed man tore a bell pepper of the plant and chomped it down in two bites, seeds and all. "Damn," he exclaimed. "That's really good."

"We're not allowed to use the word 'damn' in this book," John explained. "There is no sex, strong language, or violence tolerated at all. You are welcomed to say something along the lines of 'dagnabbit' if you require an expletive."

"Dagnabbit? I'll sound like Gabby Hays in a Roy Rogers movie."

John nodded. "Everyone appearing in this book speaks a bit oddly. The Authorial I says it's because we're inherently strange, at least as far as characters go, but frankly, I just think he's lousy at writing dialogue."

"Yes. We were warned," the man said. "The author said, in Chapter One, 'The first problem is the book itself. It is full of misspellings and bad grammar and it contains no sex (to speak of), no violence, and no strong (bad) language.'

"But I didn't think it would apply to me. I'm reasonably fascinating and fairly important. In the scheme of things."

John nodded. He had been surrounded by fascinating and fairly important people his entire life. They had all bored the tar out of him.

"Perhaps we should introduce ourselves," John said. "I'm John Heartbreak, retired bookseller, gardener, and the Fabulous Mrs. Heartbreak's factotum."

"I know who you are," the man said. "You're Problem 2. Let me quote: 'His dullness, the ordinariness of his career, the inadequacy of the town he lives in, his fear of his wife, the fact of his deafness, his age (old) and the fact that his prostate resembles a Western state of considerable size...'"

"...I get it," John interrupted. "But who are you?"

"I'm Sub-set: Problem 6X, which is the P[p]roblem of a Catholic Saint hanging out in Protestant Garden in a Protestant town. But you can call me Fiacre, or Saint Fiacre. Or you can call me Gary Marchbank. That's the name I use on Facebook."

"You're on Facebook?"

"Of course. Isn't everyone?

"I wasn't aware that saints hung around social networking sites."

"Why not? When did the world announce a moratorium on saint-making? I don't recall God saying that He was taking a break from it. As a matter of fact, I think there are a couple of prospective saints over there, in that little white church."

He pointed toward the back of the First Christian Church, behind which was the garden in which they stood. "Everyone in your church is a candidate, of course. But so far, I think I've only spotted only one, and maybe two. You're not, by the way, in the running."

[You can skip the next 3 paragraphs.]

John nodded. (This was John's seventh nod it the book. Be patient: there will be a hundred or more times when John nods. As I've explained, John has a limited repertoire of physical, social and literary skills—he is a limited man—and, besides which, I find exposition exhausting to both read and write. I mean, OMG, think about reading Susan Sontag or James Michener for more than a minute or two. KILL ME NOW!

And of course, this book is a postmodern book. Think about that too. The characters in the book know they are characters in a book. The book operates in parallel worlds which are simultaneously separate, blended, and equal. It is filled with endless parenthetical phrases and subordinate clauses that may (or may not) be diffused by the extravagant use of commas, dashes—dashes!—and (), and a nearly complete absence of verisimilitude.

This is all complicated by the fact that you are reading at 21.1 on the Flesch-Kincaid Readability Scale—which means that 87% of the folks living in Arkansas can't read it, even if Strunk and White had written it. SO:

John nodded.

"I think I'll pass on Gary," he said. "How about I call you Fiacre?"

"Aces," Fiacre said. He reached over to pull another tomato off the vine, but stopped and gave John an inquiring look. John spread his arms, palms up, and Fiacre yanked the tomato and smacked in down in three bites. Juice rolled down his chin and stained his T-shirt.

"John—may I call you John?—I'm a bit troubled by your 'dagnabbit' suggestion. Is that a commonplace expression in 'these here parts,' so to speak?"

"No," John answered. "You're free to shout out 'Fudge!' or 'Julie Andrews!' or any other symbolic marker for displeasure, surprise, or consternation that you wish."

"That's a relief. Since you're obviously 'the star' of the book that means that I'm merely your sidekick. Hence," he said, "my earlier reference to Gabby Hays and Roy Rogers. I was feeling a bit of chagrin at having to yell "dagnabbit!" for the next one hundred and fifteen pages."

"I can assure you," John sourly replied, "that you will be doing and saying things that you NEVER dreamed of doing or saying. I'm afraid that saying dagnabbit once in a while is small potatoes.

"Although," John continued, "I don't know very much about you. What kind of saint are you?"

"A minor one, I'm afraid," Fiacre replied. "I'm the patron saint of gardeners such as you, of taxicab drivers, tile makers, and box makers. Perhaps, more prosaically," he continued, "I am also the patron saint for those who suffer from venereal disease, fistulas, and hemorrhoids. May I be of any help?"

"I'm good, thanks."

"Excellent." He paused. "May I inquire as to the time?"

John reached into his pocket and pulled out his phone, flipped it open: "It's nine-thirty."

"I was thinking about something less approximate," Fiacre said. "The year?"

"It's 2014. Anything else?"

"Two things, actually," Fiacre replied. "First, are you at all troubled by the fact of my appearance? I mean, there is virtually no explanation of how or why a Saint—me—has shown up and become part of the book. You have also failed to inquire as to whether or not I am living, or an apparition, or have descended down from heaven for some special purpose in your life. Doesn't that bug you?"

"No," John said, flatly. "We're in a novel, the nature of which allows for the absurd, the perplexing, and even the fantastic to occur without much ado. True, the measure of the better writer is that she or he has the skill to make the reader believe in the possibility of the absurd, perplexing, and fantastic.

But," John continued, "I'm an experienced character in books written by a hack so, like Hemingway, I believe that 'blessed are they who expect nothing, for they shall not be disappointed.' In any case, the problems of the book were explained several paragraphs earlier in this chapter, as you know. These problems have something to do with its 'postmodern' structure—a typical, if I may say lamentable, excuse for just about any failure of quality.

"So," John said, after a pause. "You said there were two things?"

"Ah, so I did," Fiacre replied. "You said it was nine-thirty. I understand that Dr. Sloan is eager to get up to Withered Plum in time for 'The Billy Cudrup Show.' I encourage you to make haste!"

John rolled his eyes. "Let's not, and say we did. How about we just stay here and guess how many angels can dance the fandango on the head of a Televangelist instead?"

"Seventeen."

"What?"

"Seventeen," Fiacre repeated. "Seventeen angels can dance the fandango on the head of a Televangelist. Of course," he paused, "Cudrup is bald so, perhaps another two or three might crowd on.

"But enough of that, however, enjoyable. I think," Fiacre said, "you should heed Dr. Sloan's request, and aid her in any way that you can."

"And why?" John exclaimed, exasperated.

"Persons such as Billy Cudrup," Fiacre said "are evidence among spiritual fence sitters that Christianity is a confidence game operated by criminals preying on dumbbells and political wing nuts. In summary, they separate the people from Christ. Quite simply, they are the henchmen of Lucifer.

"Go forth, John, and duel with the Devil!"

Chapter 8

"I am Fiacre, born and bred in Ireland and once lived and buried in France, a monk and hermit ordained during the time of the Great Gregory and most animated—where animated means, quite simply, walking and talking and occasionally thinking—seventy-five years or so before the Venerable Bede began writing *The Ecclesiastical History of the English People*. Bede writes my name and tells my story in that book: it is the first time I 'appear' in another form (ink) other than human. Since then, I have mostly 'appeared' in anthologies of Catholic saints, or cast in plaster or cement as a garden decoration. I appear, for example, in the backyard of Peggy Gilbert, currently animated (Peggy, not me or the decoration) in a suburb of New York City.

"I am of all things the Patron Saint of Gardeners and, for entirely accidental reasons, the Protector of the Maniacs who drive taxis for money from LaGuardia to Manhattan, from O'Hare to the Palmer House, from LAX to Beverly Hills.

"Five hundred fifty three thousand and two hundred fifty six days have passed between when Bede put me in his book and my appearance in this book. Cool.

"John Heartbreak was not, as you read in the last chapter, the least bit surprised or skeptical about the sudden and animated appearance (my appearance) of a long dead and mostly forgotten man among his tomatoes. That (my) unexplained and abrupt entry into space—the space in this book; the space of the church garden; the space between your ears—was, of course, alluded to several pages back when "problems" of various types were listed, among them 'the [P]problem of a Catholic saint in a Protestant garden.'

Dan Krotz

"John was not (is not) surprised to see me because he believes that people in books, and the writers of the books, live in this Universe, and in a parallel Universe, that we identify as the "real" world and the "virtual" world. Because John saw me in Bede's book and in Father Leo Byrne's excellent *Boy's Book of Saints*, he was not surprised to see me in the church's garden. I do admit, though, that few people operate their world in the way that Heartbreak operates his.

"Many people find this strange. Often, they are the same people who believe that the Holy Spirit speaks to them in intimate and exact ways. They may believe the same things about angels. And they almost always believe that Old Lucifer slithers about in the night, and in the day, whispering sweet lies into our ears twenty-four hours a day. Yet they find it strange if, among the angels and demons that appear or might appear to John, is an entirely modest and minor saint such as me. Go figure.

"John and William Blake speak often. I can attest to this because Blake informs me of 'a dull and incessant conversationalist named Heartbreak who lives in the Americas' who bothers him several times a year. Personally, I enjoy talking with Blake, especially if I catch him on a good day; but he is himself an incessant conversationalist with several of the Old Testament prophets, and he has taken on their verbal and linguistic ticks; thus and consequently he often sounds like a crabby old fart.

"Much of the problem that people have with John speaking to the Holy Spirit, or with angels and demons and dead writers, is that these "entities" take on a physical appearance to John—much as Jeremiah and Saint Michael and the Holy Spirit did when they appeared to William Blake. I find their objection

48

somewhat odd, especially in the case of Blake, since Blake produced wonderful likenesses of his visitors for us to see and enjoy, and hardly anyone denies that these likenesses are divinely inspired.

"Such likenesses of the dead are commonplace here in the twenty-first century. Conjure up if you will Marilyn Monroe. You say she isn't real anymore, yet you enjoy the memory and the idea of her. And you have some thoughts about her, and recall a time when you watched her, perhaps with a friend, in a movie. Was that a real event? Was your friend real? Was the movie real? Is your memory real?

"You have remembered a real event and a real friend and a real movie, and you have a real memory of it. Is it only Marilyn that is unreal? Yes, of course you say that Marilyn wasn't real then. But she's as real as all these other things are now, isn't she? Reality changes over time.

"Logicians among you will quickly figure out the hole in the paragraph above, but that's because they are (you are) thinking like an old woman or an old man. Things have changed since you were young, and you have failed to change along with the times: we live through and by intelligent machines now; if you were born today—I know you are saying 'Come on, Pal! I wasn't born yesterday!'—it is probable that you will live fifty four thousand and seven hundred and fifty days. Why not five hundred fifty one thousand and two hundred fifty six days?

"We—I include myself because, please remember, I possess a Facebook account under the name 'Gary Marchbank'—we have machines that calculate our numbers for us and automatically make change; machines write code for logical routines that govern other machines; machines look at our guts and predict inevitable outcomes; machines make dating services scientific and profitable; machines...you get my drift.

"You—not me this time—are lazy and spoiled. You control the air's temperature, wipe your butts with paper as soft as a baby's kiss, and leap across countries and time zones in what used to be journeys of a lifetime (a thing that History was made of)! What labor or time saving device will you stop at, and not buy?

"What I have described (am describing) is singularity, the process where and when machines become smarter than human beings, either through the amplification of human intelligence or artificial intelligence. These machines will have greater problem-solving and inventive skills than humans possess and, inevitably the machine will design a yet more capable machine, to rewrite its source code to become even more intelligent. This more capable machine will design a machine of even greater capability, and its iterations will accelerate and lead to endless, recursive self- improvement that allows enormous qualitative change in the machine before any upper limits imposed by the laws of physics or theoretical computation kick in.

"You say this can't happen. But a machine is routinely inserted into a chest containing a bad heart, and it keeps the human being who owns the chest alive. We also modify human brains and many other organs with machines today and, pretty quick, we'll modify computers with genetic materials. In 1980, the US Supreme Court ruled, in *Diamond vs. Chakrabarty,* that biological organisms can be patented, and Myriad Genetics, a corporation registered in Delaware, the United States, did just that.

"Yes, you deny that this will happen, but how can we be so sure? What I observe is that we—you really—

simultaneously hold two diametrically opposed beliefs in your head.

"The first idea is that we will always find a solution to every problem. We are in End Times as far as fossil fuel goes, but burn it away as though there was no tomorrow, because we will innovate, invent, or discover a solution in the nick of time. Our climate is changing, our population is growing, our consumption of everything grows and grows—but we will certainly find solutions to these problems—so they aren't really problems; they are business opportunities!

"The second divergent idea is, of course, about our machines. We believe that we can escape our population and consumption problems by designing ever more efficient and intelligent machines (systems!)—and that those machines, like the internal combustion engine, the remote control, the atomic bomb, the dams and locks of the Mississippi River—are without consequence and utterly benign, especially if we are smart enough to manage them.

"Are we smart enough to manage them? Is it your observation that we are getting smarter? Oh, and let me ask again: what labor or time saving device will you stop at, and not buy?

"Because I am a Saint I am obligated to be interested in sin. No, I'm not very interested about what goes on in people's pants; organized religion, Lucifer, and politicians have got that covered pretty well; neither God nor I need to spend much time on it. There is, however, other sin that I am interested in.

"When God informed me that I was a Saint—one heckuva day, let me tell you!—I decided that the sin I was most interested in was Original Sin. Although I am a minor saint, I am not without a good work ethic, and I was willing to take on the Big O. So I did.

"I was also excited about visiting the Garden of Eden. I'm sure you can imagine my anticipation at seeing the beginnings of the World, at least the 6th day of the World when things started happening (according to us!).

"What I found was that the Garden of Eden is not a small place, and that the "6th day" is not an exact time. The 6th day was actually eighteen million and two hundred and fifty thousand days long, or about 40,000 years. It was just before the 6th day, perhaps on the morning of the 6th day, that Adam and Eve—the first people to really look, think, and act like us—began to live in Eden. They were naked as jaybirds, and buff, and had a great time doing what comes naturally when you live in Perfection with the Perfect Mate.

"So: here we have Adam and Eve—actually about 1,000 people who looked, and thought, and acted like modern people—on what was basically a Hawaiian vacation. Only it lasted for 40,000 years.

"I had a wonderful time visiting with these folks. I saw every kind of tree, enticing to look at and good to eat. A big river ran through Eden to water the garden, and then it divided into four rivers. The first river was named the Pishon River and the second river was the Gihon River. Then there was the Tigris River and the Euphrates River. These rivers never flooded and they were full of fish and the people had a fish fry every Friday night. It was a lot of fun.

"But every vacation must come to an end. Three million and three hundred fifty thousand days ago, almost exactly 10,000 years ago, the fish stopped jumping into the deep fat fryer and the fruits and nuts on the trees began to whither, and the men experienced occasional erectile dysfunction and the women began to experience frequent PMS. And God said:

"Get a job!

"Actually, what He said was, "Accursed be the soil because of you. With suffering shall you get your food from it, every day of your life. With the sweat of your brow shall you eat your bread until you return to the soil." As you probably have deduced, God was talking about production agriculture.

Times were not all bad. I had the chance to spend time with Lamech, who was the son of Methushael, and meet his wives, Adah and Zillah. Adah was, not to put too fine a point on it, bowlegged, and kind of a pill. But Zillah was a real nice looking girl, and I enjoyed watching her stoke the fire while Lamech went on and on about how lazy some of his sharecroppers were and how he might have to replace them with slaves. What did I think about that, he wanted to know?

"What I thought about that was how production agriculture led to surpluses and shortages, to management and labor disputes, to wealth and poverty, and on to politics and power struggles and war without end. These are the fruits of Original Sin; these are the fruits that have caused man to build better and smarter machines that can solve every problem that can do anything. Man's delusion in his infinite abilities is Original sin.

"Going back to visit the first 1,000 people, among them Adam and Eve, was my first adventure in Time Travel. The first 45,000 years were pretty fun, and even after things started to go bad, I enjoyed observing how folks learned how to solve problems and how to negotiate. But after that, for the next five thousand years or so, I mostly felt sad or mad. People had stopped hunting and gathering and had become production workers or owners of production workers.

Both classes are delusional and, lately, they are becoming insane.

"Prior to Sainthood I lived, as I said, in Ireland. I took holy orders in around 600 and worked mostly as an herbalist. I became famous, and a bit of a blowhard, truth be told. I had not yet had the privilege of going back in time, and I believed that I was serving both God and man by enriching my monastery by growing herbs and concocting cures for the lame, the blind, and the no-account. I did not know then how delusional I was, but I was not at peace and felt a deep trouble in my heart.

"To save my soul, I left Ireland for France and became a hermit and continued to garden. My garden became my cathedral, and in it I found God again.

"After my death I began to Travel Though Time; always at the direction of my Lord and Master *Jesu Cristo*. Through His kindness and love I have been allowed to visit many gardens in many places. That is how I have come to Berryville, and to the Community Garden at First Christian Church.

"As you can see, I am not much interested in how my presence in a Protestant garden is a problem ([P]problem)—or not. The multiplicity of churches we humans have produced is a vast silliness that has nothing to do with the love our Dear Savior and Lord *Jesu Christo* has for us, or for the love we should have for Him.

"The Good News is that the Warrior Queen Sharon Sloan and the dullard John Heartbreak prepare to do battle with Demons in Withered Plum.

"(If Mrs. Heartbreak will release her van!)"

Chapter 9

John left Fiacre standing in the garden and walked back up Church Street, turned left on to Pritchard Street, and went home. He had enjoyed talking with Fiacre and he gave him permission to stay in the old storage building at the back of the church lot in exchange for work in the garden. Their arrangement was tentative pending on approval by Dave Buttgen, President of the Church Board, but John felt sure that Mr. Buttgen would grant permission once he learned that Fiacre was the patron saint of gardeners.

Once home, John noticed that Mrs. Heartbreak had not yet returned from Eureka Springs and her visit with Stan and Jeff at Vintage Cargo: there was still no white Chevy van in its parking space.

John hoped that her transaction with the Boys had been successful, and that the rustle of their check in her pocket book would inspire a spirit of generosity, and of non-inquiry into his use of her vehicle. Dr. Sloan had called three more times while he and Fiacre had confabbed as to why and how Fiacre had chosen as unpresupposing a place as Berryville to do his next Great Work, and she was growing more, rather than less, insistent about getting a move on.

If John had been paying attention to what I am writing he would no doubt object to the fact that I used 47 words in the sentence just prior to this one. That's an awfully big number of words to cram into a single sentence. It means that you're reading at Grade 11 on the Flesch-Kincaid reading scale; about 5 grades over what *Time Magazine* requires. Are you doing okay?

John went into his back yard and patted Jane Russell, Mrs. Heartbreak's Jack Russell Terrier, and then went inside and upstairs to his office. He fired up his computer and checked his e-mail.

Caren J. Nordby, Mrs. Shogren's Hot Spanish Sister, had written in to complain about the complexity of Chapter 8. "Dear John," she wrote:

"As you know, I read the first book about you, *Coffee with John Heartbreak: A Mostly True Story of Berryville, Arkansas*, from cover to cover, and think that this second book is off to a promising start. What I find a little scary through, are the high-key philosophical moments. As a woman who was married to a philosopher for 23 years, I hope you don't mind if I just skip over those portions..."

"Oh, geez," John thought. He checked through the Shared Documents file and found Chapter 8. "I can't believe he's written nearly eleven thousand words already," he said out loud. "Doesn't he ever sleep?"

[Not much. Sigh]

John read through Chapter 8 quickly. His impression of Fiacre went up several notches—gosh, imagine meeting Zillah!—and he quickly formed a list in his head of questions to ask. Where exactly was the Pishon River, for example, and did fish really jump out of the water and into the fry pot—or was that just literary license?

John did the math and found Fiacre's calculation of years into days was pretty accurate. He didn't have any trouble with Fiacre's sequencing of events, or the time frames proposed. It jived with basic science, and John liked how Fiacre had timed production agriculture to when most Bible literalists believed Adam and Eve sinned and where thrown out of the garden. It fit together nicely.

Ms. Norby's objection was undoubtedly about the doomsday machines and singularity, but John supposed it was also because the writing was so wooden, and not because the ideas were so alien or peculiar. The Authorial I tried hard to be Schopenhauer but usually ended up sounding more like Soupy Sales. John usually skipped those parts himself. He would have to write back and tell Caron that skipping was okay by him.

When John reached the conclusion of Chapter 8 he was appalled as much by Fiacre's describing Sharon Sloan ASFKA as a 'Warrior Queen' as he was by the reference to him 'as the dullard John Heartbreak.' John, long married to Mrs. Heartbreak and for twelve years now a resident of Berryville, Arkansas, and known locally thus and only as 'a know it all Yankee' and 'an over-educated idiot' expected no respect. But that Dr. Sloan—not a real doctor but a Social Scientist and a Texan to boot—should be afforded such weighty adverbial plumage was certainly salt to his long festering self-esteem. John closed Chapter 8 with a stab and went back to his e-mails.

"Dear John," wrote Kathy Gilmore, a retired Oklahoma educator and writer…

"I suppose I'm glad that I made it into the book; I've seen my name—on a previous page, and here, two lines up. Hooray, I guess.

"It is probably the only way that I'll get published. And I like Fiacre, but I don't know about all the time travel stuff. But keep it up. Who knows where we'll end up."

John scratched his head, connoting for the less savvy reader of literary fiction, befuddlement or confusion. Why would Mrs. Gilmore read this stuff? She is a smart woman and certainly has better things to do.

As John scratched his head (again), he opened an e-mail from Jim Young, once Found in Beaver, Arkansas, but now Lost somewhere in the Pacific Northwest. He wrote:

"Dear John,

Dare I ask....who in the book is symbolic of .Jim Young? Could it be Fiacre? Ahh! That would be Lovely!

"As you know, I am an inveterate time traveler, a man with a degree of familiarity with gardens and the natural world, and am even more kindly disposed to the drunken Irish than is Fiacre himself. Perhaps, if I may suggest a plot strengthening gambit, Fiacre will be revealed to the world as Jim Young, INCOGNITO! What do you think?"

John wasn't so sure about Jim's plot suggestion. True, Jim seemed predisposed to Progressive Party politics and thus was no stranger to fantasy, but really, Jim Young, AKA, Medieval Catholic Saint Fiacre? It seemed a stretch, even for this mess.

On the other hand, perhaps Mrs. Gilmore and Young could team up and write the perfect scenario. Mrs. Gilmore had shown John a chapter from her novel in progress and it was quite good. She was certainly a better writer than the hack presently complicating John's life, but then, she probably has perfection issues and is keeping her book to herself.

John was about to write to Mrs. Gilmore to advise her to read Rona Jaffee—simply to prove that anyone can write a book—when his phone rang.

It was Dr. Sloan.

Chapter 10

"Dr. Sloan, I presume," John said into the phone. "Good of you to call. "How may I help you?"

Dr. Sloan sighed, a human behavior and literary device to connote a wide range of feelings such as sadness, frustration, despair, and etcetera. John was unable to deduce the precise feeling state in question but was sharp enough—yes, even John—to know that Sharon was somewhere in the ball park of said list.

"What's the status of the van, John?" she asked. "Is Mrs. Heartbreak back from Eureka Springs yet?"

Ah. Exasperation.

"Not yet. But I agree that we must make haste. I'm prepared to ride all the way to Withered Plum, and beyond if necessary!"

Sharon was surprised by John's sudden change of heart. And, frankly, a bit suspicious. "You're not just stringing me along, are you?"

"Not at all. I understand now that we need to intervene on Reverend Cudrup and the lovely Angel post haste. Pronto, so to speak, especially if I were Emilio Zapata."

There was a long pause on the phone. Then, "What's gotten into you, John? You've been dragging your heels all morning, one excuse after another, and now you're hot to trot. What gives?"

"I've been to the church garden and spoken to Fiacre," John answered. "He has urged me to comply with your request, and as expeditiously as possible."

"Who's Fiacre?

"Fiacre is a Saint in the Roman Catholic Church, presently visiting us from the 7th century."

"Catholic Church!" Sharon exploded. "That Whore of Babylon!"

"Tsk, tsk…tsk," John said evenly. "I see now that we can take the Baptist, however lapsed, out of Texas, but we cannot take the Texan out of the Baptist Church."

"Apologies," Sharon said sheepishly. "It was a reflex. You know how it is…"

"Indeed I do," John replied, magnanimously. "Don't give it another thought. I understand that cleaning up the mess of childhood takes some adults longer than others. In any case, Fiacre has encouraged me to help you. He said, and I quote, 'You and the Warrior Queen Sloan are on a Mission to save Christianity.'"

"What about my $6,000,000 bucks?"

"That didn't come up."

"Of course not," Sharon said, derisively. "Little Billy Cudrup swipes a fortune from the public coffers— my coffers, as a citizen—and he gets off Scott Free."

"Well, not exactly free," John replied. "I mean, he is in Withered Plum."

John, and you, can now imagine Dr. Sloan nodding slowly over her end of the conversation. "There is that," she said, dubiously. And after a pause, "What's with the 'Warrior Queen' thing? And what do you mean, 'visiting from the 7th century? Fiacre isn't another one of your dead writer guys, is he?"

"No, no," John said reassuringly. "Fiacre is a Spirit sent to assist me, both in the garden, and to guide me a bit further along on the path of Discipleship."

"Oh, God," Sloan rasped.

"Yes, exactly. And he's indicated, actually more than indicated and insisted really, that I will become a better Disciple if I aid you in Fandangoing on Little Billy's head. Apparently, Fiacre has deduced that

Reverend Cudrup, and the likes of him, cause unaffiliated Christians and Seekers after Christ to AVOID organized religion because of the propensity of its pastors to sell time shares, go to Paris, France, with male hookers, and to buy Cadillac's with 'love offerings' solicited from widows and unemployed sheet metal workers."

"Imagine that."

"Yes," John continued. "I can see Fiacre's point. He believes that Christianity is in crisis because of television hucksters and the gutlessness of Mainline Churches to call them out. Ergo, vigilantes such as *moi* and the 'Warrior Queen Sloan.'"

"I admit that I like the sound of that," Sharon said, slowly. "But I'm a little skeptical about the whole "visitor from the 7th century' deal. You haven't been abusing any pharmaceuticals, have you?"

"Some people might resent such a question, Dr. Sloan," John said, heatedly. "Perhaps you would like to rephrase your question?"

"Okay. Are you nuts?"

John shook his head, sadly. In this case, 'sadly' is no mere literary device but a sincere expression of how John's head was feeling. Hence the 'shook' part.

"Sharon," he said, (sadly). "Think about it this way. Far loopier and odder things happen in novels than the appearance of dead Catholic saints to retired booksellers. Regardless of whether you believe that such a thing has happened or not, it is enough that I believe that it happened because it furthers our plot a bit and it gets both of us closer to Withered Plum, and to the Reverend Cudrup.

"Your belief or disbelief in the matter is thus, of no importance. You, as a character in the novel, may chose to go forward as a cynical, deviant opportunist who

61

uses a delusional and vulnerable old person (me) as a tool in the execution of a fiendish and possibly illegal plan to extort money from an equally cynical and deviant televangelist. Or, you can chose to go forward as a Great Warrior Queen who saves and preserves Normal Christianity. It's your choice."

"Gosh. Which should I chose?"

"I know," John said sympathetically. "It's hard, isn't it."

"So, is the $6,000,000 definitely off the table?"

"Think of it as a test, Sharon," John replied. "A test of what kind of Queen you might be."

"I get it!" Dr. Sloan said, excitedly. "It's the Electric Kool-Aid Jesus Test!"

John smiled.

Chapter 11

While John and Dr. Sharon Sloan where confabbing on the phone about Sharon's life choices, Mrs. Heartbreak was finishing up her (successful) transaction with the boys at Vintage Cargo in Eureka Springs. She got back into her White Chevy Van and pointed its blunt nose in the direction of Berryville.

Like most Yankees, the Heartbreaks visited the Ozarks a few times before deciding to move there. Their early decision was to live out by Beaver Lake, but when Mrs. Heartbreak decided to open a bookstore she targeted Eureka Springs as the best venue for such an enterprise.

John was less sure. As a Middleclass Twit, he was bemused by Eureka Springs' seventeen hour city council meetings, by the prevalence of Elderly Trust Fund Babies, Hippies, Rage Filled Divorcees in the "business" community, and by the sheer number of Scoffers and Blasphemers dedicated to:

> Total Slack, Mockery Science, Sadofuturistics,
> Megaphysics, Scatalography,
> Schizophreniatrics, Morealism, Sarcastrophy,
> Cynisacreligion, Apocolyptionomy,
> ESPectorationalism, Hypno-Pediatrics,
> Subliminalism, Satyriology, Disto-Utopianity,
> Sardonicology, Fascetiouism, Ridiculophagy,
> and Miscellatheistic Theology.

John wasn't sure that he would fit in.

He was quite sure that Mrs. Heartbreak would not fit in. If the Heartbreaks "were" transportation, Mrs.

Heartbreak would be high speed rail, an inorganic compulsion on two rails following an exactly pre-established course, and John would be a 1953 Studebaker used on an occasional basis—perhaps to celebrate National Holidays, Geezer Fests, and as the Price of Admission to the 'I'm too tight to buy a real car' Club. This is all by way of saying that Mrs. Heartbreak is a Social Order Theorist who believes that the world operates in rational and predictable ways. No, Eureka Springs was not for her.

And while Studebaker John is, as an adherent of Chaos Theory, prone to aimlessness and a sort of organic submersion into 'whatever', he is a more or less reliable human being in so far as reliability has any meaning in the Twenty-First Century. So no, he wouldn't fit in either.

That's why Mrs. Heartbreak's White Chevy Van is headed toward Berryville, instead of to Eureka Springs, and not the other way around.

There are other places in the Ozarks to live, of course, like Holiday Island, or Green Forest, a town eight miles east of Berryville, and 16 miles further east from Eureka Springs. Green Forest has the Country Rooster Restaurant, run by the entirely admirable Willa Kerby to recommend it, and it was the girlhood home of Helen Gurley Brown, author of *Sex and the Single Girl* and editor of *'Cosmopolitan Magazine'*. If you ever get to Green Forest, though, you will quickly realize that, as Gurley Brown's Hometown, Green Forest is as purely accidental as Bill Clinton telling the truth, or George W. Bush knowing the truth. Consequently or subsequently or simply therefore, John had ruled out Green Forest; there just isn't, as Gertrude Stein commented after a short visit in 1921, any there there.

Holiday Island had briefly been in the running. John appreciated its lawn care ethic and the orderliness of its streets and public buildings. Somehow, however, its developer had managed to plop a suburb down in the middle of a nice stand of trees and, while attractive and orderly, it is still a suburb, only filled with old people who act like they are back in High School. John assumes that a hot date in Holiday Island is a prostate massage and, as appealing as that may be, it wasn't exactly, in John's mind, Prom Night. And thusly, Holiday Island missed out too. (Ho ho)

[Author's note: *I suppose I've lost the HI market.*]

As you can see, at least if your mind is as clear and bright as my mind is, that Berryville became the winner by default. Whether Berryville feels itself a winner is not known but, in any case, the Heartbreak's poured their fortune into it, and Mrs. Heartbreak opened 'Heartbreak's Pretty Good Books and Really Dreadful Coffee'. You may read about this enterprise and Mrs. Heartbreak's management of it, in the thrilling novel *Coffee with John Heartbreak: a Mostly True Story of Berryville, Arkansas*, available at Amazon.com (naturally).

Mrs. Heartbreak took to Berryville like a duck to water. Yes, I have surely missed the opportunity to invent a more interesting and creative metaphor than that tired old phrase, but none would be as exact, or as clearly understood. And be mindful, please, that I am trying to keep things at around the 8th Grade reading level, a difficult thing when you throw around terms like 'Social Order Theorist.' Anyway…

…like a duck to water did Mrs. Heartbreak take to Berryville. Quickly, she became President of the Merchants' Association, and a Progressive Business Voice. 'Heartbreak's' was a success: tourists on their way to Eureka Springs, residents of Eureka Springs, and three citizens from Berryville, made the Heartbreak's shop a regular stop. *Think and Grow Rich*, Napoleon Hill had written, and the Heartbreaks grew rich in wisdom.

And so it is that Mrs. Heartbreak is traveling back to Berryville, talking with her mother Mrs. Betty Kaiser of Lapel, Indiana, on her cell phone, unaware that her husband and Sharon Sloan are similarly engaged, but in plotting out strategies to effect a Cosmic Change in the modus operandi of a $Televangelism & Time Share Empire$.

"And did you know," Sharon said, "that there isn't a single mention of Donna Raye on the Endtimes website? Isn't that odd?"

"Do you mean that Donna has been erased?" John asked. "That's odd. Although entirely understandable."

"I find that ungallant, John."

"But understandable."

"I'm just saying," Sharon explained. "Donna Raye was the real star of 'The Billy and Donna Show.' You'd think the Little Whizzer would at least acknowledge her, like maybe naming a street in Endtimes after her."

"They have streets in Endtimes?" John asked, incredulously. "My goodness."

"John, you don't seem to understand the scope of the operation," she said. "They have streets, apartment buildings, condos, a police department, shops, and get this, an 'Angel Lane' gift store named after the current squeeze."

"Wow. What do we know about the new Donna Raye?"

"Not much. She's the author of a book that describes her fall into drug addiction, adultery, abortions, and her conversion to Christianity. I haven't read the book.

"Oh. She and Billy have adopted thirty kids. That's it. That's all I know."

John nodded thoughtfully. "I'm not surprised that she's written a book," he said. "Lots of people write books who have never actually read one. But I am surprised by the adoptions."

"Why?" Sharon asked. "Isn't adoption a thing good people do? And isn't it a thing that people who are trying to prove they're good would do?"

"That part I get," John said. "What I don't get is what kind of adoption agency lets a 70 year old divorced ex-convict who owes the IRS $6,000,000—and his former drug addict wife—adopt thirty kids?"

Dr. Sloan was at a loss for words. "Gosh," she said, finally. "It's a miracle! What if Billy is on the level! OMG!"

John nodded. "I considered that," he said. "Great scoundrels have reformed and committed themselves to new lives, new realities, and new ways of behaving. Perhaps it is the case with Reverend Cudrup and the Lovely Angel.

"One never knows, do one?" he finished.

"Do you think that? That he's on the level?"

"Probably not," John replied. "I hardly think that Fiacre would charge us with the alternative unless he had good reason. I'm sure that he didn't come to Berryville just to garden with me, Mrs. Hudspeth, and Mrs. Heartbreak. He's convinced that Cudrup is up to no good.

"But," he continued, "This is America and one is innocent until proven otherwise. We travel to Withered Plum with an open mind."

"What about my money?" Dr. Sloan asked. "Or, are you still hung up on all that 'Warrior Queen' stuff?"

John was about to answer when he heard a rumble on his driveway. "I have to go," he said. "I believe Mrs. Heartbreak has returned."

Chapter 12

Fiacre saw Mrs. Heartbreak, driving quickly, go past the Church, and turn onto Pritchard Street. He knew that John would ask Mrs. Heartbreak, in just the next few minutes, for the use of her van so that he might travel to Withered Plum and fandango the Reverend Billy Cudrup. The thought made Fiacre laugh, which he did with a deep and rumbling sound that came straight up from his belly. People were surprised by Fiacre's laugh, though it was not uncommon and heard frequently: Fiacre was a slight man but his laugh belonged to a giant, or a singer of German operas; it was that deep and rumbling.

Fiacre's amusement stemmed from the eagerness with which poor John Heartbreak now brings to the task of tipping over Billy Cudrup's ecclesiastical manure wagon. Fiacre knows that God doesn't care very much about what a church does or does not do, but He does care, and quite a lot, about what people do. Consequently, Fiacre cared too, but he would have anyway because he had immediately liked John and hoped that he would behave well. John's eagerness is a sign that he is going to behave well; so Fiacre is happy, and God is happy. This is very important to Fiacre because, well, 'when God ain't happy...

Be mindful that God has never been in the church business. Nor has God built a church or set up a building fund. And, as far as anyone knows, God has not chosen to join a particular denomination, although we have it on good authority that he most often

69

Dan Krotz

frequents churches that keep tidy lawns and refuse to play recorded music.

Notwithstanding God's indifference to churches, He concedes that churches are quite important as starting points for fulfillment of the great commandment to love one another. The main reason why God wants people to belong to a church is that such affiliation requires both faith and work, especially work because love is often a low paying job.

Many (many) people are satisfied and self-satisfied by identifying themselves as 'Spiritual,' and holding high minded thoughts about themselves. Frequently, these Spiritual Beings are excited about the potential of others to become as high minded as the Spiritual Person him or herself is high minded and, well, Spiritual. Sometimes this gives God the giggles. Other times it just pisses Him off.

According to God—I have this on good authority—a true spiritual self only emerges after often long periods of succeeding at loving the self-righteous, immoral, hypocritical wing nut who sits in an adjacent pew every Sunday for the sole purpose of depressing you. Frequently, you are the self-righteous, immoral, hypocritical wing nut sitting in an adjacent pew, and that is really depressing. Anyhoo, claiming a successful Spiritual Self without pew time is no different in God's eyes than claiming the Congressional Medal of Honor without having been in a war and behaving heroically in it.

Of course it is possible to become a spiritual being without attending to the rigors of life in a church! Viktor Frankl described Nazi concentration camps as a possible venue, and Hermann Hesse suggests the whole Siddhartha thing if you're process oriented and learn best through trial and error. But gosh, do you really want to go to Auschwitz when you've got a church handy on nearly every corner where you live?

And so it is that Fiacre's main observation is that the 'Spiritual People' he'd met in his long life had been born on third base and believed they'd hit triples. But Fiacre also observed the same thing about 'Religious People.' They too possess an extraordinary faith in their own Wonderfulness, and enthusiastically and artistically articulate it by condemning churches other than their own, sins for which they feel no temptation, science, and any governmental activity that might approximate the behavior of the Good Samaritan. Jesus was especially hard on these folks, the irony of which they seem utterly incapable of comprehending.

Fiacre had been a religious person, a Roman Catholic monk actually, which you know if you have been paying attention. And you know he was a pretty good gardener too, which is why he was interested in the Garden of Eden, and now, in the First Christian Church's garden. What you don't know but will know by the end of this sentence is that Fiacre was famous during his first tour on earth as an herbalist and curer of disease. Fiacre's occupation was one that he grew tired of and was the main reason why he left Ireland and went to France. It was also the basis for his becoming a spiritual person on top of being a religious person. It happened like this:

Fiacre and three pals were sitting around a camp fire which, in the 7th century was really just a fire because people hadn't become soft enough yet to yearn for semi-annual wilderness adventures in State Parks. In Fiacre's day a fire was just a fire.

Into the light of the fire came stumbling Seamus Cleary, terribly wounded by a blow to the head; blood flowed freely; Cleary seemed close to the end.

"O Father Fiacre," he cried out. "Mix me a potion from yer magic garden and stanch the flow of blud from me head!"

Fiacre quickly jumped up, surveyed Cleary's wound and told Heinous Fleary, one of the three pals, to fetch a shock of lambs' quarter from the garden. "By the Grace of our Lord," Fiacre exclaimed. "How did you come to possess such a wound?"

"Timothy O'Reilly came sneaking up through the forest and smacked me one with a sheleigly right on me noggin," Clearly cried. "I fear I'm doomed!"

Fiacre sat back on his heels and frowned. "Tim O'Reilly's just a little man. Could you not defend yourself? Couldn't you fill your hand with a weapon and fight back?"

"Aye," Clearly said. "I had me hand filled with Mrs. O'Reilly's breast, and while it is a fine thing, it isn't worth much in a fight!"

Fiacre was able to save Seamus Cleary's life, but both his gardening and medical career went downhill from there. He was tired of growing Lesser Snapdragon, Meadow Barley, Small-white Orchid, Opposite-leaved Pondweed, Betony, Red Hemp Nettle, Narrow-leaved Helleborine, Lanceolate Spleenwort, Annual Knawel and Basil Thyme. Mostly though, he was tired of Seamus Cleary, and tired of trying to love the self-righteous, immoral, hypocritical wing nuts who sat in front of him at every mass; who, he was certain, existed for the sole purpose of depressing him. And sadly, he knew himself as a self-righteous, immoral, hypocritical wing nut sitting among them much of the time, and that was really depressing. (See? Exactly as diagnosed a few paragraphs earlier.)

"Lord," Fiacre prayed, "I am in Your church, doing Your bidding, growing Lesser Snapdragon, Meadow

Barley, Small-white Orchid, Opposite-leaved Pondweed, Betony, Red Hemp Nettle, Narrow-leaved Helleborine, Lanceolate Spleenwort, Annual Knawel and Basil Thyme all day long, and healing one drunken Irishman after another.

"I am, Father," Fiacre finished, "in a bad way."

"No kidding," God said. "I realize the joke three paragraphs up is pretty lame, but geez, you didn't even smile. It wasn't that bad. And what's with the plant list? You keep repeating yourself. Dude, you're in a rut."

Fiacre was not surprised to hear from God. Although he did not know at the time that he would become a saint, and an inveterate Time Traveler, he took the presence of God for granted, which is how you become a Saint, and how you become Beethoven, Mozart, Lincoln, Chesterton, Dostoevsky, and Kurt Vonnegut. So: he naturally assumed that when he spoke to God, God answers back. This is a variation on the old "believing is seeing" shtick, which William Blake and Dorothy Day had down pat. Therefore:

"I know, Lord," Fiacre answered. "All I want to do is pray and meditate, and maybe hoe a row of beans once in a while. I just can't get excited about Thursday Night Bingo anymore, although Sister Patsy says we're ahead of last year by two lambs and eight chickens. At this rate we'll be able to buy a new bell for Your church."

"Fiacre, you know very well it isn't My church. It's your church. And a very fine church indeed. The bell is a nice touch."

"Lord, You sound an awful lot like one of those 'Spiritual People' we were dissing just a moment ago. Surely churches are important to You?"

"Churches are important—and necessary—to Human Beings because you would otherwise fall, as you properly note, into sort of a spiritual chaos without them. You'd all be out moon dancing on one of My magnetic fields. Pretty funny when you think about it; people who don't believe in Me will believe almost anything.

"But really, Fiacre," God laughed, "You don't imagine that Thursday Night Bingo and all the bells and smells on Sunday morning are important to Me, do you? Those are disciplines you engage in to prove to yourselves that you are following My greatest Commandment."

"And what, Lord, is it that we are proving to ourselves?"

"That you love Me with all your heart and soul and mind."

Fiacre nodded. "I do, Lord. But you have to admit that it's a big hill to climb."

"I AM WHO AM."

"There is that."

"There is that, indeed," God answered. "And don't think I'm not grateful. You've mastered the bells and smells and Bingo Night, and healed the Seamus Cleary's of the world and made long lists of plants. What you've done is very impressive, because you have faith, and you work. Be confident, therefore, that I AM pleased, because I know you did it all for love.

"Therefore again, you have accomplished a great thing, you have been tested by religion and fired by spirit: you are simultaneously religious and Spiritual and thus, ready to begin living genuinely."

Fiacre liked the sound of that. He was prepared to go on indefinitely right there in Ireland if he had to, but he was, frankly, ready for a new gig. "So, what's next?" he asked.

"Pack your bags," God said. "You're going to France and will garden a tad longer. Your church will make you a Saint after you die—which is very cool, by the way—and ladies all over the world will put little statues of you in their gardens. Then you'll become a Time Traveler and go back and visit the Garden of Eden in Early Time. Somewhere in about the Middle of Time you'll help John Heartbreak and the Warrior Queen Sloan save Normal Christianity."

"Is this one of those Crusades that is rumored?" Fiacre asked. "They seem like a lot of bother."

"It is a Crusade, but it will just be two crusaders, Dr. Sloan—the Artist and Scholar Formerly Known as Dr. Sharon Sloan—and John Heartbreak, a retired bookseller, and like you, a gardener. Their mission is to Fandango Little Billy Cudrup at his church in Withered Plum, Missouri."

"And apparently, Fandangoing will cause some effect on this person Cudrup that You, Lord, disapprove of?"

"Of course not," God said. "It won't have the slightest effect. He and the Lovely Angel are so deeply rooted in the pathology of *Self* that they cannot stop acting out one ameliorating fantasy after another. They are not in the least bit interesting.

"No," He continued, "Human Beings in general, and the Cudrups in particular, are so dull and feckless that I have to spend an inordinate amount of time in Collective Bargaining with you earthlings. Good heavens, read the Old Testament! It's one bad deal after another.

"But," God said, with a sigh, "It is what I do. However much I think about playing dice with the Universe, I won't, because I've made a covenant with its people. Whether they're Pharisees in High Churches, or Dingbats in the Human Potential Movement, they get the same deal and the same offer I made to Adam and Eve and to Lucifer and Abraham, to John the Baptist, and to the Apostles, to Martin Luther the drunkard and anti-Semite, and to his spawn the Cudrups. It is the offer I've made to you Fiacre, and to the Heartbreaks as well."

And it came to pass, a phrase Joseph Smith used in the Book of Mormon 3,187 times, that Fiacre went to France, visited interesting gardens, and is now observing life behind the First Christian Church in Berryville, Arkansas.

Chapter 13

Mrs. Heartbreak pulled her car into the driveway and shut the engine off. She was satisfied with the sale of her folk art to Vintage Cargo—she and John might have gravy for their bread this winter—but her mood was far from happy. She had just learned that her mother, Mrs. Betty Kaiser of Lapel, Indiana, would be entering the federal Witness Protection Program as part of a plea bargain that permitted her to escape hard time in exchange for testifying against corn speculators charged with rigging fructose prices. Exactly when Mother Kaiser would go incognito wasn't yet known, but it would be soon.

Mrs. Heartbreak would miss her mother, but she wasn't surprised by the turn of events. Her mother had always led a complicated life, one that bore close resemblance to a checkerboard and, since Mrs. Kaiser is so old, it is probable that she is the original source for the phrase 'a checkered past.' She, Mrs. Heartbreak, supposed that she should be grateful that Mom's penalty was Witness Protection instead of prison.

How odd, she thought, that she should be the "normal" child among three sisters, As a girl, and as a young women, and long before she had become the Fabulous Mrs. Heartbreak, she was, as her near-normal father opined, 'hell on wheels' and 'quite a handful.' But she possessed, alone among her sisters and her mother, a self-regulating gyrocompass that had located the North Star sometime during early adulthood; consequently she had steered a straight course ever since.

I am tempted to go forward with the interesting stories that represent each of Mrs. Heartbreak's sisters.

But those stories, and these arresting women, including Mother Kaiser, are not germane to this book, and they are not listed among the Seven Problems we agreed not to solve at the beginning of this novel; and so, I will not add them to the list now. Each day, as we know, has trouble enough of its own.

Why I have bothered to bring the matter of Mother Kaiser's situation up at all is that John is depending on the state of Mrs. Heartbreak's mood to regulate her decision regarding his and Dr. Sloan's request that they might borrow her White Chevy Van. For a while, all was well; she had a fat check in her pocket. Now, things look bleak: will money trump the familial ties that bind?

Of course it will! As the engine of her car tinked and cooled, she adjusted her mood to fit the reality of winter gravy. Yes, Mom might have trouble adjusting to life in Boise, or in Red Hook, New Jersey, but she always lands on her feet. It was just a matter of time before she cornered the numbers racket in whatever town the Feds decided to locate her and was back in business. Now, if only she could get John to Fly Right!

Getting John to fly right was her only occupation now that she had retired from superintending Heartbreak's Pretty Good Books & Really Dreadful Coffee. She brought to this task a skills set that ought to have been sufficient; Mrs. Heartbreak was a fine linear thinker, and would have made a competent engineer or airline pilot, especially if straight lines were required to execute a design or movement from A to B.

Sadly, John is not a linear thinker but rather, has leased space to a mind so disorganized that it more closely resembles a city dump than a source of cognition. God only knows (exactly!) what goes on inside that messy jumble sale.

Last night, for example, Mrs. Heartbreak had commented, casually—over one of her gourmet dinners—that our technology driven financial sector was in danger of imminent collapse. Money, and the records of money, would vanish!

"We're overdue, John," she exclaimed, "for getting high-jacked by Wall Street sharpies, or thrown into chaos by terrorists. They'll crash our networks and drain our bank accounts. We'll be eating grass before you know it!"

John nodded.

Mrs. Heartbreak occasionally dipped into Chaos Theory. Her dips were only occasional, however, and almost always involved the loss of money and an ensuing grass diet. Beyond that, her world was orderly and she expected it to behave predictably. When it did not, and when John did not, she tended to view these episodes as the result of moral failure rather than accident and insisted on making lists and checking them twice.

Not surprisingly, Mrs. Heartbreak was both feared and respected by public officials, neighbors, vendors, customer service workers, heads of major corporations, the President of the United States, and on two occasions, God Almighty who did not, of course, fear her, but who *had* walked away with a fair degree of respect. John, needless to say, toed the line.

It helped that Mrs. Heartbreak was exceedingly beautiful and now, as a woman of a certain age, invested with a fair degree of domestic wisdom. It was doubtful that God, or the President, or even John, would put up with the same insistency from a plain woman, or one who was organically dim.

And so it is, finally, that we have reached the point in our story where John will ask Mrs. Heartbreak for the loan of her White Chevy Van. You have waited patiently for this moment to arrive, and you deserve to have the reward of my (finally) getting on with it.

But first, a history of the Chevrolet Motor Corporation.

Just kidding.

"Dear," John greeted Mrs. Heartbreak, as she came through the gate and into the backyard. He had quickly gotten Sharon off the phone and was about to pop the question (ha ha!) when he observed the frown on her attractive face. Hmmnn, he thought. Perhaps this was not the right time.

"Are you okay? You look a bit frazzled."

"No, I'm fine. Just a bit of bother with Mother."

John nodded. He knew better than to ask.

"Things went well at Vintage Cargo, I assume then," John stated. "May I also assume gravy for our winter bread?"

"You may indeed. And perhaps the odd spud or two."

"My!"

"Yes, it was a good trip," she replied. And then, "By the way, there was a scruffy man standing in the church garden when I drove past. He was wearing dirty Bermuda shorts and a *'Jesus is coming! Look Busy!'* T shirt. Awfully tacky, John!"

"It's Mr. Fiacre, a visitor. I've given him permission to live in the garden shed. Down on his luck at the moment. On his uppers, so to speak. Broke."

"Does Dave know?" She was referring to Dave Buttgen, the man responsible for the church's upkeep, as well as for the maintenance of the church's outbuildings, and yard. "Dave will certainly not approve of that execrable T shirt."

"I haven't spoken to Dave yet," John said, somewhat defensively. "I'm sure he'll approve; he has a soft heart, and Fiacre has agreed to work in the garden and help keep the yard tidy."

"Well, please tell Mr. Fiacre to improve his appearance. I detest scruffy men. If the two of you are seen together people will think the First Christian Church is hosting a hobo convention."

Mrs. Heartbreak moved toward the house, away from John and his impending request. He took note, in an entirely salacious way, of the sway of her hips, and the loveliness of her figure. Admittedly, John's observation of these attributes might be viewed as sexual content and, consequently and seemingly a violation of the NO SVSL rules. However, the Heartbreaks have a license and are therefore permitted the occasional lapse. But I digress…

"My dear," John began, tentatively. "Dr. Sloan and I require the loan of your van. We need to go to Withered Plum, on a matter of some importance."

"Importance? What?"

John hesitated, but decided in for a penny, in for a pound. "We go on a Mission from God. Our task is to save Normal Christianity."

Mrs. Heartbreak rolled her eyes. "Sometimes I just don't understand you, John. It was a simple question."

Then: " Fine. Tell Sharon hello for me. And tell her, please, to keep you out of trouble."

She went into the house, closing the door behind with more force than seemed required. Jane Russell, the Jack Russell Terrier, looked up at John, inquiringly.

"Yes," John said. "That was a near miss."

Chapter 14

John backed out of his driveway and headed west toward the Kings River Bridge and Dr. Sloan's eccentrically tiny house and garden. I will describe the up-coming four point five mile trip in excruciating detail and use about twelve hundred words in the process. While I do this, John will be focused on the road, and will be processing thoughts, opinions, and feelings related and unrelated to our finally getting on with the story. He will spend some of the time scratching the remnants of a poison ivy outbreak on his baggy, saggy skin.

Now that I have you riveted to your chair and breathless with anticipation, we can move forward. But first, annoying commentary.

It is a political year in Berryville and campaign signs litter the side roads like pimples on the chin of an already ordinary face. John takes in the names of the various office seekers and chokes on them like doses of castor oil. He can't decide what is worse, the petty criminality of the candidates, or the accessorial wink of Carroll County's voters when they vote for these cuckoo birds.

John is widely recognized as a political snob, one of those over-educated elites we hear so much about these days. The low opinion most Berryvillians have of John's politics is derived from his insistence that the US Constitution is comprised of more than the 2nd Amendment and a bunch of meddlesome suggestions. His wide-eyed wonder at how readily the poverty-stricken residents of Berryville exercise it on election days—when they shoot themselves in the feet—affirms their low opinion.

"What a big nosed, know it all Yankee that Heartbreak is," they say.

John had been fond of quoting Dorothy Parker to these bozos on such occasions: "You can lead a whore to culture, but you can't make her think," Parker had said, with an exquisite play on the old horse and water aphorism, but it always met with frowns and looks of bafflement. "What? Explain that, will you?"

No, John didn't think so.

Mrs. Heartbreak's van was running like a top, and was as quiet as one of those new-fangled hybrid automobiles. He was pleasantly surprised that the van's gas tank was full, and that Jane Russell's hair was more or less confined to the cargo area, and not to the passenger's seat. Dr. Sloan loved animals, but would surely object to getting hair on her 'I love to Mambo' T Shirt.

As he passed Dirksen Buildings, owned by the estimable David and Shelley Buttgen, he began to feel anxious about what Fandangoing might entail. Were there, for examples, levels of fandango where great amounts of fandango should be meted out, say in the cases of Ted Haggard, Billy James Hargis, Billy Swaggart, Lonnie Frisbee, Roy Clements, John Paulk, Paul Crouch, Douglas Goodman, Paul Barnes, Lonnie Latham, Earl Paulk, Coy Privette, Michael Reid, Joe Barron, Tony Alamo, George Alan Rekers, and Eddie L. Long, all of whom had zipper trouble?

Or, was money the BIG reason to fandango, among whom Robert Schuller, Robert Tilton, Mike Wamke, Kent Hovind, Richard Roberts, Kenneth Copeland, Benny Hinn, Joyce Meyer, and the aptly named Creflo Dollar, might well be offenders? Dr. Sloan would surely focus on this extra-legal group as deserving of special opprobrium.

And what of multiple offense offenders such as Billy Cudrup himself? Didn't he have a bit of slap and tickle with a woman, in addition to defrauding the American Taxpayer out of $6,000,000? Were cases such as his deserving of a Double Fandango? Crime and appropriate Punishment was truly a matter of Dostoevskyan complexity.

John picked up speed as he slid by Wal-Mart, hiking it all the way up to 40 miles an hour in the 55 mile an hour zone. John knew that he was holding up traffic—cars and trucks began to pile up behind him—and he was not yet so enfeebled that 41 miles an hour seemed like a rush to him. But he had spent years trying to get to the airport in Fayetteville while captured behind trucks filled with chickens, or cars filled with Kansas Tourists, and he was passive aggressive enough to enjoy watching his followers go insane. Payback is sweet.

The road widened to two lanes when he got to the Out Post, 3 miles west of town. Cars and pick-up trucks hurled by him at an unseemly 60 or 70 miles an hour, and a few folks shook fists at him. John received these with a benign smile and nod. The only things he felt in response was gratitude that he is now a retired and completely unproductive human being, and amusement at the impending heart attacks of the hurried travelers who have been following him.

John had had his own heart attack way back in 1983. One minute he was an important executive standing in an elevator, eating a snickers bar. The next minute he was on his back in an ambulance with two black eyes and snickers bar smeared all over his face; he had fallen nose down and whacked himself pretty good. Shortly after that he decided not to be important any more.

As John sped—okay, ambled—past the Out Post, the van slid down a mile long decline to the Kings River Bridge. Long declines always put him in mind of Phil Black, a colleague who, with John, had labored for an endless time for the Institute for Sexual and Economic Despair, a Washington DC based think tank that Mrs. Heartbreak and her mother were certain was a CIA cover story.

I-Said, as it was generally referred to, was by no means a CIA anything. It was nothing except the place where John and Phil Black and a few other Depressives attempted to make a living while trying to instill in the sexually and economically disadvantaged the idea that Despair was a rational response to their circumstances. It was a tough job with few advantages, especially in light of the average Americans absolute faith that, no matter how bad things might get, they always *1*) could go to bed poor and wake up rich, *2*) sue a major corporation and wake up rich, *3*) get easy credit, file bankruptcy, and wake up rich, and *4*) elect a millionaire toadstool from Texas, President, blame a black guy for the toadstool's failures, and wake up rich.

The average American's faith in the certainty of waking up rich was compounded and doubly affirmed by the Prosperity Theology of Oral Roberts, Joel Osteen, Kenneth Copeland, Peter Popoff, Kenneth Hagin, and countless other Televangelists who assured listeners that God is a Magician who turns positive thoughts into money. No wonder that John and Mr. Black accomplished little in their careers, and no wonder that Phil would have his own heart attack as a result.

John considered calling Phil and getting his opinion if preaching a Prosperity Theology was a fandango-able offense. There was broad agreement, even among

Evangelicals, that zipper trouble and fraud trouble was real trouble, but how would they stand on the matter of Lies, Signs, and Wonders? Phil, a southerner and former Gentleman, was well acquainted with any number of folks who handled snakes, had been slain in the spirit, and were enabled to speak Finnish at the drop of a hat. If anyone knew, Phil would.

John was about to call him, but then saw that he was crossing the Kings River Bridge, and was seconds away from Dr. Sloan's house. He would have to call Phil another time.

Chapter 15

Sharon Sloan had adjusted to living in the Ozarks without a hiccup, much to nearly everyone's amazement. True, she was from Dallas, Texas, so jumping the cultural bar hardly required a big leap forward, but Sharon had lived in Europe, gotten smart in several schools, and now associated almost entirely with a few local Whiz Bangs and Ultra Smarty Pantses who also had chosen to settle in the Berryville area.

Why she associated with John was a mystery to her friends, and to her too, when it came right down to it. She accepted his deafness and tolerated his toad-like appearance with a fair degree of grace, but lately, she was discovering that his tendency to associate with the dead a bit unnerving. And then there was this whole Saint in the Garden business. Because of her fundamentalist roots, Sharon knew that some people felt personally stalked by the Devil, or needed to break out in fevers of Spirit filled Sway-dough Esperanto, or Urdu, from time to time.

But by and large these were decent Protestants who lived in Doublewides and were nearly current on their SUV payments. None of them, in so far as she knew, believed that you could step right up and shake an old dead Catholic's hand, and have him shake it back. Worse, John and what's his name—oh yes, Fiacre—no doubt carried on lengthy conversations in Latin, a language of little use in Berryville, Arkansas, or in Dallas, Texas, for that matter.

When John had suddenly and enthusiastically agreed to help her fandango Little Billy Cudrup, she immediately had second thoughts. When he recounted the whys of his new-found enthusiasm, 'a once in a life-

87

time opportunity to save Normal Christianity' she became even more dubious. While Sharon was fairly sure that John was not completely Woo Wee in the Mind— nor had she ever seen him ingest a psychotropic pharmaceutical—she lacked the requisite Christian excitement about the upcoming battle that one might expect from a 'Warrior Queen.'

And while John wrestled with defining 'fandango' and all that it involved, she was equally perplexed by the meaning of 'Normal Christianity.' When Doc Holiday was dying, one of the last things he said was, "Wyatt, there ain't no normal life. There's just life." Couldn't you say the same thing about Christianity? Why should the definition of 'normal' Christianity be left to a barely respectable Yankee encapsulated in the Ozarks and his imaginary Time Traveling Friend?

Needless to say, John had complicated Dr. Sloan's adjustment to life in Berryville. She had supposed, early after her arrival, that life going forward would be comprised of birding, catching the odd episode of *Glee*, entertaining her many nieces and nephews, piloting the virtually endless inventory of electronic gadgets that filled her tiny home, and executing the odd prank or two, such as punking Billy Cudrup and similar rascals. But now, she was being cast as a Warrior Queen responsible for saving Normal Christianity. All because of John, dagnabbit.

And there he was now, pulling into the parking area just east of her little house. She watched him through her kitchen window as he lumbered out of the white van and down the stone path and past a shock of bamboo to the front of her porch. Naturally, he was talking to someone who, naturally, was invisible to her. By the look on his face, John appeared to be losing an argument.

"You're talking to yourself," Dr. Sloan said, matter-of-factly. "It is an unsettling habit, John."

"But harmless. Are you ready to go?"

She sighed. "It is nearly noon. We'll have missed at least half the show."

"Mrs. Heartbreak took longer than expected to earn our winter's gravy. And," he said with a pause, "requesting her van required a nuanced approach."

"In other words, you lied to her."

"Certainly not. I explained that we were on a Mission from God and she handed over the keys. Quite expeditiously."

"Did she snort?"

"There was a bit of eye-rolling, but nothing untoward."

"I don't know why she puts up with you. The woman is a Saint."

John felt offended. "I've been an adequate provider," he retorted. "Faithful as a rock. Respectful in my requests. Clean habits. A prince, I would say!"

"Alright, Charming," she replied. "Let's get going. We've got some details to work out, including rank ordering of priorities.

"Priority one," she said, firmly, "Is my $6,000,000. Priority eight-six is an explanation of what Normal Christianity is. As far as I can see—and I can see from here to China—there isn't any such thing."

"Odd that you should mention China," John said, enthusiastically, as they walked toward the van. "Watchman Nee, one of the great men of the 20th Century, wrote a book entitled '*The Normal Christian Life*.' He was Chinese.'

"And he actually defined 'normal' in the context of Christianity? Unbelievable!"

"Believe it, or don't. But yes, he defined normal Christianity. Interestingly," John said boringly, "The word 'normal' in Chinese has nearly the exact meaning in English. How about that!"

"Fascinating," Dr. Sloan said, evenly. "What's the Chinese word for 'irony'?"

"I'm not sure. Why?"

"Never mind."

John shrugged, then got in the van, and started it up. Dr. Sloan climbed in and fastened her seatbelt. "Try not to drive anyone nuts, okay? Pay attention to the speed limit and approximate it."

"Driving slow is my only hobby," John said, defensively. "You, of all people, should permit eccentric habits."

"Just pep it up. We haven't got all day. And, against my better judgment, what did this Nee guy have to say."

"According to Nee," John said, "Normal Christianity is one church in one town. He said, 'When the Lord called me to serve Him, the primary objective was not to hold revival meetings, or help people hear more scriptural doctrines, or for me to become a great evangelist. The Lord said simply that He wants a single church where everyone loves one another, and loves Him.'"

"Ah ha! I knew it! You're part of a Vast Wing Nut Catholic Conspiracy! You want to reinvent the Holy Roman Empire!"

John rolled his eyes. "Watchman Nee was raised as a Methodist. Robert Govett, an Anglican, had the most profound effect on Nee's teachings. T. Austen Sparks, another teacher, was a Baptist. There wasn't a Catholic in the bunch."

The more John got excited about Nee's teachings the faster he talked about them, and the slower he drove. Sharon was soon aware of cars and trucks piling up behind them. When they turned off on Springfield Road to head North toward Withered Plum, there were at least thirty vehicles behind them. Sharon decided then that it was a really bad idea to have John drive their getaway car. What would happen if they ran into trouble? What would happen if Little Billy Cudrup resisted Fandangoing?

"You can stop talking now, John," she said. "You've explained it enough. I would like you to concentrate on a mile per hour rate somewhere between forty and fifty. Think you can manage that?"

"Ah, you want speed? You're getting pumped up! That's the Warrior Queen spirit I've been waiting for!"

"Uh huh."

Chapter 16

John and Sharon are traveling to Withered Plum, Missouri in Mrs. Heartbreak's White Chevy Van. They are also traveling through time. Think about it: it will "take" thirty minutes for them to go between Berryville and Withered Plum. It has taken you about three seconds to read up to this mark ~. You have travelled through a bit of time yourself. Think about it.

As John and Sharon travel through time to Withered Plum, John has been thinking about old pals; he has travelled back in time to when they were young, or at least younger than they are now. As you can see, time is dimensional and simultaneous: you can travel forward through time and backwards too, at the same time.

One of John's old pals is Rod Britten. The other is Ernest Leonard. Both of these gentleman appeared in the first book about John (that was in the past); now they are appearing here in the present and, when you read this at some time in the future, they will be in the future with you too, even if they do not "be" in the strictest sense. (I certainly hope that they "be" in the strictest sense. I am sure that they do too.)

Both Rod and Ernest are bachelors. Unlike the married John (or you, if you are a married man), bachelors have access to—or desire access to— hundreds if not thousands of beautiful women who give them unlimited amounts of wildly extravagant sex. And because the women are also modern women, they often as not go Dutch when waiters bring bills or when tickets are slid through theatre windows. Such is life for Rod and Ernest. Such is bachelor life.

Married men like John exchange bachelor life for apple sauce cake:

3 cups sugar
3 eggs
1 ½ cups cooking oil
2 cups apple sauce
5 cups flour
3 tsp. soda
½ tsp. salt
1 tsp. allspice
1 tsp. cinnamon
1 tsp. cloves
1 cup raisins, white
1 cup chopped nuts
1 cup maraschino cherries cut up

Combine sugar, eggs, oil and applesauce. Stir together dry ingredients and add to applesauce mixture. Add raisins, nuts, and cherries. Pour into 3 greased bread pans. Flour pans lightly. Bake at 350 for 1 hour.

John has enjoyed this cake several times—it comes from a cook book titled *A Taste of Hadassah*—and he thinks about that enjoyable cake whenever the lives of his bachelor friends pop into his mind, as they have now. The word 'now' by the way complicates things, not because it connotes a present moment cognition (which is "now" past) but because it is another thread of time (past time) woven into the fabric of current time that is comprised of John and Dr. Sloan travelling to Withered Plum, John thinking about Rod and Ernest at some point located in the past and now (now!) present as memory on the trip to Withered Plum, and just about…now…being read by you in the future. The cloth of life—lives—is woven in just this way.

Needless to say—but let me say it anyway—all this time biz is really about the mind body problem and how mental phenomena are in most aspects non-physical and comprised of times past, present and future. In religious terms this is a conversation about whether or not you have a soul. Do you have a soul?

If you do, keep reading. (If you don't, skip to the next chapter.)

Both St. Paul and Plato argued (argue) that we (you!) have souls, and that souls are immortal. How cool is that! More important though, is that souls exist independently of time and space; souls get to travel; through time; through space; any time, any place. If you have a soul you are a natural traveler through time.

Rene Descartes described the soul as consciousness and self-awareness. Are you conscious and self-aware? If you are, you are able to (accurately) travel to the past through your memory, and to go into the future through your imagination. If you are conscious enough and self-aware enough you can even imagine with a fair degree of accuracy what the future will be like. It is consciousness and self-awareness that puts you in touch with your soul. Your soul is who you really are.

Knowing who you really are permits you to have a soul mate who you love heart and soul. (John enjoys apple sauce cake because he loves Mrs. Heartbreak, heart and soul.)

Why this matters is because John is wondering if Billy Cudrup and Angel Cudrup are self-aware enough, and conscious enough, to know what they are doing. It is obvious to them, and to us, and to everyone, that they have strategies and plans for the future. They will say so themselves. But are these strategies and plans—time shares! End times! Endtimes Inc.!—derived from genuine self-awareness and consciousness? Can they travel to the past and to the future and then honestly attest to the rightness of now? Are they in love, and can they love?

It is possible that they are, and that they can.

The possibility that Billy and Angel are also honest, and believe that they are honest, has just crossed John's mind. Is it possible, he thinks, that they are merely delusional, but honest in their delusion, and are not the profound cynics and crass materialists that he and other Normal Christians and secular cynics think they are. Is it possible?

"No, John," Sharon said. "Such a possibility does not exist."

"What?"

"I've been reading your mind," she retorted. "It is an uncomfortable, chaotic, and frightening thing to read, but I have been doing it nevertheless. There is no—zero—nada—zip—possibility that Billy and Angel are merely misguided souls who aren't in it solely for the dough.

"You have a goofy, mile-wide streak of naivety common to poodles and socialists. You persist in expecting human beings to behave well, and for the betterment of all. It is an unattractive and counterproductive behavior in any person, but especially in an old person such as you."

"I don't know what to say. I think I'm offended."

"It is not my intention to offend you, John," she said, kindly. "But, jeepers, what am I supposed to think?

"Here we are," she continued. "I'm watching you drive twenty-five miles an hour in a fifty-five mile an hour zone. There are twenty-six enraged 2nd Amendment freaks stacked up behind you. I expect a bullet to come whizzing through the back window any minute.

"While I sit here—patiently, dagnabbit!—you've been off on a schizoid mental trip that has covered the sex lives of bachelors, a recipe for apple sauce cake, creepy, worn out musings on Dualism and the Mind Body controversy, and now...now...you want to give Little Billy Cudrup the benefit of your singular doubt.

"You, sir," she finished, "are a weak vessel."

"I may be a weak vessel, but I do have the common decency to stay out of other people's heads!"

"You're assuming I went there voluntarily."

John slowed the van. That means he dropped from twenty-five miles per hour to twenty-three miles per hour. Rednecks in the pick-up behind them started to throw empty beer cans at the back of the van. John glanced into the rearview mirror and gave a slight smile.

"I see what you mean," he answered, nodding. "But neither one of us is really in control of this book. You and I are mere literary devices."

"Not exactly," Dr. Sloan replied, hotly. "I do have a life, you know. I possess a library card, and have known associates! I'm a registered voter; I have relatives who are reading and commenting on my accidental appearance herein. I am more than a 'mere' literary device as you suggest."

John nodded.

"How are you on the whole Warrior Queen thing?" he asked.

Dr. Sloan nodded...slowly.

"I'm good with that," she said, evenly. "That part of the book rings true. I can see it."

"But, she continued, "I want my money back from Cudrup. That sapsucker owes me, and every other honest, hardworking American Taxpayer."

"What about the 'Saving Normal Christianity' part?"

"Let's just say we have mutual interests. How's that?"

"Fiacre believes in you, Sharon," John said, frowning. "I doubt that a man of his experience could badly misjudge another's character. He believes you to be not only a Warrior Queen, but a Noble Warrior Queen."

"Let's just play it by ear, John. Perhaps a miracle will occur and I'll become a raving Papist. As long as I get my money, well, 'Paris is worth a mass' as Henry V said."

John continued frowning, but increased his speed to thirty. The rednecks had started firing deer rifles into the air. They certainly looked discommoded.

John saw the entrance to Withered Plum up ahead. He would pull in there, and let the caravan of insane drivers go by.

"Withered Plum is an odd town," he said idly. "It certainly has a disheveled appearance."

Sharon nodded.

"If cleanliness is next to Godliness this must be Sodom and Gomorrah."

Chapter 17

John was used to Appalachian American ruffians hurling beverages at the back of his vehicle, and today was not the first time that those same ruffians, known within intimate family circles as Dear Uncle Dad or Dear Cousin Ma, had resorted to firearms to hurry him along the narrow, winding highways and byways of the rural Ozarks. No, John was not in the least bit flustered, although the same thing could not be said of Dr. Sloan. She was tightly gripping the van's door handle and hyperventilating a tad.

Although we have arrived in Withered Plum (and about time, too!) let's take a moment and catch our breath. The sentence in the paragraph above is 51 words long. Even if it were a well-written sentence, it would be judged challenging by modern teachers of composition. So, how are you doing? Okay?

The reason I ask is that, while a guy like Proust might natter on for 700 words—and Melville's sentences routinely topped 400 words— both Marcel and Herman are held in low regard by Rudolph Flesch, the principal author of the Flesch-Kincaid Reading Scale. Rudolph rates these boys at about 15 on a 100 point scale, which means they are VERY confusing, and maybe impossible, for most modern Americans to read (and understand) anymore. The Bible, by the way, averages 29, and this book is adhering to the biblical average. That means you're reading at the college level and are expected to handle sentences at least 51 words long. That's why I asked. In case you wanted to know.

BTW, John always had plenty of copies of Proust and Melville in the shop when he was a bookseller. He hardly ever sold any. But he is retired now and, if we are going to be honest—although I don't know why we should start now—Proust and Melville might as well be retired too. Pretty soon there won't be any copies at all.

Anyhoo, here we are in Withered Plum, Arkansas, with Withered Plum, Missouri and the gateway to the Endtimes Compound within sight.

Neither Withered Plum—whether Arkansas or Missouri—is much to write home about (apologies to Jim Long, a fine gardener and writer who lives near there). Thirty-six people and fourteen households comprise the population on the Arkansas side of the border. The Per Capita income is about $15,000 a year; consequently we can imagine that all 36 folks live on both sides of the track.

One hundred and twenty-nine people live on the Missouri side of town, and they have a Per Capita income of just over $14,000. One of the people who lives in Withered Plum (on the Arkansas side because Arkansas is an easier, funnier target than Missouri) is the fictional character Skidmore C Riley, who was invented by the pretty good writer Beaumont White.

Withered Plum, Missouri is located close to Branson, Missouri, the self-proclaimed Music Capital of the World. If you were a famous country western singer during the 1970s you are obligated to move to Branson after you kick your drug addiction, divorce wife or hubby number five, go bankrupt twice, and find Jesus on your 75th birthday. There, you will open a 'Music Theatre' and sell tickets to people named Maud and Orville. Maud and Orville will remember you as a young person and will quietly discuss how well you've aged while they stand in line, after the show, at the $3.99 all you can eat buffet.

Yes, I know. What a snooty boy Wisenheimer, you're thinking. Where does he get off, that NPR listening, Volvo driving, Negro voting, Book reading, Organic eating, Flesch-Kincaid scaling, Dim Squat?

Well, we—you, me, John, and Dr. Sharon Sloan— get off at Withered Plum, where Little Billy Cudrup and his bride Angel, the new and improved Donna Raye, got off in 2009, after a brief stay in Branson. How about that?

As John and Sharon cruise through Withered Plum, cruise through the last hundred yards of Arkansas, past the Stateline Café, and past the abandoned old school house to their left, John imagines what went through Billy's mind when he himself cruised down from Branson and first laid eyes on his future home.

What a tangled, complicated web Little Billy had woven since the days when he was growing up in Benton Harbor, Michigan, under the loving watch of Randy and Randi Cudrup. Did they know—did they know!—when they took Little Billy to see Oral Roberts—back in the day (1953!) when Oral was just a pup sweating and grunting and flailing his arms, WHIRLING his arms for the LORD in sawdust floored tents all over America—that Billy would see STARS and SEE his ordered path: GOD and SHOW BUSINESS!

Boy, did Billy follow that path. Here's a snapshot:

After graduating from Wowser Bible College in Benton Harbor, Michigan, in 1962, he and Donna Raye ran a kid's theatre on Rat Patterson's *86 Club*. In 1972 they went to California and started the Heavenly Broadcasting Network with Dan and Jan Sofa and starred (STARRED!) in a new variety show called *Lord be Praised*. After falling out with the Sofas, the Cudrups moved to Birmingham, Alabama and inaugurated the *LBP Club* and the LBP Television Network.

Imagine: from kiddie theatre to 24 hour a day Televangelism Impresario on 200 channels in only 15 years. Oral Roberts was envious; Jerry Falwell, Resting In Peace NOW but THEN still hustling, was covetous and bewildered. "How does he do it," he was heard to muse. "He wears high heeled shoes and eye make-up. What do people see in him?"

By the early 1980s Little Billy and Donna Raye were operating The Village—the 3rd most attended theme park in the United States after Disney Land and Disney World—and bringing in $2,000,000 dollars a week. Billy collected an annual $4,000,000 bonus on top of his salary—and he and Donna Raye bought a 10,000 square foot condo in South Florida. Donna bought Billy a rhino for his birthday; Billy bought Billy an aspiring hooker for $300,000. Life—Praise Jesus!— was good.

Vietnam was going on while Billy was carrying on. An old pal of John's, Jeff Dietrich wrote, back then, "On Sundays, the small [religious] community where I live gathers around the dining room table with bread and wine. We read the Gospel stories and celebrate a simple liturgy. In the context of our daily life in community, service, and resistance to the war, these stories and the liturgy come alive to me in a way that they never have in the high church environment of silken vestments, linen altar cloths, and smoky incense. I think of St. John of the Cross saying 'Where there is no love, put love, and you will find love,' and then I know, when it comes down to it, even on the natural plane, it is much happier and more enlivening to love than to be loved."

There are different kinds of Christians.

Jeff went to jail. He was arrested for pouring blood and oil on the steps of a US Federal building to protest the Gulf War, for cutting a fence around the Nevada Nuclear Test Site to protest nuclear weapons, for occupying the bell tower of the Los Angeles Cathedral to protest the Church's extravagant building projects, for blockading the toilets in City Hall to get port-a-potties for those who sleep on the streets, and for laying beneath the wheels of a dump truck to protest the destruction of a sleeping area for homeless men. In all he has been arrested over forty times.

Some years ago, as part of a court-ordered sentencing report, a federal probation office wrote, "Mr. Dietrich is a sixty-year old man who works in a skid row kitchen. He makes fifteen dollars a week and has no bank account or assets and is incapable of paying a fine.

"Over the years he has been arrested scores of times and seems undeterred by incarceration. It is my opinion that further incarceration of Mr. Dietrich would serve no purpose, and in fact, would be a waste of the government's resources."

Billy went to jail too. In 1987 he was convicted of three counts of mail fraud, twelve counts of wire fraud, and one count of conspiracy. Evangelist Farber Hall called Little Billy a liar, an embezzler, a sexual deviant, and the "greatest scab and cancer on the face of Christianity in 2,000 years of Church History." Farber went on to raise $10,000,000 to keep The Village Theme Park solvent and even installed a spectacular water slide.

There are different kinds of criminals.

Although Billy had been sentenced to 25 years in prison and ordered to pay a $400,000 fine, another judge, while upholding the rightness of the convictions, reduced Billy's sentence to six years and allowed Billy out of the slammer in 1992. Billy's Federal Bureau of

Prisons (BOP) number is 666-666-666-0 (just in case you ever need it).

The people defrauded by The Village time share scam—on average $1,000—each received $3.40 as the result of the class-action suit.

Donna Raye sued Billy for divorce (the slut!) in March of 1992, and she married Roger F., formerly Billy's best friend. She died on June 6th, 2009—just about the time that Little Billy and Angel arrived in Withered Plum—the day after she appeared on *Larry King Live* to announce her death, scheduled for the next day. Whatever else we can say about her, Donna was a show biz super trooper right to the end.

And let me say it again: here we are—you, me, John, Sharon, and Billy and Angel—in Withered Plum.

How about that.

Chapter 18

During the time Dr. Sloan lived in Germany, a time annoyingly referred to as 'The Lost Years' by friends and family, she had fallen into German Habits and required frequent intravenous injections of fatty acids and cholesterol. Consequently:

"I'm feeling peckish," she said. 'It is past noon and I would enjoy a bit of strudel and an espresso. How about it?"

John nodded.

The chance of finding 'a bit of strudel and an espresso' in Withered Plum was as likely as finding purity of heart at Goldman Sachs, or functional brain cells in the Arkansas State Legislature. Never the less:

"How about the State Line Café?" he suggested. "We're within eleven seconds of arrival."

Dr. Sloan nodded.

Over chicken fried steak and lukewarm Dr. Pepper, Dr. Sloan queried John about his fitness for the task ahead. As a Social Scientist—not a real doctor—Dr. Sloan was at least as interested in the theoretical and artistic dimensions—the Gestalt, if you will—of the matters before hand, as she was in the mere application of the theory. Fandangoing was all well and good, but she required that the fandango function as a far-reaching Statement, and not simply result in denting Little Billy's balding pate.

In *la' Affaire Cudrup*, the Statement must serve not only the punkstering interests of Dr. Sloan herself, but the fiduciary interests of the American Taxpayer as well. In a nutshell—and what other hackneyed, over-used cliché serves so well?—the statement had to be

104

worth $6,000,000, plus the nearly $1,100,000 it had cost taxpayers to try, imprison, and parole Pastor Cudrup.

Sloan was no stranger to Statements, and spectacular ones at that. During the Lost Years she had, in typical Germanic fashion, acquired a taste not only for strudel, but also for the finely honed turn of phrase, the well-turned ankle of language gloriously fitted into explication both neat and crafted. Imagine then, her distress at appearing in this book (of all books!), and at reading the sentence just before this one. Yes, John is certainly a weak vessel and, very likely, a poor source for the manufacture of spectacular Statements.

Among the Statements kicking around in her head just now—kapow!—are Descartes' *'Cogito ergo sum'*, Niccolo Machiavelli's, 'I desire to go to Hell and not Heaven. In Hell I will enjoy the company of popes, kings and princes. Heaven is full of poor people and boring beggars, monks, and Apostles', and the Yippie Abbie Hoffman's "Never Trust anyone over thirty!" Kapow!

Would a Strong Statement, a Memorable Phrase, emerge from her encounter with Cudrup and his Endtimes Minions? Could the retired bookseller John Heartbreak be relied upon to help facilitate the making of such a Statement?

Looking at him now, stuffing gravy into his slowly masticating mouth, Sharon was not sure. There was nothing about his placid, elderly face that inspired confidence; he shuffled when he walked, he talked to himself, and he bumped into things. Was there a clumsier man in all of Arkansas? And the deafness! Talking to him was like conversing with a lilac bush…

…and the fact that he habitually discussed the ins and outs of his day with dead people, among them purported time travelers, was disconcerting, to say the least. And what was she to make of this Fiacre Business, and the whole, warped 'saving Normal Christianity' agenda? If the Strong Statement emerging from the upcoming confrontation became simply a headline in the *Carroll County News*, 'Local Social Scientist Poor Guardian of Vulnerable Adult,' she would become a laughingstock among friends and family; the Lost Years in Germany would certainly be forgotten and subsumed by The Nutty Years in Berryville. She could hear her niece Talia laughing now.

"John," she began, tentatively. "We haven't exactly worked out the details of our little expedition. I'm wondering if you have a plan in mind. So far we've identified mutual interests; you want to save Normal Christianity, and I want to locate my $6,000,000—and counting. But how, exactly, are we going to do those things?"

John nodded.

So like a Ph.D., he thought. Good with Grand Visions and Noble Thoughts but, when it came down to the nitty gritty, the actual in-the-trenches 'Fire when ready, Gridley' stuff, then by golly it was, 'Oh by the WAY, John, WHAT did YOU have in mind?' time. He smiled a generous smile and patted her hand.

So like a D.O.R.K., she thought. What a condescending, middleclass twit. Good with bromides and platitudes but, when it came down to the hard work of thinking, then by golly it was 'Oh by the WAY, Sharon, let's SAVE Normal Christianity while YOU punk Little Billy for spare change', time. She smiled and pulled her hand away.

"Let's play it by ear," he said. "We've got Mrs. Heartbreak's White Chevy Van, and we're on a

Mission from God. All we need is half a pack of Chesterfields. We've got nothing to worry about."

That sounded familiar. And not particularly comforting.

"So, no. You don't have a plan."

"Let's say that I've got the idea of a plan," he said, confidently. Why not speak to Sharon in the language of an Academic, he thought? Mollify her a bit?

"Perhaps we should develop a preparatory Strong Statement as a guiding principle?" he said. "Something along the lines of, 'Kill a Commie for Christ' which, while not particularly edifying, was effective enough to secure billions of Military Industrial Complex Cold War Moolah—*and* keep the John Birch Society in business for decades."

Dr. Sloan nodded thoughtfully. Perhaps the Boy Dunder was on to something? "Hmmn," she mused.

"It is possible that a Strong Statement could attract reinforcements. Say like, some of your church buddies?"

"Church buddies?"

"Yeah. Surely, they're interested in saving Normal Christianity, aren't they? I mean, how about that old Nazi, Ratzinger? Could we count on him?"

"Are you referring to His Holiness, Pope Benedict XVI? I hardly think referring to him as 'an old Nazi,' is much of an invitation."

"That's the guy! How about him?"

"I'm afraid the Vatican is run by a new man these days. Francis is now Pope. A moderate. Not a Nazi."

"Well, how about the Episcopalians or the Presbyterians? Methodists? Congregationalists? Any of the Mainline folks?"

John shook his head. He looked dubious.

"I guess we could ask them," he said. "Although, I have to admit that it is a mystery to me why Mainline denominations have abandoned Evangelism, and allowed themselves to be co-opted by the Billy Cudrups' of the world, and Shake Rattle & Roll denominations."

"The absence of the Mainline on every important issue today—the Gulf War, the widening income gap between social classes, immigration—is shocking. Almost incomprehensible, really. It feels like they've forgotten Christ and are afraid to live and preach His message."

"I suppose then, that that means, no, you can't rely on them to help us save Normal Christianity, and I can't rely on them to help me get my dough?"

John smiled.

"No, oh Noble Warrior Queen. We can't rely on them. We'll have to rely on ourselves."

"Gotcha."

Chapter 19

Fiacre has been amused by the conversation between the Warrior Queen Sloan and the retired bookseller Heartbreak. He appreciated Dr. Sloan's amusingly quixotic ambition to possess or repossess Taxpayer assets from the Cudrup Person, and he was gratified by John's passionate embrace of the challenge to save Normal Christianity.

The truth of the matter is that Fiacre judges both endeavors as approximately silly, about as consequential as his own hopeful desire that God might rethink the eating habits of squash bugs, and direct the little bug(ger)s toward the common dandelion, and away from zucchinis. Wouldn't that be cool?

There would, of course, be an unintended consequence of such Godly rethinking. From time to time, as in the case of squash bugs, Fiacre indulges in a bit of intelligent design argumentation, and deludes himself into imagining that the Universe is a watch, and that God is the Watchmaker. Obviously, he thinks, the intricate workings of a watch requires the skills and intentions of an intelligent designer to make it tick and tock, and as with a watch, the complexity of X or Y or Z—an organ or organism, or the solar system and the Entire Universe Itself—necessitates an Intelligent Designer. Surely, God could tweak The Watch a bit and redirect the pest in question without causing another Ice Age?

But Fiacre knows that Darwin—knew Darwin, actually—put the Watchmaker idea to bed to nearly everyone's satisfaction. Of course, and as you certainly know and probably think about often, perhaps even ceaselessly, there is the whole Infinite Monkey

Theorem to deal with, to say nothing of Hume and that tiresome busybody Richard Dawkins.

But it feels good to revisit an elegant old argument, even if it is flawed, and that's mostly why he had foisted the Save Normal Christianity strategy back onto John; Human beings almost always require a lighted path to follow if you want them to get anything done, and this one had predictably—but elegantly too—done the trick (Ha Ha).

The beauty of it all, Fiacre thought, was Sharon Sloan's consternation and confusion about Heartbreak's sudden and unexpected descent into delusion. She had imagined a mostly fun filled adventure focused on polishing Little Billy's bald head with an emery cloth, and perhaps delivering a Fake $6,000,000 Demand Note in front of his television audience.

But no.

Heartbreak had begun hearing voices, had accepted a Mission from God, and believed he was under the protection of the Patron Saint of Gardeners—who was not only a duly appointed representative of that Great Whore of Babylon—the Roman Catholic Church—but who, John also believed, was a sentient Time Traveler presently and physically located in the Community Garden behind that little white church he went to. *Mon Dieu!*

Fiacre laughed. He had punked the Grand Mistress of Punk and, Coming to a Chapter Near You Soon! would reveal himself to her in all his 7th Century glory. Sometimes it is just so neat to be me, he thought.

He walked over to the short row of apples trees that John had planted three springs ago. They had looked just awful for most of the summer—covered with rust and nearly leafless—and could do with a bit of rain and cooler weather. Fiacre took a leaf between his thumb and forefinger and carefully rubbed it back and forth. The little tree snapped straight toward the sky and apples appeared on several of its spindly branches. Yup, he thought, it is definitely neat to be me.

During the Enlightenment there had been about 7,000 varieties of apples in Europe and North America. Today, there are only about 90. Fiacre was not sure of what the number of Chinese and Middle Eastern varieties had been then, or now, for that matter. But he thought they must be fewer too.

Conversely, there are 38,000 Christian denominations active today in the 21st Century. Every century, people have added about two thousand seven hundred fourteen Christian denominations—since Fiacre had lived in the 7th Century—when there had been one. Among Berryville's seven Baptist churches is a Primitive Baptist church which, by itself is divided into the Predestination Baptists, Old-School Baptists, Regular Baptists, Particular Baptists, and the Hardshell Baptists. Fiacre couldn't help thinking that it would be a better world with fewer denominations and more varieties of apples.

Fiacre was impressed by the First Christian Church's little garden. It was nearly weed- free and the soil looked rich and productive. He noticed with approval that the tomatoes and peppers looked particularly robust, and the okra, a slimy modern invention in his view, at least produced spectacular stocks and beautiful blooms. The First Christians, at least some of them, knew how to grow food.

Mrs. Hudspeth, perhaps the most knowledgeable of the gardeners, had focused on flower production, and the garden was riotous with color, bees, and butterflies. Fiacre knew that John did most of his praying while he worked in the garden, and it was easy to see why that was so. God's presence was there for everyone to observe (except of course, for the annoying metaphysicians and pantheists among you; roughly 13% of Americans), especially as manifested by color and smell and the soil's fecundity. John was thusly and particularly susceptible to conversational interludes with dead writers and angels because of these smells and blushes and farragoes of insects and birds.

If there had been, for John, a thorn among the roses, it was the former Garden Manager, young Kari Keever. This person, who had attended Berryville High School (BHS) but who also habitually and simply referred to the high school, simply as BS, had been a stern task master and a meddlesome stickler about adhering to and maintaining organic production standards. Consequently, the First Christian Church's Community Garden was an *organic garden.*

As a veteran of a foreign war that took place mostly in a jungle, John was an admirer of napalm, both for its efficiency and for the dazzling light show it produced upon impact, and so he was inclined to live better through chemistry. Young Keever, however, had different ideas and because John was afraid of her—as he was of most women—John carefully toed the organic line, even now, long after Kari had fled Berryville for the rarified air of college. Fiacre, however, was himself an organic gardener and thus and consequently solidly in Kari's court.

Kari was, John remembered, that most annoying of adolescents, a studious over-achiever who got your obscure but incorrect references to Tolkien or T.S. Eliot (and corrected them), was well-groomed and respectful toward adults (except to John), and who also worked hard and did what she said she would do. These ordinarily admirable traits, especially in one so young, were annoying because you knew she knew that most adults are full of it—but is too polite to say so. One also hopes to be admired in return by such a fine person—and it was extremely annoying when you were uncertain of what her opinion might be.

John's role in the garden—a role which Fiacre knew that John hoped to pass on to him—Ha Ha—had been to be Kari's Yard Boy. If something needed watering or weeding or winnowing—any W serves here—Kari would inform John of the need and expect him to respond appropriately and cheerfully. John thought that Fiacre could—would—seamlessly assist him in the same way.

John excelled in his Yard Boy role. After all, he had had decades of training by an expert—Mrs. Heartbreak—and now that he is retired his occupation is listed as Factotum. 'Lift that Bale, Tote that Barge' was a tune that John was most familiar with. But John is getting older and he would like a little help taking up the slack.

Fiacre eavesdropped in on Sharon and John's conversation at the State Line Café in Withered Plum while he inspected the garden in Berryville. Dr. Sloan continued to focus on the money—'show me the money!'—she was shouting at John while John nodded placidly and hummed.

"Perhaps you're familiar with Watchman Nee," he was saying (again!) to Sharon.

Fiacre was familiar with Nee and fundamentally agreed with him—that there should be only one church per town. After all, there was only one God, right?

The disputatiousness of modern Christians was a continuing surprise to Fiacre despite his nearly 14 centuries of human observation. He understood that people would have disagreements about what was and wasn't a sin, but when you got down to it, there really weren't all that many sins to fret and argue about. What, about 10, right?

What was all the Hub Bub about?

Much of the problem, as Fiacre saw it at least, was the American tendency to achieve perfection—and then try and improve on it by making it a money making proposition. Billy Cudrup was a good example—which we'll get to, by and by—and guys like Joel Osteen, who assures his flock that God wants them to have money, fame, power, and multiple orgasms. Not only does belief in Christ mean eternal salvation and everlasting life at the Right Hand of God but, according to Joel, double coupons and that cute blond on the cheerleading squad. Talk about prosperity!

Fiacre had holed up at the Motel 6 in Eureka Springs before coming to Berryville. He watched the Trinity Broadcasting Network the whole time and logged in about 30 hours with Joel in between times dodging the maid. She kept coming into the room to turn the TV off and, since she couldn't see Fiacre concluded that the room was haunted after eight failed attempts. After that, Fiacre was not disturbed.

What Fiacre learned from Joel was that an awful lot of blonds live in Houston and about 17,000 of them go to Joel's church every Sunday morning. Imagine: Joel preached a sermon to that many people—and never mentioned Jesus Christ. Fiacre came away from each sermon wishing he had the names of Joel's broker and barber.

What was it that Joel said to all those people? It might as well have been 'God is dead and my hair looks great' for all that it mattered. It reminded Fiacre of a sermon he heard Father Devine give back in the 1940s: 'God is not only personified and materialized. He is

114

repersonified and rematerialized. He rematerialized and He rematerialates. He rematerialates and He is rematerializatable. He repersonificates and He repersonifitizes.' Wow, huh?

Fiacre looked over the squash plants. They looked pretty miserable, and were covered with borers. Fiacre knew that even he wouldn't be able to do much with them. God can be so unreasonable sometimes.

Chapter 20

John stepped out of the Stateline Café while Dr. Sloan paid for their chicken fried steak and Dr. Pepper. Herman Melville was leaning against Mrs. Heartbreak's van, a dyspeptic look on his face.

"Who's that gal, you're hanging around with?"

"The artist and scholar formerly known as Sharon Sloan," John replied. "She won't appreciate your calling her a gal, by the way."

"Modern gal, is she?"

"In the sense that Louisa May Alcott is a modern gal, Herman. She's a bit of a transcendentalist but with Baptist antecedents. A Texan, actually."

"Good God."

"Exactly. Everyone has a row to hoe and some rows are harder than others. She has, however, taken to Arkansas like a duck to water, and that unfortunate Texas braggadocio diminishes by the hour. She is a good egg in my view."

"You have fowl on the brain, sir. Ducks. Eggs. I'm embarrassed to be a party to such dialogue. If I'd written such dribble I'd have starved to death."

John was too polite to point out to Melville that starvation would have been the likely result if the Melville family depended on Herman's literary income for survival. Instead, he said, agreeably, "There are a number of disadvantages to appearing in this novel. Hackneyed dialogue is certainly one of them, and the extravagance of run on sentences and verb-noun disagreements are three and four. The list of disadvantages goes, frankly up to a hundred and four— and counting.

"But I have no control over what, or how, the Authorial I writes," John continued. "Yes, I admit to being embarrassed by my appearance herein, and doubly embarrassed by the book's postmodern construction and points of view. But what can I do? Surely you can see that we are both victims of circumstance?"

Melville sighed. "It is a sorry set of circumstances that brought me to Arkansas. Look at this place," he grumbled. "If this dump was in New England the Governor would declare a state emergency and seek Federal funds."

"If you step this way," John said, pointing to a patch of dirt about a yard north of where Melville was standing, "you'll be in Missouri. The 'Show Me' state."

Melville sighed again and slouched even lower against the van's hood. Then:

"What are you doing here, John? What has brought you and the artist and scholar formerly known as Sharon Sloan to such a low place?"

"We're here to Save Normal Christianity," John said, forthrightly. "The Warrior Queen Sloan and I are in route to Endtimes Church to confront the Televangelist Billy Cudrup and the new Donna Rayee, Angel. A 'Mission from God' actually."

Herman's eyebrows lifted, questioning and surprised:

"You ain't exactly Ahab, John, but I admire an Odyssey, and epics of all kinds. I see that you see America as a holy place and as eschatology rather than a mere nation. I also like the sound of 'Saving Normal Christianity.' It resonates with my transcendental roots but confirms America—including even Arkansas!—as a New Jerusalem, the setting for final salvation, and for its people, who have rejected the Old World (Old

Europe, I think secretary Rumsfeld called it) and are determined to create a New World. America, in their eyes—in our eyes, John!—has a sacred mission to fulfill biblical prophesies!

"There are many arguments to persuade us that our Glorious Lord will have a Holy City in America," Melville recited, recalling Cotton Mather's 1790 sermon, *'God's City: America.'* "A City," he continued, "the streets whereof shall be pure gold."

John was gratified to see Melville so animated. Usually, the old seafarer had sailed so far out into the Slough of Despond that it was impossible not to be similarly afflicted. But now, he absolutely radiated cheerfulness.

"Your endeavor reminds me of what I wrote in *White Jacket*," he continued. "We Americans are a peculiar chosen people, the Israel of our time; God has predestined great things from our race, and great things we feel in our souls!"

Melville was just winding up. He was about to say that the Puritans were also on a Mission from God, charged with creating a new society and a new church that would fulfill His plan for the human race—but Dr. Sloan exited the Stateline Café, toothpick in mouth, and said, rather rudely John thought, "You're mumbling John! Most unattractive!"

Melville shrugged and slipped back into the van and the copy of *Billy Budd* that John kept stashed in the glove box. He had to tolerate Lizzie, his intolerable wife, but he was not commanded to tolerate other orders of female.

Sharon smiled. "I think I've come up with a Strong Statement. One that will cause a grand rallying around the Anti-Cudrup flag."

"And…"

"Taxpayers, for Christ's Sakes!" she said, loudly. "I think it's a pretty neat synthesis of both our aims. Whaddaya think?"

John did not nod. True, it succinctly captured the cruel spirit of the country's mood, but he had been hoping for a more elevated statement along the lines of say, well, 'Saving Normal Christianity One Normal Christian at a Time.'

He said so and was treated to a lot of Jerry Colonna and Marty Feldman type eye rolling. Since both of these guys are dead, and you don't know who they are anyway, let me just say that Sharon mimicked them to mock John in a particularly mean-spirited way. And, of course, it is fun to think of Sharon imitating these guys—so let's just leave it at that. Okay?

"Are you done?" John asked. "Could we discuss the idea rationally?"

"Sure," she said sarcastically. "As soon as you define 'normal Christian' for me."

John was stunned. He and Sharon had known one another for several years now, and she knew him to be a practicing and happy Christian. He had even invited her to attend services at the First Christian Church with a degree of sincerity and resolve that had almost (but not quite) effected the deal. Wasn't it a certainty that he, John Heartbreak, in the flesh, was an exemplar of the Normal Christian? Was he not the archetype from which she could draw the firmest conclusion?

Dr. Sloan shook her head. "I know what you're thinking, John. You think you're a normal Christian and that you're the normal or near normal example sufficient to the cause. Am I right?"

John nodded. (If you're keeping track, this is the 18th time John has nodded. That's less than once a chapter, so I don't think I'm over-using it; it is neither an exhausted transitional device, nor simply a sign of creative exhaustion. Besides which, let's also keep in mind the fact that Heartbreak, while a good enough bookseller and outstanding at yard maintenance, is essentially a dull human being with a limited repertoire of expressions and, moreover, is more or less, certainly more than less, emotionally constricted and inherently rhythm-less. All this nodding business then is, strictly speaking, consistent with his character. Personally, I wish—as I'm sure you wish—that he was handsomer, richer, more famous, and more inclined to action hero antics. If he was it would certainly make for a more interesting book. But: you dance with the one you brung. So:

Sharon laughed, but not unkindly. She knows that if Mrs. Heartbreak hadn't rescued John from the Horse Latitudes of the early 80s, he would be living in rural Iowa, hoeing a Trappist cornfield, looking unattractive in a dirty calve length nightshirt, brown. The Trappist's loss was Mrs. Heartbreak's marginal gain, but the impact on Christianity as a whole was surely nominal, and on its normality completely unknown.

His habit of talking with angels, and his belief that the Holy Spirit was a frequent tourist to Berryville, also separated him from the town's average Christian on the Street. Sure, many of them could be counted on to witness to the presence of both while under the influence of high caliber ecclesiastical horseplay at Wednesday night services, but they would drop dead in fright or enroll in a psychiatric bin if the Holy Ghost appeared in the passenger seats of their cars on Thursday morning to discuss, as he frequently did with John, the fortunes of the Minnesota Twins.

John was also of the opinion that Lucifer was no more than a spectacular failure, a fallen and therefore unsuccessful angel. Why be so afraid of such a Big Loser? Yet preacher after preacher, church after church, Christian after Christian, poured enormous time and energy into making Christianity a never ending celebration of Halloween. So focused were they on the Devil and Hell that they scarcely had time for Christ or Heaven.

These signs are the minimal degrees of separation between John and the majority of other Christians in Berryville, Carroll County, Arkansas, the United States, and the World. There are other signs, of course, perhaps too numerous to count, but these will suffice for now.

Sharon believes that the rise of televangelists and of fundamentalist deniers of science and philosophy and art and Christ's command to love one another is due to the average American Christian's Cosmic Blondness, and to the fact that his material goods are the sole fixed point, the sole incontestable value amidst the uncertainties of life, that he really believes in.

John does not, insofar as Dr. Sloan can see it, fit into that normal mold. If he is to Save Normal Christianity it will probably have to be done without the aid of Normal Christians.

Naturally, the burden will fall to her. Isn't that just the way it always is!

Chapter 21

Dr. Sloan and John simultaneously reached for the handles of Mrs. Heartbreak's van—to get into it and toddle along the last three hundred yards to Endtimes—when the chicken scented air of Withered Plum erupted with the roar of penis augmentation devices. Sharon and John clamped hands over ears and turned to stare dully at a large crowd of paunchy, late-middle aged cases of arrested development, passing through town. They were undoubtedly on their way to Eureka Springs for the bi-monthly Annual Blues, Bikes, and Beer Festival.

Each member of this unsightly, noisy crowd sported an important black T-Shirt bearing a slogan. John read 'Rehab is for Quitters' and 'If you can read this the Bitch fell off' between blinks. Ah, America, John thought: inventor of Prozac and Viagra, expensive orthodontia and Fankenberries, boob jobs and competitive cheerleading. Only here would authentic low-lives riding their only asset be so democratically synthesized into a pack comprised of suburban accountants and insurance salesmen (excuse me, Estate Planning Executives) playing dress-up.

John recalled Matthew Arnold's worry that 'America will rule the world by their energy, but they will deteriorate it by their low ideas and want of culture.' John wondered what Arnold, who might justly be called the bridge between Romanticism and Modernism, would make of the parading bikesters. The hilarious meat of Arnold's observation would certainly fill the yawning gap of time falling between *Easy Rider* and the Marketplace Swashbucklers passing by. Within that gap would be James Dobson and Gore Vidal,

Kenneth Copeland and Noam Chomsky, Ted Kaczynski and Glen Beck, Susan Sontag and Kathryn Kuhlman, yowling cheek by jowl in harmony, each and every mother's son and daughter conjoined in grief over the destruction of civilization as we know it.

Yes, they fill the gap with song: the left-wingers, of shaking the dust off their Birkenstocks of the ravening consequences of the Free Market, of the stupidity of global warming deniers, and of religious fundamentalists everywhere. And there is the conservative counterpoint: yodelers of bourgeois mediocrity undermining the classical virtues and turning us into comfort loving, irreligious consumers and hedonists; hear the hum of freelance pessimists on both sides denouncing the latest vacuous realm of unreality: wasteful government spending, lack of government spending, over regulation, under regulation, the sanctity of marriage, the guarantees of the Constitution and Bill of Rights, the...Mathew Arnold's gap is wide and aromatic with the stink of complaint.

The underlining hilarity of the moment, John thought, was that the racketing procession of Harley Davidsons was made possible and even acceptable, by the Puritans and the Protestant Reformation. These merry noise makers were simply expressing their individuality, their triumph over the darkness of mere authority, and their pride in personal freedom. They might belong to—probably belonged to—a church back home that roundly condemns *On the Origin of the Species* and all that it entails, but is otherwise faithfully committed to Social Darwinism.

Puritan leadership—the Cotton, Mather, and Winthrop families—insisted that personal witnessing and individual, private salvation, were the signs of the genuine Christian. This viewpoint is comprehensively covered in a sermon delivered by John Cotton on January 19th, 1637 and further explained with his issuing of '16 points of clarification'. This was met with *'An Elders' Reply'* clarifying the matter even further and, running true to the Protestant experience, resulted in an additional 82 clarifying points later that year.

While we can be certain that Increase, John, and Cotton Mather would roll over in their graves at the sound of Sinatra singing *'I did it my way'* or learning that 90% of Americans have 'high-self-esteem' (you other 10%: God, what losers you are!) they would not deny that individualism itself is the offspring of the Reformation.

Consequently, subsequently, and therefore, that's why Dr. Sloan and John now observe a mostly tubby parade of freely-expressing Estate Planers playing dress-up on high powered machines in the beautiful Arkansas Ozarks. They have the money and the God-Given Right to be as dorky as they want to be, and screw you if your elitist values are appalled by the noise and the narcissism of the moment.

Chapter 22

John and Sharon got into Mrs. Heartbreak's van, and Sharon buckled up as John switched on the key. The long parade of bikers finally ended. John cranked his body around to see if anyone else was behind him. His neck was barely mobile; it had begun to fuse up with age and even small acts of observation like looking left and right involved twisting his waist, followed by much huffing and puffing from the expended energy. Sharon began to feel like a hostage; she made a note to never be John's passenger again.

A large and spanking new Winnebago bearing Iowa license plates rolled through Withered Plum and slowly passed the rear of the van. From John's contorted position he was able to read the Iowa State motto on the plate—'I Brake for Hogs'—and a bumper sticker with 'In Case of Rapture this Car is Driverless.'

Because John was wondering why people felt compelled to publish gibberish and rude sayings on flat but unlikely surfaces, he missed seeing the driver. It was Clara Jane Staley, also known as Clara Jane Smith *ne'* Clara Rinker, in casual flight from her home in Forrest City, Iowa, where she and her husband, retired FBI Agent Orin Staley, owned a Winnebago dealership.

Had John seen her, he would have been delighted. When Clara Jane lived in Berryville—gosh, what, five years ago?—she had engineered and delivered a successful plan to reconstitute the legions of dour and tightfisted Iowa based tourists—who visited the Ozarks during the off season to take advantage of the discounts on hotel rooms in Eureka Springs—into consumers, with the happy result of a significant increase in purchases of dollar books at Heartbreak's Pretty Good Books and Really Dread Coffee.

John believed that Clara Jane's success was due to the intervention of the Holy Ghost, Who had begun appearing to John, off and on that spring and summer, wearing a Wartburg College sweatshirt and short shorts. The matter of the shorts stuck in John's mind long after the event because the HG's knees were visibly double-jointed, and His legs were really (really) hairy. John also remembered how delighted the HG was by Clara Jane's leading the group of Iowans he'd commanded to appear on the Berryville Town Square in a stirring rendition of that old hymn, 'In Heaven There is No Beer.' Memorable events indeed, friends.

These exciting happenings and the aftermath are completely told in the book *Coffee with John Heartbreak: a Mostly True Story of Berryville*, Arkansas, available at www.Amazon.com and better bookstores everywhere. It is sufficient to say here, however, that John and Clara Jane had a productive, reciprocal, and warm friendship. He had missed her when she had moved to Forrest City with Agent Staley.

I suppose, if you have been paying attention to the four paragraphs above this one—where I introduced you to Clara Jane and gave a brief summary of her and John's relational highpoints—that you're thinking that I have complicated our story by bringing Clara Jane into it.

You have no idea.

Let me go over the back story as quickly as possible, even as I assure you that the details are necessary: it makes possible our understanding of how Clara Jane and the Warrior Queen Sloan will become mortal enemies, conspire each to do away with the other, and in a thrilling, novelistic climax, wrestle at the high sharp edge of a precipice—in a scene so similar to the one Conan Doyle penned about Holmes' final duel with Professor Moriarty that it seems stolen (so, of course it is). (PS, this is BS; none of this will happen). (Just so you know). (Well. Maybe it will. Stay tuned).

Clara Jane was born Clara Rinker in the little town of Tisdale, Missouri. Her upbringing, social class, and geographical location (20 miles NW of Withered Plum), had made her a fully vetted Appalachian American at birth. As Lyle Lovett would sing, a *'Redneck Woman.'* Needless to say—but let me say it anyway—she fit into Berryville as seamlessly as a Tim LaHaye novel fits into the mind of a Schizophrenic Conspiracy Theorist. So:

Clara Jane is five feet four inches tall, give or take a couple of inches. She weighs 130 pounds, give or take five pounds, and is exactly thirty-five years old, give or take five years. She is an occasional brunette, sometimes a blond, but never a redhead unless you count strawberry blond as redheads. She wears glasses although her vision is 20-20. When she is not AWOL from her husband and driving a Winnebago Motor Home (not the Winnie-Minnie but the Big Expensive one), she drives a Toyota Camry or, when she previously lived in Berryville, that most non-descript of automobiles, an aging Ford Taurus. She is, if you get my drift, an expert at being and not being: now you see her. Now you don't.

Although Clara Jane is completely real to John Heartbreak, neither of us can be sure that she is real—in the strict sense of real. But than, what is? Is John real? Is Ishmael real? Is the Bible's Abraham and Isaac real? No, no, maybe you say. What they all have in common is that they are in books. They all have a creator (Creator) and at least one of them thinks exactly like his

Creator (creator) wants him to think. And because he thinks, well, *Cogito ergo su*—especially since she herself feels unreal at times.

But John can see her. That's good enough for him and, isn't it good enough for you too? Five four—give or take an inch, dishwater blond, funny eyeglasses? BIG Winnebago. Pretty in a sort of indefinable way. You can see her, right? Oh. Clara Jane is also a serial killer. Did I forget to mention that?

Or, as John will tell you, Clara Jane is a retired serial killer. When she first came to Berryville, she and John ran into each other at the Evil Retail Giant. John was buying a pair of socks—get this people: there is only ONE retail outlet in the entirety of Carroll County where you can buy a pair of socks!—and Clara Jane was testing the comparative tensile strength of a couple of bowie knife knock-offs back at the gun counter. She knew that indentation hardness correlates linearly with tensile strength for most steels, and hardness testing is a fairly economical substitute for...oh. You don't care. Okay, then.

So...Clara Jane was buying a knife and happened to see John staring at her in recognition. John, an inveterate reader of John Sanford mysteries, instantly knew who she was despite (in spite of?) her see me, no see me regalia. She, recognizing his recognition, immediately began planning how to kill him— defenestration was a favorite method, but since there are no windows in Berryville big enough, or buildings high enough, to make defenestration practical, she settled on the most economical tensile strength test of all (sticking) and chose the off brand bowie knife (Chinese, but it was nearly $20 cheaper, can you believe!) to do John in.

Clara Jane was about to move in for the kill when she was uncharacteristically disarmed by his directly approaching her with the offer of employment. He had some pesky, cheapskate Iowans to deal with, you see.

Here's where it gets complicated.

Clara Jane assumed that John's job offer—help me get rid of these Iowans!—involved killing them. While it is true that John had briefly considered that maximum option, the book in which this whole mess is thoroughly described is also handicapped by a NO SEX, NO VIOLENCE and NO STRONG LANGUAGE (NSNVNSL) clause, thus mitigating that satisfying but ultimately Legion of Decency disallowing opportunity.

How frustrating, she'd thought at the time. Since her first killing, let's see, she was seventeen and had whacked Besom Slider with a hatchet, Clara Jane had killed twenty nine men and three women by various means, including that old favorite, defenestration. That would make a yearly average of 1.88 dead ones and, with all that practice, she'd gotten really good at it. Too bad, so sad, that John hadn't permitted her to boost her average a tad!

This account may lead you to think that Clara Jane is a bad person. To her credit, the folks she'd 'hit' would make nearly everyone's short list for elimination. Besom Slider, for example…well, considering the NSNVNSL clause, I can't tell you why Besom deserved to die…but he did. And so it was with each of the other 31 people Clara Jane laid to rest; they had spent their lives victimizing mostly defenseless people and, if you are an eye for eye sort of person, or a Dirty Harry, Charles Bronson, Dexter, Quentin Tarantino fan well, there you have all the justification you—and Clara Jane—need.

John's, and subsequently Clara Jane's problem, was that Iowans didn't really qualify for the death penalty. True, they were tightfisted and self-righteous and Lutheran to the core and wouldn't pay full price for a book even if it was a church approved copy of the *Kama Sutra*. And though nearly all of them had grown wealthy on Corn Welfare from Uncle Sugar and were (are) the First Cause of why 80% of your diet (no kidding—you can look it up) contains corn (which is why Americans are obese), those facts by themselves didn't really meet Pitch from a High Window Criteria. So, how were they to change the disgraceful behavior of Iowa Tourists?

Ultimately John and Clara Jane opted for a SHAZAM-like, miracle based strategy that worked okay (just okay), but had the unforeseen and unintended consequence of causing Clara Jane to reform and become a Methodist. Yes, she followed the advice Walter Scott developed and did the old Five Finger Exercise: she found faith, repented, confessed her faith, was baptized, and began living the Christian life.

John and Mrs. Heartbreak had been hopeful that Clara Jane would choose their church, the First Christian Church Disciples of Christ, as her home church. But Clara Jane had, like so many new Christians, gone church shopping. After weeks of observing the local vicars, she picked the First Methodist Church of Berryville. Clara Jane knew that the Methodists were Arkansas Razorbacks fans and thus, soft on felons, and she felt reassured that the expansiveness of the Methodist's parking lot would facilitate quick getaways on the off chance that such need would arise.

Clara Jane stayed in Berryville after the successful Iowa Tourist Miracle. It was a safe town to hide out in—who would believe that a serial killer would live in Berryville, Arkansas?—and in no time at all she was tightly woven in the fabric of the Community. She kept a tidy yard on Pritchard Street right across from where John and Mrs. Heartbreak lived, opened an 'Iowa Welcome Center' on the Town Square with support from the local Merchants' Association (thank you, Melinda Large, and all you Merchants!), and like most residents, shopped at the Evil Retail Giant an average of 3.5 times a week.

As she became more and more real, at least as real as anyone in Berryville is real, she met and fell in love with Orin Staley, an agent of the Federal Bureau of Investigation assigned to the Ozarks for the purpose of guarding Beaver Dam from terrorists who might be vacationing in the area. What cock-up had caused the Agent's tenure in the Berryville area is not known, but soon after falling head over heels for Clara Jane, he retired from the Bureau, married her at the First Methodist Church, and took his bride home to Forrest City, Iowa to meet Mother Staley. They stayed, they opened a Winnebago Dealership, they joined another First Methodist Church, they settled in, they settled, settled…settled…

It is not known to John, nor do I know for that matter (I mean, it could go either way) if the Holy Ghost remained in contact the new Mrs. Staley after she and Agent Staley settled into married life. What I do know is that Clara Jane found the Forrest City Methodist Church sufficiently lacking that she went church shopping again; she was looking for 'something more,' some indefinable 'thing' that might salt the otherwise bland stew of flat Methodist theology, flat Winnebago sales, and the flatly relentless but uninspired needs of the retired federal civil servant she had haplessly become latched to.

One night, Mother Staley invited Clara Jane to investigate a new church in town, The Church of God with Signs Following, which had rented a storefront in Forrest City's devolving downtown. She had felt oddly comforted by the small group that had assembled that Wednesday evening and, for a moment, felt as though she was back home in Tisdale, Missouri, when the preacher, Sincerely Dwayne Wayne Darby—'They call me Sincerely because I am!'—bounded onto the small stage set up at the front of the store and said:

"Thank God, I will get a view of the Battle of Armageddon from the grandstand seat of the heavens! All who are born again will see the Battle of Armageddon, but it will be from the skies! Let us remember one thing, we Christians are sheltered from the coming of the approaching storm!"

In a matter of minutes Sincerely Dwayne Wayne held the small audience in the palm of his honest, working class, callused hand. Clara Jane was not exempt; she had been transported back to her childhood, with all its known comforts and primitive impulses. She felt a hot flash run up her spine and chills roll down her shoulders and into her hands. Oh, what a switch from Methodist hot dishes!

Pastor Darby's sermon was an encouragement to be ready for the Rapture, which he compared to NASA Thusly, he preached:

"You know we're spending a fortune on this space program. A fortune! If they'd just shut it down, see, and wait for the sound of the trumpet, that, my friends, is going to be one space program! I've got my name, by the grace and help of God, in that other space program.

You know the one where you don't need no big missile over in Florida to put you in the air?

"Why don't you do it tonight, Jesus? Do it tonight!"

Mother Staley was unmoved by Sincerely Dwayne Wayne's exhortations, but Clara Jane was. She joined The Church of God with Signs Following, and even convinced her husband to donate a reconditioned Mini-Winnie to the church so that Pastor Darby wouldn't have to sleep in his car anymore.

"You feel better, don't you," she said to Agent Staley. "Really. Right?"

Agent Staley Ret. nodded.

After months of attendance, she found the courage to confide in Sincerely, and told him all—all—about her past. Sincerely, who Judged Her Not, chose that moment to share his Dispensationalist opinion that, "it was all going to come out in the wash pretty quick, and didn't the scum need to die anyway?

"God Blesses you, Clara Jane", he said, "For doing His work, when Local, State, Federal, and International Law Enforcement—and all them other lily-livered Liberal girly men—are too Godless and Jesus-less to do it!

"You should think of your past as glorious, Clara Jane. Don't ever regret doing the work of the Lord. Not now, not then, not in the future. Jesus is coming soon, and with his Raptured Saints, he will slay millions with the power of his words, and the hem of his robe will be stained crimson as he wades through the oceans of blood he sheds."

Life within The Church of God with Signs Following, and within the sight of Pastor Darby, was exciting and made everything without it second best. Pretty boring in fact. She needed to make some changes.

After services last Sunday, she told Sincerely Dwayne Wayne that she needed to go back to Berryville for a few days. She felt called. He smiled and nodded.

Today she is driving through Withered Plum.

Chapter 23

John watched the Winnebago leave Withered Plum on the south bound road to Berryville, and waited a twenty second count before backing onto the road headed north. He timed his reversal to achieve maximum annoyance to a short line of vehicles also headed north, probably to Branson. So perfectly had John scheduled backing up that the lead driver, who was now directly behind him, had to slam on his brakes, and then, of course, gasp in alarm. John looked into his review mirror and smiled.

"Have you ever thought about opening a Detective Agency?" Dr. Sloan asked, seemingly—no, obviously—out of nowhere.

John nodded.

"I had a sign in the bookstore window for a long time announcing *'Spade & Archer—Private Investigations, Strictly Confidential—Inquire Within.* I originally put it there as a kind of a joke, but then people came in—not a lot, maybe one a month—and wanted to talk to Mr. Spade or Mr. Archer. I always shrugged and said 'they're out on a case, but I'll have them call you if you leave a number.'

"Some of them did."

"I guess that proves,' Sharon said, "that even Berryville has a few mysteries needing solution."

"Especially Berryville," John stated emphatically. "You have no idea what skullduggery unfolds every day. Why, you should hear what people talk about during Fellowship on Sunday morning. It would curl your hair, Madam."

"What do you think? Should we do it? I mean, open a detective agency. I kind of like the sound of 'Sloan & Heartbreak'!"

John nodded.

"I've got time on my hands now that I'm retired. A little excitement wouldn't hurt. The name needs a bit of tweaking, of course. I suggest we go with the standard alpha order, of course."

Dr. Sloan harrumphed. Then frowned and said, "You'll have to get over this religious kick you're on. It really slows things down. And, hopefully, any cases we take on will include some sex, and certainly some violence. We have future books to think of, after all.

"And another thing," she continued. "I refuse to go through these books using asinine non-expletives like 'dagnabbit'. It is so out of character. In real life, as you well know, my vocabulary is colorful and well-rounded. I can even cuss in both Low and High German."

"No doubt a product of the lost years in the Fatherland," John said dryly. "If you need to cuss so badly, how about something like *'Mater tua caligas gerit'*? My German is poor, and I prefer to know if you're cussing at me, or someone else."

"What does *'Mater tua caligas gerit'* mean?"

"Your Mother wears army boots."

"No! We need something with hair on it!"

"*Futue te ipsum?*"

"Meaning?"

"I'm not at liberty to translate. You know the rules."
"What a pointless conversation!"

John looked into his rearview mirror again and saw the driver behind him, an Appalachian American in an immense Dodge pickup truck, shake his fist and yell,

"*Futue te ipsum.*" John put the van into Drive and smoothly exited Arkansas and entered Missouri.

Dr. Sloan pouted, an unexpected behavior in both Dr. Sloan, and in a prospective gumshoe. Annoying as Miles Archer was, John could not recall him ever pouting. Stealing and smirking, yes, but pouting? He didn't think so.

"If you wish to be a principal in the firm of Heartbreak & Sloan, you'll have to give up pouting," he said. "It is not a look that will assure clients."

She decided that it was good that John was driving instead of her. If she had been at the wheel it is probable that she would have accelerated and driven into the immense oak that hovered next to the highway as it changed from Arkansas 12 to Missouri 68.

"I'm quite sure," she said sternly, "That you never had this sort of male dominant conversation with Clara Jane Smith. As I recall from reading the first book, she was seldom at a loss for words and you, Sir, never bested her in a conversation. I am becoming unsatisfied with my roll herein. I expect a few changes, and PDQ!"

John was taken aback. No, not by Dr. Sloan's Prima Donna behavior, but by her mention of Clara Jane. For the last minute or two he had an uncanny sensation that she was close at hand.

"John!" Are you listening to me?"

* * *

Clara Jane rolled out of Withered Plum at exactly the posted speed limit and read that she was 17 miles from Berryville. It would be good to see it again, she thought, although why she'd felt compelled to leave The Church of God With Signs Following, and Pastor Sincerely Dwayne Wayne Darby—just as her feelings, for both the church and Pastor Sincerely had grown pleasantly heated—she didn't know.   Whatever the reason, she felt called to Berryville and, since joining the church, and after many counseling sessions with Pastor Sincerely, she had learned to pay attention to her feelings.

As your garden variety hit woman slash serial killer, Clara Jane was, not to put too fine a point on it, less in touch with her feelings than you might imagine. Yes, I know this is surprising, but murderers, even those specializing in societal housekeeping, are astonishingly out of touch with every day sorts of emotions.

That had changed when she began working with John; she had done a good thing—reformed rather than killed a large number of Iowans—discovered the pleasures of relationships and community affiliation, and joined a church and committed (to herself) to change her ways.

She had even fallen in love, or what she assumed falling in love was all about, and married Agent Staley. She was happy to go to Forrest City, Iowa, with him, and she was sorry to leave behind the friends she had made in Berryville.

But life had gotten dull. Agent Staley, although a good enough person, was quintessentially a Federal Employee and exactly as dull as anyone who had followed rules precisely for twenty-five years could possibly be. Even the excitement of selling Winnebago Motor Homes to retiring corn farmers had eventually paled and become ordinary. Clara Jane often felt as though she was a bystander in Forrest City, waiting alongside the road for a ride out of town.

Once in a while she thought back to when she had planted a small explosive device inside Manny Richter's cell phone and blew his head off, or the time when she ran Chuckles Lachine through a wood chipper until he was just a tidy red pile of popcorn-sized matter; she just had to smile.

But then she felt—not exactly guilty—but not good, and tried to stop thinking about those happy days of yesteryear. Sure, life in Forrest City was pretty flat, and Agent Staley, Ret. was as boring as a forgotten jar of something at the back of the refrigerator, but life wasn't all car chases and dismemberments. Life was taking the flat days and the boring days in stride…after stride.

But that was before she attended The Church of God With Signs Following and learned, from Pastor Sincerely Dwayne Wayne all about the imminent arrival of Jesus, about how he was coming with a Sword, and how he needed her experienced hand to wield that same sword of Righteousness that she was so expert at using.

"Clara Jane," Pastor Dwayne Wayne had said, "Jesus is returning to take up Christians into heaven by means of a rapture immediately before a seven year worldwide Tribulation.

"And are we not living in a time of worldwide Tribulation? Are you going to stand with Jesus?"

"Oh yes!" she had breathed. "Oh yes!"

She smiled as she headed south. She wasn't exactly sure why she was heading back to Berryville. But there had to be a reason.

Chapter 24

Fiacre bent over and plucked a Japanese beetle off a squash vine. He studied it for a moment and, noting the skeletal leaves of the squash plant, thought about how seriously *Popillia Japonica* had gone about his work. It was serious like all animals, cows, snakes, grizzly bears, and platypuses are serious: they work and root and chew, but fail at poetry writing and religion making; they lack the sense of humor required to start religions, or to form governments.

It is human kind's lack of seriousness that allows them to escape their animal natures. Fiacre's main reason for appearing in this book, this dreadful post-modern mishmash, is his sense of humor, that and the occasional gush of sentiment for the silly seriousness of the people who are appearing in it with him.

He squashed the beetle between his forefinger and thumb. "Another dusky Hindu bites the dust," he said, laughing.

Brooke West, who was going into the back door of the church, looked up at the sound. He was startled a bit by the sound, and observed Fiacre's disreputable appearance, in semi-consternation. No doubt, he thought, the bum in shorts and the '*Jesus is Coming, Look Busy*' T-shirt was a friend of John Heartbreak's. Who else but John would permit access to the garden of such seediness?

As Brooke entered the back of the church, Elvis left through the front door, and Fiacre paused in squishing to think of John's and the Warrior Queen Sloan's whereabouts. As an expert in time and travel Fiacre was pretty near certain that they had just made the right turn off Highway 68N and onto the road leading to the main Endtimes Compound. He clearly saw the Endtimes sign to the left of the van as John and Dr. Sloan irrevocably tootled past it, and toward their rendezvous with destiny.

Fiacre knew the conclusion of their rendezvous, but he was uncertain about how John and the Warrior Queen would cause it. All he knew for sure was that, somewhere during the coming Fandango, she would say, "Elementary, my dear Heartbreak" in response to one of John's queries. It was moments like that that made being in the book worthwhile.

He squashed another beetle and thought about the Reverend Billy Cudrup. The two events are not unrelated, he thought. How like *Popillia Japonica* is Little Billy, he thought. "For Christ's Sake," he said out loud. "Billy, you're 70 years old and you're still munching away at The Rumor of God. You're buying and selling The Rumor like He's a corn future! May The Rumor have mercy on your soul for your seriousness!"

Fiacre meant that sentence—the one just above—to be a prayer for Little Billy's soul, for the repose of Billy's soul, when repose was the inevitable fact. Like Chesterton's Father Brown, Fiacre knew that the great victory was not in discovering the murderer, but in helping the murder discover his sin, and repent of it. Fiacre's mission for Heartbreak and Sloan was fulfillment of that prayer.

If they were successful, Billy would stop munching, start acting his age, and take occasional husbandly advantage of Angel who, not to put too fine a point on it, was a considerable step up from Donna Raye in the looks department. He would know that God is not a Rumor, that old age is not a rumor, and finally understand that enough is enough. "Get a life, Billy," Fiacre prayed. "Beat your time shares into ploughs and plant a garden. Get a life. Relax."

God is not a rumor to John, but John often lacks playfulness and overindulges in seriousness. Hopefully (yes, I know it's a silly adverb so, okay: 'with hope'), Sloan's Fandango will result in not just Cudrup's redemption, but in an increase of John's silliness quotient. He is peevish much of the time, and a victim of Catholic Orthodoxy most of the time. John could lighten up and, with hope (happy now?) Sloan is the lamp.

Among John's peeves are patriots who have not been to war, church services—especially on Wednesday nights—that resemble television variety shows, angry middle-aged women with Indian Guides, tight pants, small slices of pie, Ted Cruz's wet mouth, Appalachian American's with poor lawn hygiene, Administrative Overhead, corn subsidies, people who say 'it smells like money', authors who have never read a book, Country Music radio stations, modern dance, waiting rooms, raisin shortages, public service unions, Liza Minnelli, illiterates and felons on college football teams, Olympic snowboarding, cats, lap dogs, lap cats, weak coffee, Administrators—male and female—nicknamed 'Mother Tucker' by subordinates, the culture of France, substitutes for cream, linguists masquerading as philosophers, bending over, modern dentistry…

…and then there was the whole Catholic thing he had to muddle through. Last week in Sunday school, for example, Loretta Tanner led a discussion of James' Letter. Among Catholics, James' Letter is the most important 'how-to' source for engaging the Christian life. It is also among the simplest of the books and the least abstract: 'If you are in trouble, brothers, pray. If you are happy, sing a psalm.' Pretty straight stuff, right? And easy for the mostly non-bible reading Catholic to follow.

Naturally, the criminally insane Martin Luther named James' Letter a 'straw epistle', and condemned it for its focus on good works rather than on faith. This got up Catholic noses and caused them to turn red in the face and to say things like, "Well, I guess we'll just stop feeding the poor and close our hospitals! I guess we'll just roll around on the floor, high five each other in pseudo Urdu, and sing trashy Country Western music instead!"

John was a little nervous when Loretta announced that James was that Sunday's lesson. He hoped that folks would note the value of what James had to say, even if he was a little light on the whole faith deal—and they did. In fact, the outcome of the lesson was that all Christians have work to do, regardless of age, health, sexual preference, and nationality, and that such work is often a reliable sign of the genuineness of the worker's faith. John was certainly relieved that he wouldn't have to point out that Luther was a drunken anti-Semite and lickspittle to German Aristocracy.

Fiacre had to laugh at John's nervousness. Although Luther really was a certified jerk, he was small potatoes in the scheme—God's scheme—of things and hardly worth all the trouble people had decided he was worth. A church, 'the church', is not God, a fact that Fiacre had learned over the past thirteen centuries, and which God certainly Knew from the beginning. Finally, the trouble people made over it was part of human kind's charm, and yeast for all the songs, poems, pictures, architecture, and hot thoughts about Sophia Loren they were given to. No, John needed to lighten up, re-peeve and de-peeve, and work a little less. He needed more faith that things would work out just fine.

The Warrior Queen Sloan AKA Sharon Sloan AKA Dr. Sloan also known as the artist and scholar formerly known as AKAASFKA Sharon Sloan felt a pulse of anticipation as they left Highway 68N and turned onto Endtimes Drive. Little Billy Cudrup, high heels and all, and the new Donna Raye, Angel Cudrup, were minutes away. The roof top of the Endtimes Compound peaked over a ridge just east and ahead of them and, within it, the lair of Pastor Cudrup himself. She hoped that they would arrive after the taping of *The Billy Cudrup Show* so they could accost him without interference from the crowd.

John hoped for exactly the opposite (of course he did, the contrary fool). He had only observed Pastor Cudrup on the television and was looking forward to hearing him in person. It was possible, he told himself (again), that Cudrup was sincere in his beliefs and was not the villainous, unrepentant self-excusing sociopath and ex-con that Normal Christians were sure that he was. What if Billy was an honest God Broker, and had only answered yet another call, a post prison call, from the Lord. Had God said to him, "Go you, Billy, to Branson, Missouri, that Graveyard of the Country Western Has Been, dine at the $3.99 All You Can Eat Country Buffet, and grid your loins to preach the Time Share Gospel!"

Well. Why not?

Sharon glanced at John. His bovine like expression gave no indication of readiness for the battle ahead. She found this rather disturbing.

Chapter 25

As you know, John is aware that he is in this book and that it represents a parallel life that more or less approximates his actual life. You, however, are probably not in the book (yet), but you are aware of John being in the book. You are imagining things about John—and he is imagining things about you (really) as you read along. Imagine that. The oddities and indignities of being both fictional and human are material concerns to John, and they would be to you too, if (when?) you were/are in fact, in the book.

These ideas may be fiction; and one, or all of them, could be true. More or less.

What about you? Are you aware that you are operating in parallel lives, realities, and Universes? Plutarch was probably the first author to think about how lives are intertwined and woven by threads of recognition, imagination, awareness and lack of awareness, and faith in God, or lack of faith in God. If you dream yet another strand is woven into your subconscious and, if you are tuned in enough the strand may be a conscious one. Plutarch nattered on about this at great length—he was a Platonist after all—but you are tired of this thread...so we will drop it.

However:

Suppose you are married. Suppose you are a Christian. Suppose you have purchased a car or a pop tart this morning.

As a wife or husband your husband or wife understands you and your world in a completely different way than you do, even though he or she observes your operation and navigation of the world in as intimate a way as possible. She or he may be thinking of you as a pop tart, which should make you happy! Or, maybe he or she purchased some other pop tart this morning. Boy, that would cause something else.

If you are a Christian than you know that God knows you. Does God know you in the way you know yourself? Is God's opinion of you lesser or greater than your opinion of yourself?

The car salesman knows you as a chicken to be plucked, or as a $400 commission check. If the salesperson is of a salacious bent he or she may imagine knowing you in a salacious way; imagination is another (3rd) way of knowing. The complexity of others is something that car salespeople overlook; they may have active imaginations, but they are always at the center of the action: they only imagine themselves.

Dr. Sloan knows Dr. Sloan and she knows John. John knows John and he knows Dr. Sloan. That's at least six levels of knowing if you count imaginative knowing, which you should count since you are reading this book, in itself proof of parallel lives, realities, and Universes.

Imagine how complicated this becomes if we factor in God knowing Dr. Sloan, and knowing John too. He knows them perfectly (a God thing) and consequently knows them as perfect—or as utterly contemptible; at the end of the game the knowing door swings only one way—and everyone will know what there is to know.

The word 'complication' however, hardly covers it when we might suppose that John, for example, does not know himself very well. Perhaps John does not know that he is not old, or deaf, not a bumbler, not a famous timewaster and village know-it-all. Maybe John is, if he bothered to look, vigorous, patient, peeve-free, and open to suggestions and new ideas. Perhaps the 'Out of Business' sign visible to most people who look into his eyes says something entirely different. Maybe it says 'Dime a Dance' or 'Hot Cha Cha.' That would be a surprise to John. But it would be cool.

Sadly, John *is* old, and deaf, and a bumbler, a timewaster and village know-it-all, but remember that he may not know that for sure, or maybe he only suspects it. In his present mind's eye he is rather heroic: on a Mission from God and charged with saving Normal Christianity. This re-imaging has puffed him up a bit; you may be able to see a glimmer of 'Hot Cha Cha' in his dull brown eyes. (Try and imagine it.)

Dr. Sloan does not suffer fools gladly. She has made an exception in John's case because he can surprise her once in a while; say with the whole Fiacre slash Warrior Queen Deal, and once by insisting she travel with him to Kansas City to confab with a band of relocated Somalis farming on some abandoned slum land. That was unusual. Today, watching him brown-off hoards of Appalachian American ruffians in pick-up trucks was simultaneously hilarious and terrifying, especially with the AARs' started firing rifles in the air. That was unusual too, and not something you see every day.

She is aware of John's many peeves and accounts him to be a peevish person. She is herself, however, not without a few ticks; more than one person thinks of her as a sort of Princess and the Pea character; consequently, she could be kinder in her assessment of John and what she views as his crankiness.

Among Dr. Sloan's cranky peeves are College and University Deans, sloppy design work, prima donnas other than herself, fructose, imitation vanilla, camouflage pajamas, trust fund babies, hymn singers, complainers (other than herself), Anton Webern, small 'c' Conservatives (i.e., Texans), blondes named Ann Coulter, the blond Meg Ryan, professional blonds, dry bread, tax cheats, uncomfortable shoes, banana republics, squirrels, margarine, society ladies and Junior Leaguers, anti-immigration morons, drunken anti-immigration morons and drunken Junior Leaguers, the fleshpots of Egypt and anything related to Odessa, Texas.

Naturally Dr. Sloan believes that John and all other right thinking people hold these same advanced views—that would be peeves—and that agreement on these matters and ideas, constructs, and conditions signals intelligence and possession of at least a baseline appreciation of culture.

The fact of the matter (this matter anyway) is that John is largely in favor of blonds, drunk or sober, and usually is willing to give them the benefit of the doubt. He would also hold out for a field trip to the fleshpots of Egypt prior to making judgment. That said, he is entirely in agreement in the matter of Odessa. My God, have you been there?

The question of course then is how well does Dr. Sloan know herself? We see that she does not know John exactly and, if she did, she would hold him a bigger fool than she already imagines him to be. So: in the matter of self, does she know herself better than she knows John?

Who knows?

She does, of course. We can agree that Dr. Sloan knows herself very well and it will help to know that the listing of her peeves is purely imaginative. (Maybe. Maybe not.) But as imagination specifically related to Dr. Sloan, it takes on an entirely separate and functional reality—just as *Plutarch's Lives* shaped our knowing of

Pyrrhus of Epirus, Romulus, Numa Pompilius, Coriolanus, Aemilius Paullus, Tiberius Gracchus, Gaius Gracchus, Gaius Marius, Sulla, Sertorielus, Lucullus, Pompey, Julius Caesar, Cicero, Mark Antony, and Marcus Junius Brutus—all real people who, if we understand science correctly, stood in the same rain you stand in, breathed the same air, and are integrated into our personal DNA.

If you were John and had seven years of Latin taught by Nazi Brown Shirts disguised as Dominican nuns, you would know these 'lives' to be real lives. But truly, they only exist in John's imagination, and there only by way of Plutarch's imagination. Yet they are as real as Dr. Sloan is real—and as John is real.

Isn't it cool to think that their lives run parallel to yours?

What is left to discover, of course, is how Billy Cudrup sees himself as an actor in all of these distinct and separate lines of existence. How does Billy see himself? How does God see Billy? Do God and Billy see Eye to eye? How does (will) Billy see Dr. Sloan and John? How will Dr. Sloan and John see Billy? How will Dr. Sloan see John see Billy? How will John see Dr. Sloan see Billy? Most importantly, will Angel Cudrup be wearing a push up bra?

A fandango, as you can see, ain't beanbag.

Chapter 26

For a while, Fiacre couldn't get enough of Tony Orlando and Dawn. There was something about *'Take a Letter, Maria'* that really got to him. Maybe it was the song's concrete stereotyping of men and women?

He didn't really know why, but he loved the song's story. It was about a hard-working, strong and silent business executive whose wife done him wrong. While he stoically cuts the B off, the loyal secretary Maria stands by adoringly. Mr. Strong and Silent observes Maria's loyalty and—when she took her glasses off—how hot she is. Fiacre concluded that the businessman delivers Maria from the obscurity of office work, that they make ceaseless heart stopping monkey love and live happily ever after.

If Fiacre cared about John's opinion (he does not) he would not admit to enjoying Tony Orlando and Dawn. But he had enjoyed them, and he probably would again sometime in the future when he stopped by the 1970s. The last time he was there he caught six or seven of their concerts in a row and loved every one of them. So, sue me (Fiacre would say).

Fiacre is as much a Time Tourist as he is a Time Traveler, and he has sampled some of the best and worst of times. You may regard this as unseemly behavior in a saint, but regard also please Fiacre's Catholic context. Unlike Protestant culture—with the fine exceptions of Episcopalians and Unitarians—Catholics aren't opposed to a good time, can tell and laugh at a joke, and will take a drink now and then. One of Fiacre's fondest memories is hanging with Hilaire

Belloc on a tramp through France. Belloc would take a drink now and then and there was probably no fiercer or more devoted Christian than he.

Consequently, this trip to Berryville, Arkansas has, frankly, the makings of a dud. John is as dull as advertised and, while the Warrior Queen has promise, she has yet to perform. True, that isn't her fault. The Authorial I (howdy!) is certainly taking his time getting to Endtimes and the Grand Fandangoing of Pastor Billy Cudrup. I'm sure you wish he'd hurry up.

But as you know, dear hearts, life unfolds one day, one hour, one minute, one…at a time. By and by, okay?

One of the hold-ups is trying to figure out who Billy Cudrup is. Because his behavior is so predictable, so routine, and so utterly banal, it is quite possible that he is not even a human being, but is some kind of animated machine, and one of the first observable examples of singularity.

Singularity will happen at a specific point in time, and in a flash, like the sun setting in Key West. Sometime, maybe soon, maybe in the case of Little Billy Cudrup, the vast machined system obeying our every command will effectively stop, turn around and say, "No, I don't think so."

Fiacre has no idea when that will happen. He supposes that he could travel far enough forward in time to a world given over to singularity, and then work his way backwards to the finite moment it 'happens' and find out that way. But, frankly, he isn't really interested in the idea of singularity enough to do that.

There had been improvements to the wheel during his earthly life that had impressed him more, and there had been a couple of theological conflicts that had caught his fancy and gotten him hot under the collar, but they ultimately turned out to mean nothing much.

Nothing at all, actually. God was still in His heaven and all was right, more or less, with the world.

It has occurred to him, however, that maybe Cudrup *is* a machine and not really human any more. How else could it be possible for someone to talk constantly about God and not know anything about Him? Billy was like one of those manure extruding machines where you pour a lot of wet cow flop into one end of a pipe and it comes out on the other end as an eighteen inch pine-scented Yule Log. Odd, don't you think?

If Cudrup was a machine it would explain a lot; Fiacre couldn't understand why a human being would live the way Little Billy has chosen to live. It looked like such a rat race to him, and why bother for heaven's sakes, if you had to hide the dancing girls, the Nubian limo drivers, and the household lackeys that are the usual fruits of successfully milking delusional, greedy, ignorant mendicants?

Chesterton, a great friend of Fiacre's, had said 'a man must be very dull indeed to want a lot of money and spend all his time getting it', yet that barely explained why Cudrup had chosen God as his product when selling erectile dysfunction drugs or guns or dirty pictures paid at least as well, and perhaps better. People seldom went to prison for selling that stuff; and, surely, you just had to meet a more jovial crowd of customers than the depressed, broke, and dim-witted fundamentalist who comprised the bulk of the pigeons Billy seemed to be plucking again.

Machines operate in an entirely 'yes' 'no' universe. Objects or information goes into the machine; the object or information shuttles 'in' or 'out' of one or a series of gates; ultimately it is spit out as a transformed object or answer. Is that what goes on in Billy's brain?

Desperate or impaired Christians poured sorrow, pain, dreams, wishes, complaint, laments, pathologies, diagnoses, hatreds, phobias—and money, into the machine that is Billy Cudrup and out comes...

...What? Who knows?

Is the transformed object or answer the product of Little Billy's Christian Extruder as contained in the *Book of Revelation*? He advertises his expertise as a Revelations scholar and teaches weekly classes on its meanings. Fiacre has planned on attending a class, but has somehow not found the time. Perhaps all would be revealed after such edification.

'Not finding the time' is an odd excuse, and perhaps even an incredulous excuse, for a Time Traveler, especially one as experienced as Fiacre is. It is a real excuse actually, and if you press Fiacre about it, he will sigh and say:

"Every Televangelist I can think of claims to be an expert on *Revelation*. I suppose that's because *Revelation* can mean anything to anyone; it can scare the pants off you if you want it to.

"I am mostly confused by it," Fiacre will admit. "Nothing in it reveals a thing to me—and I've consulted some real experts.

"None of them mentioned Billy Cudrup as a peer."

Deciding if Billy is simply a Revelation Machine, or any other kind of machine for that matter, is material to the outcome of our story because machines are not culpable. If Billy is a machine it would let him off the hook, leaving the question 'Who is operating the Billy Cudrup machine?"

Perhaps Dr. Sloan will find out.

Chapter 27

I wish we could say that Endtimes appeared wreathed in a malevolent fog, or in a dampening mist on a distant, skull littered hill. It did not. To Dr. Sloan, it looked more like a half-completed nursing home where the developer had run out of money and all the grannies had been parked outside on the sidewalk. In the most charitable view, it resembled nothing so much as a derelict, bankrupt ski resort slumped on the side of a depleted, snowless molybdenum mine.

If you possessed a jar of candy hearts and those hearts have gotten wet and the dyes have all run together and clumped in a sticky wad you know then what Endtimes looks like. It was a Precious Moments diorama, but one that had been dropped on the floor and severely discounted by a discontented retailer. It lacked the tacky grandeur of Elvis on velvet, but was otherwise well centered in the Land of Kitsch.

The repossessed doublewide that is Endtimes disappointed Dr. Sloan. On the short drive from Highway 68 to the parking lot of the Compound, she had subconsciously prepared herself for battle. She was hepped-up for a moat guarded by Visigoths or, more precisely, Appalachian American Visigoths slapping billy clubs into slap reddened palms. In her imagination these AAVs had small dark holes for eyes; they were all high on a methamphetamine-like substance administered in ever increasing doses each morning in the communion grape juice by a *Capo di tutti* sort of person. We won't begin to describe how unattractive Mr. *Capo di tutti* is in Dr. Sloan's mind, but he is one ugly Mother Tucker.

What she saw instead of Visigoths was a twenty-five year old security sedan with a single revolving jelly bean on its bowed-in lid. There was no moat, no billy clubs.

There were a few abandoned aluminum walkers though.

As Dr. Sloan peered through the windshield of Mrs. Heartbreak's van, she felt a thick stab of disappointment at the utter banality of the place. Truth be told, she had been day dreaming, just a moment ago, that she was wearing a golden breastplate and bearing sharp Fandangoing dirks in either hand, her face radiant with the Power of the Holy Spirit. Rather like—no, precisely like—Jean Auguste Ingres's 1854 painting of Jeanne de Arc, she was girded for holy, bloody war.

"Cruise the parking lot, John," she commanded in a dispirited voice. "Reconnaissance is probably not necessary, but it is always prudent."

John immediately complied (duh. Of course he did) and slowly wended his way through the sparsely occupied parking area. Middle-aged automobiles of largely American make straddled white lines marking the designated allotment of space per vehicle. Endtimes' visitors were obviously careless or impaired or rebellious of rules and rule making. But it made sense in a way: why bother with details when the world was ending PDQ?

John failed to pick up on Dr. Sloan's dispirit. He hadn't known what to expect from Endtimes, but he was far more familiar with the world of Television Evangelists than was Dr. Sloan. What he saw more or less confirmed his experience. After all, Televangelists lived in make-believe worlds, had graduated from make-believe colleges, had make-believe doctorates, and performed mostly as hosts of variety shows.

Endtimes would certainly look different on television than it did to the naked, untelevised eye.

"Michigan," John said. "Michigan again. Oklahoma. Texas. Texas times two...three...four. Ohio. Kansas. Arkansas. Arkansas. Arkansas again. Ohio again."

John inched through the parking lot, reading the plates of cars in a monotone. Dr. Sloan had to resist the urge to flick a quick forefinger against the geezer hair in his right ear. How obtuse he is to my feelings, she thought.

"I can read, John," she said, rather loudly. "Are you at all aware of how crummy this place looks? It's like a mobile home park for retired K-Mart employees. Frankly, I was hoping for something more, well...

"...something out of Harry Potter? Lord Voldemort's castle, perhaps?"

"Yes! Exactly. This is so...so anticlimactic."

"That's the beauty of it," John said. "Remember Hannah Arendt?"

"Ah. 'The banality of evil,'" she exclaimed, then recited: "'The great crimes of history are not executed by fanatics or sociopaths, but by ordinary people who accept the ideas of their leaders and therefore participate as though their actions are normal.'"

Dr. Sloan paused for a moment and squinted at the cheaply constructed façade surrounding the entrance to Endtimes' lobby.

"You've nailed it!" she yelled, excitedly. "This place looks exactly like a tarted up grandmother thinking about drowning her grand children in the family bathtub!"

John nodded.

"OMG. This place is really spooky!"

John nodded.

"You knoooooowwwwwwwwww," Dr. Sloan said, slowly, feeling her very real hand tighten on her very metaphysical dirk, "Endtimes is kind of like a Stephen King clown. Kind of...TERRIFYING!"

John jumped at Dr. Sloan's sudden exuberance. A moment ago she was slumped in an existential End Zone; now, mere seconds later, she was bouncing in her seat with what John judged to be a level of excitement unseemly in a person of her age, gender, and country of origin. She looked uncannily like a Jack Russell Terrier on the heels of a snack cat.

"Calm yourself, my dear," he said. "We go incognito from here."

"Park the car, Heartbreak," she snapped. "If you use that condescending tone with me again, I'll twist your nose off."

John parked the car. He reddened. He held his hands up in a placating gesture. He gave her a questioning look. And said:

"I accept your apology. I appreciate your desire to quickly confront Pastor Cudrup, to ascertain the whereabouts of your $6,000,000, and to inform him that his chickens have come home to roost. But I suggest that we engage the enemy in a nuanced and thoughtful manner.

"Look," he said, pointing at the roofline of the Compound. "See the cameras? We're under surveillance as we speak."

Dr. Sloan raked her eyes across the front of the Compound. John was right. Even though no Visigoths were immediately visible, every square inch of the parking lot and adjacent grounds were covered by security cameras. She saw them swinging right and left, up and down, as routine and intent as birds of prey drawing a bead on scampering mice. There was, obviously, a highly sophisticated force watching their every move, even if they weren't visibly on the ground around them.

She nodded, and calmed herself. They would need to blend in with the elderly pilgrims gathering for the Billy Cudrup Show, and move in Cudrup's direction slowly and methodically, with apparent good humor and smiles of admiration. Serpentine was the word that best describes the strategy emerging in her thoughts.

"We'll need to move in a serpentine manner," John said, jolting her. "Try and appear devout."

What does devout look like, she wondered? She had seen Marie Osmond pray over lunch one time at a Dallas restaurant, but it had just given her the willies and made her nervous. She wasn't sure if it had been the praying, or Osmond herself, but the feelings were sharp in her memory. She made a very serious face and looked off into the far distance.

"How's this?" she asked, modeling.

John jumped back. "Holy smokes. Stop it!"

"What?"

"They'll check us for weapons for sure."

"I'm doing the best I can!"

"Well, try and think beautiful thoughts."

"That's a little hard, boyo. You got me all whipped up with the whole Hannah Arendt thingy. I've got clowns on the brain."

"Alright," he said, nodding. "Just make a blank face and purse your lips like a Baptist lady. Think about Karen Carpenter singing *Rainy Days and Mondays*. That'll take your mind of Cudrup."

"I'll have a stroke."

"Sharon!"

"Alright, alright. Baptist lady. Karen Carpenter. Blank face. I think I can do it."

"Good."

John opened the van door and stepped out onto the mottled pavement. He faced the Endtimes entrance and took a step toward it. Now would be a good time for the Holy Ghost to show up, he thought.

Dr. Sloan thumped her chest with her forearm and heard the satisfying thunk! of muscle against metal. A small smile played on her lips. Then, her face went blank.

Chapter 28

As John moved in the direction of Endtimes' entrance, he crouched and walked quickly in a zig-zag pattern. Dr. Sharon Sloan, the Artist and Scholar formerly known as Dr. Sharon Sloan, watched him with increasing alarm.

"What are you doing, for God's sakes?"

"Serpentine," John said in a hoarse whisper. "We move as the snake."

"Epileptic," Dr. Sloan replied. "You look like you're having a seizure. Knock it off, okay? You're going to draw attention to us."

"Well." John's feelings were hurt. "I assumed we were traveling incognito. I'm just trying to fit in."

Sharon shook her head and looked at her feet. The asphalt in the Endtimes' parking lot, while new, was already beginning to crack and fissure. She could see that small shoots of chickweed had begun to root. It wouldn't be long before the parking area looked like it belonged in a ruined first tier suburb. She walked over to where John was crouched and pulled him upright.

"If we want to fit in,' she said, in a calming voice, "we have to look like Orin and Luella Parsnips, from Bum Squat, Missouri. We're retired chicken farmers, and I clerked at Wal-Mart for several years after our no good kids took off."

"Why are our kids no good?"

"We need a compelling reason to belly up to Cudrup's bar and drink the joy juice," she said. "We are victims of hateful, willful children who only want our hard earned money to spend on unsuitable pursuits.

"Our son Donald left home to study ballet at the University of Central Arkansas. He is currently employed as a part time toe dancer with the Fort Smith Ballet and lives with a black guy named Maurice who lifts weights and is a performance artist.

"You know what that means, don't you?" she asked.

John nodded.

"Our daughter Ella lives with a person named Hog Dog and is herself known as 'Easy On, Easy Off' Ella. She smokes cigarettes and drinks whisky when she isn't incarcerated.

"Both our kids hate us and we never hear from them unless they need money. Donald says that you are a homophobic racist and Ella believes that I am a self-righteous Jesus freak church lady...our children are, of course, absolutely correct."

"Without putting too fine a point on it," John observed.

"No point on it at all," Dr. Sloan replied. "We're here because we're Naturalized Citizens of Billy World. We, like Billy, are victims of a rotten Universe, and we hate everything in it—including our rotten kids. You and I—as Orin and Luella Parsnips—are lonely, old, and sickly. We're filled with bile, ignorance, intolerance, self-pity, rage, bigotry, delusion, xenophobia, rightwing ideology, anti-Semitism, sexual repression, cholesterol, depression, fanaticism, apparitions of Mandingo on a rampage, acid reflux syndrome, chauvinism, prejudice, vitamin A, C, & D deficiencies, self-righteousness, vitriol, ire, wrath, fury, cruelty; we harbor an infinite well of certainty that we are oppressed, subjugated, dominated, and controlled by a vast leftwing conspiracy of limp-wristed, oral sex addicted, multi-culturist college graduates. You, Orin, secretly struggle with an unspeakable desire to dress in women's clothing. God only knows what you've done with those chickens out in the shed."

"Good heavens!"

"Precisely. We've come to Billy World because all of its cherubim and seraphim sing in grand confirmation of these beliefs, feelings, pathologies, and yips. For us, for Orin and Luella Parsnips, it is heaven indeed!

"So, John," Dr. Sloan admonished, "We don't have to zig and zag to the front door. Just stand tall and be an ordinary, everyday maniac."

Fiacre chuckled. The Warrior Queen really cracked him up. He was enjoying eavesdropping on her, and the direction in which her conversation with the dullard Heartbreak was headed. She'd nailed the human conditions of Pastor Cudrup's targeted market pretty fast, but the funny bit was that Normal Christians *were* mostly a vast leftwing conspiracy of limp-wristed, oral sex addicted, multi-culturist college graduates; more or less the average High Church Episcopalian and recovering Baptist...and about every fifth Roman Catholic Fiacre had run into.

He stooped to pluck a habanera off the vine and popped it into his mouth. "Hokey Smokey!" he exclaimed. Dull as he was, Heartbreak could grow peppers!

It should not surprise you that Fiacre can be working in the First Christian Church Community Garden in Berryville, Arkansas, and simultaneously listen in on a conversations taking place in and near Withered Plum, Missouri. Time Travelers are tridimensional in nature—they often meet themselves in their to-ing and fro-ing—and as a soul and Saint as well as a Time Traveler, Fiacre is an especially gifted chrono-locomotive. Every conversation is an iTune in the world of the Departed Present.

He momentarily lost track of what Sloan was saying; tears streamed down his face from the heat of the pepper; he was tempted to spit, not that it would help. Fiacre pulled the hem of his T-Shirt up and wiped his eyes, then bent down to see what other fresh hell John had planted.

"Serrano Del Sol," he muttered, impressed. He was looking at a fairly stout, squatty pepper plant with dozens of 3 inch fruits varying from very dark green to scarlet. Fiacre knew the pepper well; it was hotter than a check from Lucifer and had to be taken in small doses, and then only when surrounded by tomatoes and cilantro.

Next to the Serrano, John had planted a Mellow Star and, just next to it, a really lovely *Corno di Torro* that would be perfect for roasting. The Mellow Star is an Asian variety, the *Corno* is Italian, and the Serrano is, of course, Mexican. Whatever Heartbreak's deficiencies in the charm and excitement departments, he more than made up for them as a gardener.

Fiacre recalled a conversation about farming he'd had with Dorothy Day, the founder of the *Catholic Worker*, back in New York City sometime in the middle of the Twentieth Century. Day had called on him, in a prayer of intercession, to go knock some sense into a cadre of over pious intellectuals trying to garden on the Catholic Worker farm in Elmira, upstate.

"Dorothy, please. No," he had said. "It will be no fun at all. You've got three angry women at constant odds with three lazy men, each haranguing the other— and each other—over their character flaws. All manifestly real, by the way.

"And they've taken up Bible quoting, for God's sakes. Some of the passages they quote are so obscure even Isaiah hasn't heard of them."

163

Day sniffed. "What kind of saint are?" she asked. "'It will be no fun' he says. For crying out loud, Fiacre, religious life isn't a cake walk, you know!"

He had hung his head in shame, a feeling that surprised him given his transcendent, supernatural, been there done that man of several world's experience. Yet, he also knew that Day would soon become a Saint herself, one that would show up Fiacre and several of his other saint pals for the saintly punks they actually were (and are). He sighed.

"Okee doakee, Dorothy," he acquiesced. "Where shall I begin?"

"Begin by telling them they're all guilty as sin and that the Bible is not a gun. Tell them to stop thinking so much; a little more 'head down and butt up' positioning is exactly called for. Say 'God loves a cheerful giver, and scorns the pickle puss…'"

"…I'm not sure that appears in Corinthians," Fiacre interrupted. "Perhaps you mean to say…"

"…I mean to say what I'm telling you to say," Day said sternly. "They need to pray more and talk less and worry about the devil not at all. The devil can take care of himself and they can depend that he will.

"Tell them that God rides the lame horse. He carves the rotten wood. Finally," she said, "Tell them to grow some decent peppers. I am especially fond of *Corno di Torros.*"

"Is that it?"

"One more thing," she had said. She reached into the pocket of her house dress and pulled out a paper. "Here are 10 rules they should follow. I think these came from Watchman Nee…but you can tell them it comes from you. Give the list to them."

Fiacre scanned the list, which was headed:

Fiacre's 10 Rules for Getting into Heaven

1. *Think about God all the time. It gets easier with practice.*

2. *Listen when God speaks to you. PS: If God talks to you about someone else's sinfulness, it isn't God Who is talking.*

3. *God respects manual labor. He especially expects at least a little of it every week from federal employees, priests, pastors, and intellectuals of every stripe.*

4. *Guilt is a sign of good mental and spiritual health. Deal with it.*

5. *God does not belong to your church. If you get mad at your church and start a new one, God won't join your new church either. You might as well stay where you are.*

6. *The Book of Revelations is an important book. It is also The Book of Scoundrels. Watch out for people and preachers who spend too much (of your) time there.*

7. *Unless they're holding a gun, everyone you meet gets a fresh start. Every time you meet them.*

8. *Pray for a peaceful death every day. If you go with a clear conscience you have lived well.*

9. *Read holy books. There are a lot of them, including some novels.*

Dan Krotz

10. The devil is a spectacular failure. People and preachers who spend all of their time talking about the devil worship a false god and are behaving scandalously. They should worry more about what God wants and less about what the devil is up to.

Fiacre nodded. He would deliver the list.

"Anything else?" he asked, dreading an answer. But he had to ask, of course; Dorothy was not a woman you plied with half measures.

"Sometime," Day began…"sometime early in the next century, you will go to Arkansas, also as is New York City a part of the United States of America—though I know you'll find that hard to believe when you get there—but once there you will direct a man named Heartbreak and a Warrior Queen named Sloan to Fandango the apostate named Cudrup. He is selling indulgences. Make sure you give them this list so that they in turn can give it to Cudrup.

"Cudrup's receipt of the list will be his last chance for redemption. If he rejects its message the Warrior Queen and her companion will initiate Operation Fandango."

"Dorothy, I have two questions," Fiacre recalled asking. "First, who is the Cudrup person? Second, what is a Fandango?"

"Cudrup is a counterfeit hell robber; he pretends to save people from the fires of hell. As to the exact nature of a Fandango…well, I don't exactly know what that is. I am sure," she concluded, "that it is a spectacular thing to observe."

Now that Fiacre was where Dorothy had predicted he would be—in Berryville, Arkansas, America, he suddenly remembered two things. First, the list that he had presented to the Elmira gardeners made absolutely no impression on them. They went on arguing, blaming, and failed to raise a single spud.

Secondly, he had forgotten to give the list to John. He reached into the right hand pocket of his Bermuda shorts, pulled out a wrinkled slip of paper and, *Wah La*, there it was.

Dang.

Chapter 29

Since Mrs. Heartbreak's retirement as President and Chief Executive Officer of Heartbreak's Pretty Good Books & Really Dreadful Coffee, she has been able to devote herself almost exclusively to the task she best loves, to wit, the management and supervision of John Heartbreak.

One might assume that Mrs. Heartbreak finds this retirement-age obligation an onerous one but, truth be told, she takes to it like a duct to tape, like a Democrat to graft, and like a Republican to corporate handouts.

The **bold** *italicized* underlined fact is that Mrs. Heartbreak, like Social Order Theorists everywhere, such as say, Joe Stalin, Otto Preminger, Captain Bligh, Eleanor Roosevelt, Carrie Nation, Albert Ellis, Sylvia Plath, Bobby Knight, Barnum & Bailey, George Meany, Joan Crawford, Albert Shanker, Lawrence Welk, Jane Austen, Vito Corleone, Margaret Sanger, Martin Dies, Scarlet O'Hara, and Rand McNally, was born with a lust for supervision. She would have it (all of it) no other way.

A secondary but quite important post retirement obligation has been her propagation of phrases such as 'ain't it awful' and 'we'll all be eating grass for sure'.

These key phrases respond to articles appearing in the *Arkansas Democrat Gazette*, and to accounts hurled past the amazing dentistry of photogenic people on the television: *exempli gratia...*

"Ain't it awful how Congress is ruining the economy? Mark my words; we'll all be eating grass for sure...before Christmas...before sundown...before etc!"

The whole 'we'll be eating grass' and 'ain't it awful' stuff was Mrs. Heartbreak's natural and all-purpose utilitarian rejoinder to any event, circumstance, occasion, body in motion, locution, Act of God, Supreme Court ruling, accident, juncture, conjecture, or atomic and other sub-particle reactions or chain reactions that was contrary to her notions of fair play and honest brokering. (If you happen to be a Social Order Theorist yourself—you may be a retired person with a public service pension, or a Sociologist, Unitarian, vegan, or a Self-Made Man or Woman— you'll understand the panicky relish with which Mrs. Heartbreak spouts such rejoinders without further explanation.

But how does one explain Mrs. Heartbreak's attachment to John?

Well:

John was the result of a moment of weakness, moments that Mrs. Heartbreak's mother, Betty Kaiser, described as "one of my daughter's rare 'Josephine Baker Moments' (JBM). JBMs are, BTW, characterized by succumbing to twisted, tempting, thundering, toe tapping, Thorazine infused brain infarcts which look an awful lot like Chaos Theory Moments as they temporarily transcend the normal locus of, in this case, the philosophic and operating frames of reference of Mrs. Heartbreak's Social Order Theory.

John (as you must know by now) is a Chaos Theory Advocate. As a CTA, his belief is that everything is connected to everything else and that no reordering or restructuring or planning by Social Order Theorists can or will successfully change our inevitable free-fall into whatever. Consequently or subsequently or therefore, his and Mrs. Heartbreak's marriage was inevitable.

Factors leading to that inevitable outcome may have been Mrs. Heartbreak's desire to *1*) leave behind an unfortunate maiden name, i.e. 'The Fabulous Miss Kaiser' and exchange it for one that more deeply resonated with her causative potential, i.e. 'The Fabulous Mrs. Heartbreak; *2*) confidence (long since proven to be both misplaced and delusional) that the raw material that was John could be refined into a useable product and; *3*) trust that his unflagging love of, and deeply held devotion to her, was reliable and would last until the end of (his) time (and why wouldn't it, considering who she was and is?). But: whatever; it was inevitable.

During the Heartbreak's by now long and successful marriage, Mrs. Heartbreak's application of the principles of Social Order Theory had softened a wee bit, at least around the edges. Had softened so much, as a matter of fact, that she hardly gave John's current whereabouts—-he, stranded now in the Endtimes Ministry parking lot with Dr. Sloan (much to Dr. Sloan's annoyance)-—much thought throughout this admittedly lengthy and discursive description of her World View and Operating Philosophy.

John's management free moment was not due to any lessening of interest on Mrs. Heartbreak's part but, rather, was rooted in her continuing distress at the Problem of Mother Kaiser and her imminent entry into the Witness Protection Program (WPP). As she got older—my goodness, no longer 39!—it became more difficult to multi-task, and to simultaneously manage more than one potential miscreant at a time. Thus, her concentration was 89% focused on Mrs. Kaiser and only 9% focused on John.

The remaining 2% was allocated to what Carl Rogers annoyingly labeled 'the on-going experience' which, at this precise moment is the Problem of the Bum in the Garden (1%) and the Problem of the Honking Big Winnebago (1%) just now weaving up Pritchard Street.

The Bum in the Garden Problem is Fiacre who, just now has found a crumpled note that he had forgotten to give to John. Mrs. Heartbreak is unaware of Fiacre's consternation—one might conclude that Mrs. Heartbreak is not always in touch with the complexity of others—or that he has a tremendous belly ache from the consumption of John Heartbreak's jalapeño peppers. Consternation plus heartburn has become distress, a notably rare feeling state for Saints, unless of the Martyr variety, in which case the bellyaching was professional, loud, cacophonous, and infinite.

"Dagnabbit," Fiacre muttered (while Mrs. Heartbreak stared at the Winnebago poking up the street). "I guess I'll have to go to Withered Plum and mosey over to Endtimes to deliver the note."

Fiacre was discommoded, but edified that such a swell word would describe how he was feeling. Edified and confirmed that, however he might wish to remain among the vegetables, a Mission from God is a Mission Indeed; he had to play his part and would play it. So:

Fiacre prepared himself to become tridimensional while hoping that the Warrior Queen Sloan and Heartbreak were still in the parking lot. He didn't want to waste time slumming around Endtimes looking for them.

Poof!

Pritchard Street's narrow boundaries barely accommodated the lumbering Winnebago as it pulled to a stop in front of the Keever's bright yellow house, and directly across the street from the Heartbreak residence.

Mrs. Heartbreak was not feeling fabulous or charitable about the proposed parking situation.

"My goodness," she exclaimed. "I certainly hope Mr. and Mrs. Keever will ask their guest to park elsewhere!"

Mrs. Heartbreak's alarm turned to astonishment, and then delight. "Oh Clara Jane," she exclaimed. You've come back!

Chapter 30

John and the Warrior Queen Sloan are frozen in time. This is a literary device—we left them standing in the Endtimes parking lot a chapter or two back—but it is also a hard truth of memory, of organization, and of how the Universe spins and connects no matter our intentions or plans…

At any given instant
All solids dissolve, no wheels revolve
And facts have no endurance
And who knows if it is by design or pure inadvertence
That the present destroys its inherited self-importance?

…wrote Auden, and ain't it the truth, Honey?

When time freezes catfish jump out of the water and are suspended in air. Bees mysteriously evacuate their hives and drop to the ground. Hens stop laying in mid squawking squat. Mice appear dazed and roll to a dead stop in an open hand. Snakes crawl from hibernation burrows and lie as sticks on the snow. Packs of dogs begin   to   howl   simultaneously—and   cease simultaneously.

This happens in a millisecond, or a century, yet who knows for how long it happens? Gum pausing in mid snap snaps, vowels severed from consonants regroup, mephitis hangs in the mist, then wafts; the center ceases holding, then holds.

In the nick of time, so to speak.

John listens to Sharon's cautionary tale, Mrs. Heartbreak grins: Clara Jane grins back. Mr. Eddie Keever is suave and charming on the Tradio Radio while daydreaming of a California beach; each is true: Tradio Radio, the dream and the beach.

Mrs. Gilmore observes a female cardinal land on the rail of her Eureka Springs porch and thinks about visiting Kathmandu, a thing she has never done before. *Cardinalidae Paroaria*, as she calls herself now, but who is really Gujeshwari Prachanda Deva, a human girl once living in Kathmandu, hopes Mrs. Gilmore will lay out some salt.

Gujeshwari Prachanda Deva *ne Cardinalidae Paroaria* has entirely forgotten about the husband who held her head under the water of the Kantipur River until she became a cardinal. But now—this minute, this second—Mrs. Gilmore reads it and remembers it, or can at least think about remembering it. Such is time becoming memory.

John Heartbreak, Dr. Sharon Sloan the Warrior Queen, The Fabulous Mrs. Heartbreak, Clara Jane Smith-Staley, Mr. Eddie Keever, Mrs. Gilmore, Gujeshwari Prachanda Deva, and *Cardinalidae Paroaria*, all share this exact moment, this exact time, this stuck in-between go there time from here time.

Between there and here an Endtimes Suit straining at the seams from angry steroids and Sermons from Revelations, is walking stiff kneed in a perfect line drive toward John and the Warrior Queen. The Suit has a small head, and rubies for eyes that rapidly revolve in deepening sockets.

There is a bulge under the jacket where a heart would be if 'be' can be deciphered in a Clintonesque way. The bulge should be unnoticeable, except that the suit surrounding it and under it is cheaply made and badly tailored. Pinned to the bulge is a plastic sign signifying 'Chet Chandler Endtimes Security'. Chet is caught somewhere between 'is pushing' and 'was pushing' a wheelchair. He has joined John, *et al*, in-between there and here.

Dogs barking, bees dropping, beach dreaming and suave and charming on Tradio Radio, grinning exchanges, bird sightings, river murders, wishes for salt, all of it, was started and stopped and started again by Fiacre's travel from the First Christian Churches' Community Garden (there!) to the Endtimes parking lot (here!).

Time Travel is not seamless; it is not a fabulous run of modern gutter, or a realized advertisement for a Caribbean Cruise, nor even the *poof there to here* suggested in the last chapter. Fiacre hopes to approximate the time and place where John and the Warrior Queen Sloan reside now, but it is entirely possible that he will miss them and it by an hour and a mile; perhaps by even a day and a league.

I'm sure you get it, especially if you are a traveler. John himself expected to arrive in Minneapolis at noon one day, but a weather glitch put him on a bus in Rochester, Minnesota instead. A flat tire, a revolution, a clerical error, all of these and a few more, have made John a day late and a league short more than once. Often, actually.

Sometimes the earth heaves or weeps, has a small seizure, shifts a plate, forms a Continental Rift Zone, or simply ignores the atomic clock and hitches a notch off center and back for no reason at all. Then Fiacre's trip heaves and weaves, seizes up, shifts and hitches a notch off center; it happens to every time traveler. Fiacre has learned to sit back and enjoy the trip; perhaps he'll get there a day before John and Dr. Sloan.

But:

Let us consider Chet. Suppose a man in a bad suit with steroid shot eyes, lumping muscles, and who is packing a gun, approaches you, led by a determined, angry stare. Suppose he believes that the world is ending, and that the ending will be supervised by a chosen few, he among them. You are not among the chosen few, according to him. You. Are. A. Problem.

So here is you, and there is Chet, and Fiacre is somewhere between here and there. What do you suppose will happen, you not being chosen and all?

Chapter 31

The hitch in time that caused Chet Chandler to pause in mid wheelchair push unhitched, affording him and the chair permission to roll forward; he and it did. All the while, Chet's revolving ruby tinged eyes zeroed in on John and the Warrior Queen Sharon Sloan: the left eye on John, the right eye on Sloan.

Strabismus, thought Dr. Sloan, diagnosing Chet's eyeball action (even though she is not a real Doctor). She had seen the condition before, once in Oliver Wendell Haldenstein, an impoverished German Prince working as Faye Dunaway's stunt double in the film *Chinatown*, and once again in her cousin Arietta Basket, an assistant manager at the Taco Tyco in West Fort Worth.

Neither of these cases, however, was accompanied by the blood apparent in Chet's eyes, nor were the eyes set in heads quite as small and round and malevolent as was Chet's. As a matter of record, by the way and just so you know and for future reference, both Arietta and Oliver Wendell are, despite their strabismus, decent, law abiding taxpayers; they wouldn't hurt a flea if it nested in their ear.

That last paragraph is a digression (I suppose) we could live without, yet it sets the stage for our introduction to Chet Chandler, and several important facts about him that provide much needed verisimilitude to our story.

First, Chet was for a brief and shining moment famous for having caught a fish with two heads—one on either end—when he was fourteen years old. A picture of Chet and the two-headed fish testified to this happening in the *Springfield Ledger* and it was accompanied by a 200 word story 'Boy Catches Two-Headed Fish'; CHIK TV ran film at both 5:30 and 10:00. It was a proud moment for Chet and his extended family.

Sadly, that was the high point of Chet's life, and like so many young people who achieve fame early, he began to experience adjustment problems as he neared adulthood and, both he and his family became despondently frustrated as he failed to realize the potential foretold by that earlier, exciting accomplishment.

You, as a reader of literary fiction by high-toned folk such as Alice Sebold, Joan Dideon, or the terrifying Anita Brookner, may find Chet's initial accomplishment and subsequent failure to capitalize on it insufficient cause to warrant or justify the unmitigated hell that his life became for him afterwards, but our story is told in the Ozarks, focuses on the lowest common denominator, and responds sensitively and I believe persuasively to life as it is lived in them thar hills.

Let us also, consider, Honey Bunch, that the last sentence was 80 words long and rated a hard 20 on the Fleisch Kincaid reading scale. I'd like to see Anita Brookner do that, and with only four commas!

But let's cast Anita Brookner aside for the moment:

Chet smiled, first at John, then in the direction of the Warrior Queen, never in the meanwhile, taking an eye off either one. Dr. Sloan noted that Chet gripped the handles of the wheelchair as though wringing the necks of two recalcitrant chickens; that is to say: his knuckles where white with tension and the handles wept (creak, creak) under pressure.

"You folks look like yer havin' a little trouble," Chet said evenly. "I noticed yer hubby weaving around the parkin' lot like a drunkard. But he ain't drunk, is he. Is he?"

"My dear man," Sloan protested. "Lips that touch liquor have rarely touched mine, and not at all for the past 35 years. There was a short period of time, I will admit, when I was a reckless, wild youth, but I soon came to my senses and settled into a Righteous and Formidable Baptist Existence! Yet, even that period of heedlessness was to a purpose: I now KNOW sin when I see it, and can and will CONDEMN it as the occasion arises.

"Which, as I am sure you know," she finished, "Is all too FREQUENTLY!"

"Beggin' yer pardon and amen, Sister," Chet stammered. "We got a lot of strange birds flocking our way these days. And as you may well understand, Pastor Cudrup has many enemies."

"Indeed I do!" boomed Sloan, peering at the security agent's badge. "You are, I see, Chet Chandler, 'Security.'

"Are you qualified for your work, Mr. Chandler? Can you be depended on to protect the Reverend from Secular Humanists, Godless atheists, Episcopalian do-gooders, New Dealers, dope fiends, proponents of open marriage, Unitarian Universalists, Gay, Lesbian, and Transgender Performance Artists, Moderate Republicans, all Democrats, Herbert Buckingham Khaury imitators, Wetbacks, Museum Attending Opera Freaks, Catholics, Jews, Muslim Presidents, Rachel Maddow, fluoridation activists, booksellers, book readers, book reviewers, Harvard University professors, New York Times editorial writers, Richard Simmons, National Public Radio reporters, IRS agents, Certified Public Accountants, and Warrior Queens on a Mission from the Anti-Christ purporting Himself to be God?"

Chet reached into his jacket, pulled out a Magnum .44 and cocked it and aimed the barrel at John's forehead. He said, "Locked, loaded, and ready to kill!" His eyes began to revolve in an extravagant and wildly entertaining way in their sockets. Dr. Sloan applauded.

"Good man, Chet," she said with a delighted laugh. "I believe you'd have Lucifer himself on the run."

"Including this jumped up, Yankee," he muttered, moving the barrel of the gun in a circle a bit smaller than John's head. "I don't like the looks of him."

"Hardly any one does," Dr. Sloan, replied. "But I can vouch for him. He's my husband, Orin Parsnips. We're from Bum Squat."

Chet looked dubious, but lowered the barrel of the gun. "If you say so, Ma'am. But he looks suspicious to me. Why was he weaving around the parking lot?"

"As you should plainly see, Chet," Dr. Sloan said, "My husband suffers from limosis. It causes him to stagger about, bump into things, and lick blackboards. I would guess that today's episode is the result of over-excitement. It's not every day that we get to see Billy and Angel tape their TV show."

Chet nodded and smiled—his teeth resembled millet—and his revolving eyes slowed to a moderate 10 kilometer an hour pace. He drew a deep breath and holstered the .44.

"Sorry if I scared you," he said to John. "You look like one of them intellectuals from Chicago, or Sioux Falls. We just can't...we have to..."

"...maintain eternal vigilance!" Sloan finished for him. "The devil walks the earth and stalks the innocent. We just can't be too careful."

Chet nodded quickly, repeatedly. "Mrs. Parsnips, Ma'am, you are a powerful and truthful speaker. I admire your warrior spirit."

"You too?" she said in surprise. "Well. I had no idea that side of my character is so obvious to everyone. Why haven't I been in touch with it, before now?"

John cleared his throat. "Perhaps Mr. Chandler would let me ride in his wonderful wheel chair?" he said. "I feel another bout of limosis coming on." He stuck out his tongue to demonstrate. "Buhhhhh…"

"How about it, Chet?" Sloan asked with a winning smile. "Shall we wheel hubby into the studio in style."

Chet felt confused. He wasn't actually used to helping people. His original plan for the wheel chair was to slam it into the legs of the old man as a diversion, while he plugged the woman in case she started acting uppity.

"Well, okay," he said slowly. "Let me help you."

Chet grasped John's arm and began to ease him toward the wheelchair's seat. He didn't notice Dr. Sloan stealthily move behind him. Silently, she put her hand on his neck and pressed her forefinger into a fleshy spot just below the beginning of his jaw line. She etched her thumb into the base of his skull and gave it a quick poke. Chet slumped over and fell into the wheel chair.

"The old Tasmanian Devil Detonator," she said proudly, blowing a bit of mythic smoke off the tip of her forefinger. "Works like a charm."

John was speechless. "How in the world did you do that?"

Dr. Sloan shrugged. "We're on a Mission from God," she said. "These things happen."

Chapter 32

Dr. Sloan began to wheel Chet Chandler toward the front door of Endtimes. John followed along behind her, sputtering in protest. Chet lolled in the chair, all dead weight, and dead to the world as well.

"What do you think you're doing?" he said with a rasp. "How are you going to explain this mess?" He was pointing at Chet's slumbering, muscle bound frame and tugged urgently at Sharon's sleeve.

A covey of Endtimes pilgrims stopped near the front door just before entering and stared at John as he queried the Warrior Queen. Their eyes were narrow and sharp with suspicion; it was a practiced look; obviously, they were Free Will Baptists. Dr. Sloan smiled in their direction and nodded pleasantly before turning back to John.

"There's nothing to explain," she whispered to him, smiling for the benefit of their audience. "We'll merely report finding this man *hors de combat* in the parking lot and angrily inquire if the Reverend Cudrup routinely employs drunkards."

"Fine. But what do we do when he wakes up?"

Dr. Sloan laughed. "No worries, my Dear Heartbreak. Or should I say, 'Elementary,' my Dear Heartbreak? Let me educate you.

"The Tasmanian Devil Detonator is," she began, "a secret wrestling hold that, when applied correctly by professionals such as me, render its targets comatose for 15 minutes. Upon awakening, Vics immediately begin exploring their innermost and secret desires. In Chet's case, I'm betting he'll be in bunny slippers and a housedress by the time the dinner bell rings. By sundown he'll be feeding the choir a tuna hot dish."

"Good Lord," John exclaimed. "You've turned him into a Methodist!"

"In the meantime," the Warrior Queen continued, ignoring John's interruption, "you and I will be forgotten in the general shock and awe over Chet's transformation from steroid raging lunatic into a kindly Methodist auntie. The entire Endtimes Security Force will descend on Chet like white on rice—to use an old Texas favorite—thereby providing exactly the diversion I need to raise the curtain on Act One of my Grand Fandango."

John nodded.

Then:

"May I ask how you know that this...this...preposterous scenario is possible?" he asked, in disbelief. "And what's with the Tasmanian Devil thing? I've never heard of such a thing!"

Dr. Sloan sputtered. "Well...," she began, confidently...and then stopped. She looked upwards, then left and right for an answer, but came up empty.

"I guess I'm as mystified as you are," she said, after a lengthy pause. "I have no idea how I knew about the Tasmanian Devil Detonator, or why I can apply it with such authority. But let me say," she continued, "that I'm enjoying my Warrior Queen Powers, however they're derived."

"I think this entire episode is absurd."

"Let me remind you," she said, "That we *are* appearing in a novel. Many things are possible in novels.

"But it is complicated," she agreed. "What's happening right here—right now—in Withered Plum, Missouri, is occurring simultaneously with my writing a snotty letter to the State of Tennessee about the new Sand Hill Crane hunting season. I'm really back in my cottage along the Kings River slapping the heck out of my keyboard. Can't you hear the muffled clacking?"

John cocked his head and tried to pick up the mushy sound of fingers striking a keyboard. He wasn't able to, of course, but counted that as a blessing. Clara Jane Smith—now Clara Jane Staley—had often complained about hearing the Authorial I (that would be me) typing away off stage while she tried to carry on a conversation with Mrs. Heartbreak, or to hear one of Pastor French's fine sermons. Sometimes, it nearly drove her to distraction.

John couldn't pick up on the typing because of his deafness, of course, and other characters in the book, like Mrs. Heartbreak or Alexander Virden, assumed the subtle racket was something happening at the Tyson Plant just north of Berryville. After a while, it was just white noise to them. But Clara Jane, who was constitutionally incapable of ignoring subtle environmental messages, heard every single key stroke.

John simply missed everything.

"Are you able to hear the Authorial I typing?" he asked.

"Of course I can," the Warrior Queen answered. "Between his clacking and my own clacking it's a wonder I can hear anything else. The background noise is the worst part about being in the book, now that you mention it. I wish he would give it a rest, frankly."

John shook his head. "You don't really want that," he replied.

"The minute he stops typing, we're stuck. If he goes to the bathroom—we're stuck. If he pops a cup of Earl Grey into the microwave, we're on hold for at least two minutes and twenty seconds. Imagine standing here forever, me with my hand on your sleeve, and you shepherding Chet's wheelchair. Not pretty to think about."

"I hadn't thought about that," Dr. Sloan said. "What happens if the ugly old toad dies?"

"You don't want to think about it," John said. "But I'm sure it doesn't help calling him an old toad. How would you like fall in love with Pastor Cudrup and become the new Angel?"

"He wouldn't dare!"

"One never knows, do one?"

"I did not volunteer to be an object of ridicule! May I say that I suddenly find the whole idea of parallel universes to be rather odd, especially when my parallel self is subject to the random whims of Whatshisname?"

"The Authorial I," John corrected.

"Whatever. Obviously, I should have consulted with an agent prior to making an appearance in this book. At the very least I should have negotiated some agreement about the minimum amount of Cudrup's ill gotten $6,000,000 that is acceptable as payment to me.

"Hear it now, Heartbreak! I won't take a dime less than four million two. Otherwise, I'm walking right off the page!"

"I can't see what you're complaining about," John retorted. "You get all the best lines, say all the smart things, and you get to be a Great Warrior Queen. I am constantly referred to as dull, old, and deaf. I've become your dagnabbit 'sidekick,' gosh darn it. Which, I'll have you know, I resent!"

"What's your point?"

"It's not fair!"

"But you *are* dull, old, and deaf, while I am witty, bright, and courageous. Surely you see our leadership *Zeitgeist* as entirely rational and natural?"

"I see no such thing. I have half a mind to walk off the page myself!

"Don't be too hasty," Dr. Sloan said. "If you weren't in the book all you'd do would be going to funerals and thinking that doctors' visits are recreational. Certainly, you prefer hobnobbing about with fierce Warrior Queens, such as me, to that?

"I mean," she continued, "the fact that I can render a Neanderthal such as Chet unconscious with a single Tasmanian Devil Detonator is really rather splendid. I'm having a great time, actually."

"Hmmn," John mused. "It is sort of fun…

"…but when we open our detective agency we're going to call it 'Heartbreak and Sloan'. My name first!"

Neither John nor Dr. Sloan was aware that the staring Free Will Baptists had gathered forces and were staring even harder. Who was this insistent woman? And why was she berating that apparently vulnerable old chap, and with large words too?"

Luckily, Chet began to moan, quietly at first, and then rather loudly as his revolving red eyes popped open.

"Ohhhh, my neck," he said, rubbing it with his hand. "What happened?"

Moving quickly, Sloan reached under Chet's elbow and jerked him to his feet, then propelled him into the middle of the approaching crowd.

"Chet," she said with a cheery bray, "let me introduce you to the newest group of Pilgrims come to see Reverend Billy and the lovely Angel!

"Darlings," Chet exclaimed. "How are you? Welcome to Endtimes! Oh my God, you look famished! Can I get you some hot dish! Tuna?"

Sloan smiled as Chet ushered the by now bewildered Free Willers into Endtimes.

"See?" she said.

Chet called out to them, "Where did I get this awful suit!"

Dr. Sloan smiled again.

Chapter 33

Fiacre woke up with a start. He was in a fetal position, arms locked tightly around his knees and head tucked into the fold between his shoulder and the crooks of his elbows.

He was not alarmed; veteran Time Travelers get used to the various and myriad ways in which they land forward or backward away from the moment departed. Poor Procopius, the Roman historian, always woke up grasping the ball on tops of flag poles. Fiacre was grateful enough for his relatively comfortable arrival stance.

You might well imagine that streaking through wormholes and five and six dimensions at a leap, plus general management of time dilation itself and velocity specifically within the context of special relativity, exemplified by the twin paradox—along with gravitational dilation as required by general relativity— is complicated and requires special training; and so it does, unless you're a Saint, RC, in which case it's a snap. (Feel free to consult E.U. Condon and Hugh Odishaw, *Handbook of Physics, 2nd ed.* McGraw-Hill Book Company, 1967, for the particulars. Or, just take my word for it.)

Time Travelers commonly share several initial seconds of disorientation after arrival, along with a bit of nausea. Fiacre was no exception and was experiencing both right now.

Happily, the feeling of disorientation falls away rather quickly, and Travelers can dose themselves with a couple of newt's eyes and an image of Barry Manilow to ameliorate the nausea.

Clinical trials show, however, that Manilow side-effects may include esophageal hemorrhage, naughty thoughts about your sister-in-law, depression, suicidal ideation, barking, objects appearing smaller in mirrors, increased worries about spontaneously combusting, sudden weight gain, dementia, road rage, and desires to dress like Joan Collins. Discontinue use of Manilow if you experience any of these side effects, and consult your physician immediately.

Fiacre, experienced herbalist that he is, simply ignored the nausea; he knew it would dissipate in a minute. He used the minute to uncurl and take stock of his surroundings.

He was in a small, very dark room. He knew it was small because he could feel the hard surfaces to his right and left with his hands. When he stretched out feet they bumped up against another hard surface; he pulled his right arm in and then raised it out in front of his body as far as it would go, and hit another hard surface. He deduced that he was either in a closet, or stuck in the trunk of a 1976 Lincoln Continental Mark V.

The Mark V came to mind because he'd been locked in the trunk of Imelda Marco's Lincoln back in '76 and it was full of shoes, as was his current space. He hoped he hadn't miscalculated and ended up back in Manila instead of Endtimes.

Back then, Imelda's security force had roughed him up quite a bit before stuffing him into the trunk of her car for safe keeping until an execution date could be set. It was an altogether unpleasant experience and not one he wished to repeat. He raised himself up to his knees and felt the soft brush of fabric against his cheek. Ah: not a trunk; he was in a closet.

Fiacre stood and fumbled around for a door. When he found the knob he cracked the door open quietly, and squinted against the sudden onslaught of light. Angel Cudrup was sitting at a dressing table, brushing her hair. Her back was to him—brush, brush—and he quickly pulled the door shut. Oops.

Fiacre was an experienced avoider of women. Like many men of the 7th century his views of the fairer sex have and had been shaped by culture and custom. On one hand he, like the fool Heartbreak, idolized one woman—in John's case the Fabulous Mrs. Heartbreak, in Fiacre's case the Blessed Virgin, for whom he had built an oratory and hospice in the province of Brie near Prodilius. On the other hand...

...suddenly the closet door opened! Mrs. Cudrup and Fiacre stood nose to nose, she with a puzzled expression on her pretty face that morphed into a gasp. She quickly stepped back.

Fiacre quickly stepped forward. "Behold a pale horse!" he shouted, thinking fast.

"His name that sat on him was Death, and Hell followed with him! And power was given unto them over the fourth part of the earth, to kill with sword, and with hunger, and with death, and with the beasts of the earth!"

Mrs. Cudrup fainted dead away; Fiacre stepped over her body with a chuckle.

"Jeepers," he laughed. "That worked out pretty good! And now, for a quick get-a-way."

Fiacre scanned the room. He was probably in Dilly and Angel's bedroom. There was a frilly canopy bed in the center of one wall and two night stands on either side of the bed. Fiacre resisted the urge to peek inside the drawers, but he did notice several pair of platform shoes, including a pair of tennis shoes, on Billy's side of the bed. Fiacre estimated how tall Billy might be; maybe five one, five two tops, but it was so hard to tell by watching him on television. It was possible that Reverend Cudrup was only eleven inches tall in the middle, and the top and the bottom was platform shoes and toupee. Maybe he would stay at Endtimes long enough to catch the show.

There was a door to his left, flanked by a Thomas Kincaid painting. Fiacre glanced at the painting and felt a post trip nausea burble, but gulped it back and hurried from the room. Twenty feet beyond the painting lay another door that was probably a way out of the Cudrup's living quarters. Fiacre hoped that it was in, or adjacent to, the Endtimes Compound; he needed to find the dullard Heartbreak and the Warrior Queen ASAP.

He opened the door and stepped out into a hallway that looked sufficiently like one in a Motel Six to warrant a nausea ameliorating burble of confidence. The trouble with time travel, he thought, and with being a Time Traveler itself, was the approximations of time and space that signaled the end of a journey. He had talked to God about some improvements, but the conversation had gone a predicable route:

Fiacre: "How about when I Time Travel I get to exactly where I want to be, at exactly the time I want to get there?"

God: "Where's the fun in that?"

Fiacre: "It's not about fun!"

God: "Oh, yeah?"

But it was looking better and better that he was at Endtimes. When he got to the elevator there was an 'Out of Order' sign taped to its door, and he noticed that the hallway carpet was fuzzy and delaminating, even though the Compound itself was less than eighteen months old. Cudrup was, no doubt, of the opinion that it made no sense to invest in 30 year construction if the world was ending in five.

He cocked an eye toward the end of the hall and saw an EXIT sign over a door to what he hoped led to a downward staircase.

As he neared it, the door opened and a kid walked through it. The kid had lank brown hair cut to look like Justin Bieber's, and was similar to the mod shags Fiacre saw when he visited London during the' 60s. He smiled and flipped a peace sign toward the kid.

"Wow," the kid said. "I love your shirt."

Fiacre looked down and nodded. *'Jesus is coming! Look busy!'* he read. "Yeah. It's pretty cool. I took it off a guy when I was at a Tim LaHaye book signing. He whined like a collie."

"Cool."

"Say," Fiacre asked, "have you seen a dull looking old guy and a fierce Warrior Queen anywhere?"

The kid shook his head. "I dunno," he said. "One of our security guards went nutso and threw away his gun. He keeps screaming for tuna hot dish and is running on and off the television set. Pastor Cudrup is going crazy.

"Anyway, security locked the front door and they're trying to nab the guy. They're not letting anyone in or out of the building until they grab him. Maybe your friends are in the parking lot.

"It's pretty weird around here, today," the kid finished. "Maybe today is the day?"

"What day?"

"You know," the kid said. "The day we ago *ku-bluey*. End times?"

"Nah, it isn't today," Fiacre said. "It isn't going to happen for a long time."

"Really?" the kid asked. Hopefulness mixed with doubt.

"Yeah," Fiacre said. "The world can't end until Sarah Palin marries Dennis Rodman and they have Korean triplets."

"Dude?"

"Word."

"Does Mrs. Palin even know Dennis?"

"Not yet. But I had a vision, and they are always on the money. Dennis repents, Palin refudiates, and they bump uglies."

"Wow."

"And then Dennis becomes President."

The kid nodded thoughtfully. "Yeah. That would be end times."

"So you see," Fiacre said, "you've got lots of time. Time enough to blow this pop stand; maybe go to California. Have some fun, maybe?"

The kid nodded. "Wow."

"So," Fiacre said. "How do I get to the television studio?"

The kid pointed down the stairs beyond the open door. "I can show you," he said.

Chapter 34

Nothing in this book is a coincidence, or everything is a coincidence. The boy leading Fiacre down the stairs is from Tisdale, Missouri, a snarl of a town seventeen miles southeast of Withered Plum, and thirty seven miles northeast of Berryville. Clara Jane Smith now Staley, who is now—right now!—in Berryville receiving a hug from Mrs. Heartbreak, is originally from Tisdale.

[If you think this is more than a coincidence, cue in some scary organ music.]

Organ music is a good thing to cue in right now—can you hear it?—because the boy from Tisdale is Endtimes's organ player, although maybe organ player isn't quite what he is; he has never had a music lesson and he doesn't play so much as he blitzkriegs sheet music. He has certainly never played a thing that folks in Tisdale heard before he started playing it—and they never ever wanted to hear what he played a second time.

One day the boy started to peck at his Uncle Delta Sartell's electric keyboard; a week later he was whacking out Boellmann's Toccata. I guess he is a savant.

What the boy played was church music. Church music *is* more or less okay in Tisdale as long as the tune in question sounds like Barber Shop Quartet singing, or something Wynonna Judd might twang to death after a debauched night and a shame glutted morning. But the boy played 'ungodly church music', 'music to murder hogs by' according to Uncle Sartell, who nervously snatched the keyboard away from the boy after hearing him play the *Suite Gothique*. "You're scaring me, boy," Sartell told him. "You're reminding me of Clara Jane."

The boy, whose name is Lawrence Biggs, is at least twenty years younger than Clara Jane, and although he has never met her, he knows her story very well, and he knows what remains of her extended family since they still live in Tisdale. What remains of them.

Like the boy, Clara Jane is also a savant, probably Tisdale's first savant as a matter of fact, which is probably why folks in town get the willies over any kind of specialness, specialness not being abundant in any local sense, whether it takes the boy's ghostly form of hog killing music, or Clara Jane's unrequited killing of kin, which hardly ever involved music at all unless you're a John Cage fan and see the point and counterpoint of gags, yelps, groans, weeps, whines, grinds, crackle crackle, and the suck splat sounds of person centered mayhem, to paraphrase Carl Rogers, as music.

Only 47% of the people who live in the Ozarks—that would include Tisdale and Withered Plum, Berryville and Eureka Springs—are born and bred there, stay there, and live there now; the 'Others' are Yankees like John and Mrs. Heartbreak, or Appalachian American Look-a-Likes from adjacent southern states or the regrettable Texas. These 'Others' have no idea what the large minority that surrounds them, engulfs them, cheats them, resents them, and laughs at them, is up to (except for the surrounding, engulfing, cheating, resenting, and laughing parts. They get that.).

But there is only so much moonlight and magnolia, so much Shepherd of the Hills hoodoo a person can swallow before they're forced to slap themselves sentient and slink back to the Continental United States from whence they came, or become Pinball Wizards: deaf, dumb, and blind. Welcome to The Natural State!

And so it came to pass, as Joseph Smith began 926 sentences in the Book of Mormon, that 53% of Tisdale's population was completely unaware that residents were disappearing at the rate of about one a week, while the other 47%, the 'Naturals', knew that folks were disappearing at a higher than average clip, but reserved judgment because the disappeared weren't missed all that much. Their absence, in fact and not to put too fine a point on it, enhanced property values and improved Tisdale's admittedly dismal but overall quality of life. So it was all good. More or less. Depending on your view of such matters. Anyway:

They—the disappeared, the absent, the here today gone tomorrow—the departed, had in common one thing; they were blood bound to Little Clara Rinker, now Clara Jane Smith Staley: cousins, uncles, a brother, and Peyton Knobsgobble, not a blood relative but a partner in the methamphetamine sale and distribution business with Ray Bob's Tisdale Tap, Clara's brother and first cousin.

It wasn't long after Peyton, Jimmy Joe, and Joe Jimmy disappeared that they were followed by Billy Willy Rinker and then by Charles Ray, Ray Billy, Billy Ray, and Ray Charles Rinker (the Appalachian American Ray Charles, not the African American Ray Charles). If you're counting, that's eight little Rinkers gone to ground (plus one Knobsgobble).

It was only when Bobbie Rae Postwhistle, the wife of Billy R. Postwhistle and the sister of Bobby Ray Rinker disappeared, that the Rinker family started to talk about the suddenly departed. Bobbie Rae was the barmaid at Ray Bob's Tisdale Tap and, when she didn't show up for work as scheduled, and Billy R. Postwhistle didn't know "where the expletive deleted" was, all the Rinkers began looking over their shoulders and jumping at the sound of cat scratches.

The 'Others' in town, that lamentable pack of pansies and over-educated elites from the outside, continued to be oblivious to the dwindling number of Rinkers, and except for noting the pleasurable decrease in high speed methamphetamine fueled 4x4 traffic on the single road through town, kept to themselves and their Fellow NPR listening Travelers. Nothing bothered them at all…except for that horrible smell!

On occasional basis the foul odors of industrial chicken production, processing, packaging and transporting abated through some climatic miracle; perhaps the wind shifts a degree or two, the temperature pauses between degrees, and the barometric pressure takes a dose of Prozac and napped for a while.

The confluence of such happenings will, for an hour, a weekend, ameliorate the habitual stinkyness of The Natural State, that Land of Opportunity, long enough for Realtors to tour visiting Others about the place—a Window into the Land of Opportunity—to laud its beauty, celebrate its low property taxes, to encourage the myth that its poverty is mere quaintness, and to get the Others to sign on the dotted line.

"What are you doing this weekend?" Realtor One asks.

"Wal, if the wind dies down I guess I'll go trawlin' for Others," says Realtor Two.

If at closing the wind has shifted and the Other sniffs and becomes alarmed, be not surprised if the Realtor feigns befuddlement:

"Smell? I don't smell anything… here just sign there… and there… and…"

After a while the Others become about as indifferent to the faint smell of carcass permeating the environment as are the Natives. Once in, oh say, a blue moon, an Other who is teetering between sentience and Pinball Wizardry might sniff and ask, "What's that smell!!?"

To which Natives have been trained to invariably reply, "It smells like money!"

This from a guy who makes twelve bucks an hour gutting chickens on 3rd shift.

But the air had become intolerably meaty in Tisdale, and let's says it was on Robert E. Lee's birthday, 1996, just to pick a day, that those gone missing was finally acknowledged. Several Natives had gathered outside the door of Ray Bob's Tisdale Tap, preparing to go in to celebrate the General's birthday, when Ray Billy Rinker Jr. exclaimed, against all rules of training and eleven years of indoctrination, "What's that smell!!?"

"It smells like money," replied a chorus of Natives.

"No it doesn't!" shouted Ray Billy Jr., pointing. "It smells like Bobbie Rae Postwhistle! There she is!"

And there was Bobbie Rae, in plain sight, crucified on the hood of an abandoned 1976 school bus parked across the street from The Tap, the bus currently serving—well, current to mean for the last eleven years—as the home of the Prekel Beantop family. Mrs. Postwhistle's body was partially obscured by a small flock of buzzards which, sensing the approaching crowd, lifted off and flew away in a crabby, buzzardly manner, leaving the body in plainer view.

"Yep, that's the wife," said Ray Bob Postwhistle. "I guess somebody should call the High Sheriff."

The preceding violent passages are unfortunate, and you have my apologies for this seeming violation of the NSVSL rule. But it is, frankly, impossible to say much about the Ozarks without at least a *soupcon* of skullduggery. Bad dentistry and Wal-Mart can only take you so far, literature wise. In any case, please be advised that the next two paragraphs are a bit graphic.

It took the sheriff's deputies almost four hours to get Bobbie Rae's remains off the hood of that old school bus. She had been thoroughly Super Glued to the sheet metal and, because the glue had hardened into an almost glass-like substance during the five days the sheriff estimated the body had reposed there, his deputies had had to chip, chip, chip-away before they could stand her up, and then put her down and into a waiting ambulance.

Although it would be five days before they determined a cause of death—Bobbie Rae had had the living delights scared out of her—the Sheriff's Department, and then the Missouri State Crime Investigation Unit with back-up support from the Tisdale Fire Department, wasted no time in locating the remains of the missing eight Rinkers and the unfortunate Peyton Knobsgobber.

They found Jimmy Joe Rinker's body hanging by the neck from the town's water tower. Joe Jimmy's body was lashed (tidily) to the 'Arkansas 33 miles' sign on the south side of town. His feet and hands were missing, causing investigators to surmise that he hadn't tried to walk out of town, or hitchhike. That left only foul play or, so at least, they concluded.

Most of Billy Willy Rinker was found leaning up against the wall of the Antioch Primitive Holiness Tabernacle on Main Street; Charles Ray was in the hog roaster in City Park; Ray Billy was going up and down on the elementary school's teeter totter; Billy Ray was sitting in the backseat of the town's squad car, and Ray Charles Rinker slept the big sleep on a lime green velour couch on Mrs. Ajax Freeway's porch.

The time between the first death—that would be Jimmy Joe Rinker, and the last death—Bobbie Rae Postwhistle, was eleven weeks. You may be wondering how it is possible for ten corpses to hide in plain sight for so long. How, you may ask, was it possible for residents not to see a moldering corpse tied to one of the town's two traffic signs? Or, how about that crazy guy Ray Billy, going up and down on the teeter totter? Didn't the kids out on recess wonder about him as he bobbled up, down, up?

Obviously, alls ya'alls don't get off the main roads much. You haven't tried to get an Ozark based town council to enforce building codes, or cut its grass, those amber waves of weeds thriving along all its public byways. Nor have you experienced the collective blindness of the Natives as their towns become like the Sears and Roebuck couch painting Aunt Tillie bought in 1963; no one has really looked at it since the Kennedy assassination.

The fact is that dead bodies could positively festoon the streets of Berryville or Withered Plum or Green Forest, Arkansas—to name just three—and no one would notice. If an Other pointed it out, the Natives would just resent it. No kidding: take a look around; be especially tuned into groups of buzzards; you never know what you might see if you look closely enough.

When folks got around to telling fourteen year old Clara Jane of the deaths of her eight relatives, of a close business associate of theirs, and of a neighbor, the barmaid Bobbie Rae Postwhistle, she was remarkably dry-eyed. No one suspected that the small statured teenager had had anything to do with the killings, but everyone who talked to her commented on the cold chill that ran down their spines.

"Sumpin' ain't right about that gal," everyone said. "When she looks at me I hear music to kill hogs by!"

When Ray Bob Postwhistle began looking around for a replacement wife for the now deceased Bobbie Ray Postwhistle, he naturally sized up 14 year old Clara Jane.

"Dang," he said, licking his lips.

And therein lay the solution to the eleven murders— Bobbie Ray soon joined the eight Rinkers, Peyton Knobsgobber, and the late Mrs. Postwhistle; Clara Jane had plans opposed to those of her close and extended family that did not include the mailing of those Ozark inspired greetings cards such as 'Happy Birthday, dear Uncle Dad!' or 'Merry Christmas, Brother Cousin Otis!"

Clara Jane's plans also excluded early marriage to the likes of Ray Bob and Ray Bob's Tisdale Tap. She, like so many other young people from small Ozark towns, hoped to become a beautician—Sheer Delight!—or to move away to Branson for a job in the Hospitality Industry—"do you want fries with that?" Certainly then, Ray Bob's lusts, and his hopefulness for free labor, had to be thwarted.

Ray Bob's intentions toward Clara Jane were well known in Tisdale. He discussed his options in comprehensive detail with Tap regulars—should he wait until she was 15?—should he let her finish the 9th grade?—but ultimately concluded that neither important and loudly announced his intentions to proceed post haste.

"Ain't you scared of her, Ray Bob?" folks asked. "I hear hog murdering music when she walks by."

"She'll be squealing like a little piggy this time next week," he said, with a grin. "That's the only music you'll be hearing."

201

Ray Bob was thwarted by 5,000 volts from an arc welder; his remains were stored in the Out of Town mailbox in front of the post office. He would have remained there indefinitely except that Ray Bob was the single source of beer in Tisdale and, when he failed to open at 7:30 AM for Bertha E. Wheatley, an Episcopalian Other and problem drinker, or again at 8:45 AM for Hymer E. Crull, a Native and Tisdale's Designated Town Drunk (DTD), a hue and cry was sounded and the search began.

By now, both Natives and Others shared whispers about Clara Jane, and more than one Tisdale resident had spoken to the High Sheriff about the spooky girl.

"We'll keep an eye on her," he said. "But if she's done it, she done it good. We ain't got no proof."

To Clara Jane's satisfaction, there was a precipitous drop off in proposals, regular or otherwise. She began also to grow in self-awareness, and recognized that she possessed talents that were not only highly specialized, but in short supply as well. Perhaps there were persons outside Tisdale of low moral character who would not be missed if they became Departed? Perhaps there were persons willing to pay for the pleasure of not missing someone?

Please buy *Coffee with John Heartbreak: A Mostly Truth Story of Berryville, Arkansas*, to learn if such a supposition is true.

Thus, when nearly twenty years later the boy Lawrence Biggs started playing Boellmann, and then that old Bach goody in *D Minor*, folks in Tisdale began having trouble sleeping at night. When they turned corners they stopped first and peered around it before proceeding; they took to checking the water tower for swinging men. Every note Lawrence played stirred up a

Clara Jane memory. Folks got the Chronic Willies so bad they put new locks on the doublewide.

When news of the new Endtimes Ministry in nearby Withered Plum got to be common knowledge, Roberta Yates, a member of the Living Word Full Gospel Pentecostal Whole Truth and Real Deal Church of Revelation reported a vision of Lawrence playing his music there for Billy and Angel Cudrup. Not surprisingly, Mrs. Yates' vision was widely accepted as a Command from God, and Red Yates, husband of Roberta, was designated to haul Lawrence Biggs over to Endtimes and drop him off there. The Tisdale town council providently gave Red $50 to cover expenses, which worked out to more than $1 a mile, high cotton indeed.

Lawrence was delighted to have a real organ to play, albeit electric rather than pipe, and auditioned for Endtimes's Music Minister Dr. Randy Starr by playing *Bach's Trio Sonata, 3rd* movement.

Dr. Starr was worried about the Communist music he was hearing, but recognizing that Lawrence was a savant, and not a true musician, played a recording of 'Jesus, You Rock My World' by the Bob Jones University Glee Club, and asked Lawrence if he could replicate it. Of course he could; Endtimes offered Lawrence a music internship providing free room and board; Red Yates and the Tisdale town council accepted the offer on Lawrence's behalf.

It is not the nature of savants to have strong feelings about their savanting activities. Like Clara Jane before him, it was enough that Lawrence could do a thing that was in short supply. Clara was able to kill with ease and impunity; Lawrence could play anything on the organ, easily and with the same impunity.

And so:

As the boy and Fiacre head down the stairs, he tells Fiacre that his name is Lawrence Biggs, "but everybody calls me Little Biggs 'cause my sister Roberta is Big Biggs and she ain't the small one in the family."

Fiacre nodded. "Okay," he said. "Little Biggs it is." He liked Little Biggs, and how unafraid the boy with the Justin Bieber haircut appeared, when they had nearly collided outside the Cudrup residence near the staircase door. Fiacre didn't know that the boy was a savant, perhaps an idiot savant, and assumed that the boy, like Fiacre himself, operated mostly by instinct and grace and wouldn't care anymore than Fiacre did that Angel Cudrup was lying in a deep fearful swoon on the mobile home grade carpet in Billy Cudrup's boudoir.

After all, Fiacre thought, what had Angel ever done for Little Biggs or, for that matter, what had Reverend Billy Cudrup ever done for Little Biggs, except rob him of his precious teenage time and scare the ever-loving shineola out of him with lies about end times?

Fiacre and Little Biggs did share the opinion that most of what bad could happen to Angel had already happened. Surely her chance meeting with the harmless Time Traveler Fiacre was a small thing against the bigger, tragic, Whoop Dee Doo of marriage to a 70 year old time share salesman who wore high heels and owed the IRS $6,000,000.

Fiacre was sure that Angel would snap out of her current swoon and, if Little Biggs came to know that Fiacre was the cause of Angel's current circumstances, well, he wouldn't think it amounted to much. After all, Little Biggs had, coincidentally or not, grown up in snarling Tisdale in the shadow of Clara Rinker now Clara Jane Smith Staley, and was no stranger to life in the Lower Depths.

"Where does this stairway lead, Little Biggs?" asked Fiacre. "Will I find the Warrior Queen at the bottom of it?"

"It goes down to the Grand Hall."

"Grand Hall?"

"Yeah. It's just a TV studio with some stores around it," Little Biggs reported. "There's the Holy Bunker Café, the Angel Travel Shoppe, Randi Chapel which Pastor Cudrup named after his mom, some kind of grocery store and a bookstore, a sewing shop, and a place where they sell houses and condos and stuff."

Fiacre and the boy reached the second floor. He could see the bottom of the stairs, one flight down, and felt a shiver of anticipation for the fun he expected to have once he got there. He wanted to give Heartbreak Dorothy's note of instruction, and then sit back and watch it all unfold.

"What's the Warrior Queen?" Little Biggs asked. He was at the bottom of the stairway, looking upwards toward the slower moving Fiacre.

"The Warrior Queen is a who, not a what," he answered. "She is here to Grand Fandango the Reverend Cudrup and seek the return of $6,000,000."

"Cool. Can I help?"

"I don't see why not," Fiacre said with a smile. "Why don't you open the door?"

Chapter 35

As Fiacre and the Little Biggs reached the bottom of the stairway and where about to enter into the Endtimes's television study—and the electronic lair of Reverend Billy Cudrup—Dr. Sharon Sloan, AKA The Warrior Queen and the dullard John Heartbreak—stood rapping at the now locked front door leading into Endtimes.

Dr. Sloan had attempted to follow the Baptist visitors, who had initially appeared so threatening and suspicious of her and John. But John had slowed her down, and an Endtimes security guard had literally slammed the door on her foot and pushed her back before locking the door.

She was not entirely surprised by the guard's obstreperous behavior, and acknowledged, with a chilly grin to John, that the guard was simply another weak as water male appendage unable to cope with, or accept her, as a more dominant, vibrant female figure than were the women he habitually shoved around back at the trailer court. No doubt the guard would be similarly rude to Jeanne du Arc, Mae West, Boudicca, Belle Starr, or even to the household goddess, Martha Stewart.

"I believe," Sloan said, thoughtfully, "that I'll turn that little man into a fire hydrant as soon as we get inside, and then turn the dogs loose on him."

"Can you do that?" John asked. "I was unaware that mastery of the Tasmanian Devil Detonator included the anthropomorphic power required by such a boast."

She raised her eyebrows and turned to face him directly, *vis-à-vis*, as it were.

"You have no idea, Heartbreak, of what I am capable." She cracked her knuckles and seemed to enjoy the sound of thunder emanating from each digit. "Let's get this show on the road, shall we?"

Dr. Sloan cupped a hand over her brow and pressed a noble nose to the door's window, peering into, so to speak, and through, a glass darkly. "Dagnabbit!" she exclaimed. "We're missing all the action.

"Chet Chandler's running, being chased by a cadre of Endtimes Minions. It looks like they're gaining on him."

"Is Chet still packing a gun?" John asked. "I'm not exactly sure what a minion is, but I don't want anyone to get plugged unnecessarily."

"Oh, wow," Sloan said. "I can see Billy! He's walking over to the Head Minion and shouting at him. This is so exciting!"

"What does he look like?"

"He's about five feet tall without the shoes, five six with them, and has a face like a Winesap apple left over from last year."

"No, no," John said. "Not Cudrup! I mean the Head Minion. I want to know if we're going up against large, angry Blackwater Consulting types, or garden variety Appalachian Americans? Does he have missing teeth, or appear to be dropping his Gs when speaking?

"Or, as might be the case under a Blackwater Consulting scenario, a Head Minion who would possibly speak with a Slovenian accent and carry an automatic weapon? These details," John finished, "are germane to the task at hand."

"Oh my," Sloan said, ignoring John's question. "Chet's taking his clothes off. Jeepers! He's thrown his underpants at Cudrup—and scored! Billy's wearing Chet's panties around his neck. This is so great!"

"Sharon, it appears that your diversion is working," Jon said. "But we need a quiet moment with the Reverend and, locked out as we are, I don't see that we can seize the advantage."

"Hmmn. You're right, Heartbreak! There is a time to cut bait, and a time to fish! A time to sow, and a time to reap!"

"You sound positively biblical."

"Don't get carried away," she said dismissively. "I still have my eye on the money. Go back to the car and get my deer slayer hat," she commanded, suddenly. "We are about to mince Minions and ream Reverends!"

"You worry me," John said.

He backed away and peered into her face. It seemed to glow preternaturally and, if he wasn't altogether mistaken, wore an expression of manic enthusiasm that belied the important religious and spiritual intentions of the endeavor. John was usually willing to go along with the demands of women—after all, he was still married to the Fabulous Mrs. Heartbreak—but asking him to run and fetch a hat was too much! Is that what being on a mission from God required? That he become as docile as a Labrador Retriever? He didn't think so.

"My dear Dr. Sloan," he began. "Let me remind you that I am a man of some substance. Simply because I choose to keep my lamp under a bushel basket is no cause…"

"…Heartbreak! Hat! Move."

As John jogged over to the White Chevy van to retrieve (ha!) the Warrior Queen's deer slayer hat, she moved stealthily along the front wall of the Compound and began testing window latches.

"Drat!" Each was securely locked. She began tapping on what looked like an apartment or condo window, first to ascertain if someone was inside and secondly, to break the glass adjacent to the lock if no one was home, and force entry. She sneered; that would give John a few worries.

John showed up, huffing and wheezing like an antique combine. He pushed his arm forward and watched the Warrior Queen take her hat from his hand and slap it on her head.

"Perfect," she said, with satisfaction. "Now, do you mind breaking the glass, right about…" pointing…"here?"

"Madam, I am not a common criminal!"

"Break the glass, John. We're on a mission from God. Did Isaiah quibble over details? Did Jeremiah wimp out over simple legalities?"

"Jeremiah had a few objections!"

"He may not be the best example. My point is that these are extraordinary times. You say you want to Save Normal Christianity, which you say you are commanded by God to do, but you whine about spilling a little milk. My advice to you, Heartbreak, is to man up and move out!"

John closed his eyes and gave the window a tentative tap. Tap. Tap. Tap again.

"Oh for Gosh sakes," Dr. Sloan hissed. She pulled the deer slayer hat off her head and covered her elbow with it before smashing the window, then reached inside and forced the latch open.

Sloan ignored John's shock and pushed the window open. "After you, John," she said. "Let's go Save Normal Christianity."

Chapter 36

John is stuck midway in the newly smashed window in an imaginatively undignified manner. Imagine it.

Dr. Sloan has her hands on his enormous ass, pushing and shoving and grumbling uncharitably about John's bulk and the inflexible, not to say brittle, composition of his body's advance toward entropy. His stomach is an unbudgeable fulcrum.

John stares at an unmade bed festooned with throw pillows and an afghan depicting cats engaged in varieties of cute cat behavior. It is hideous and frightening because John knows that a person who would purchase such an article is capable of almost anything.

The more Dr. Sloan shoves and heaves, the faster John rocks. His forehead nearly touches the floor on the downward cycle before snapping upward to the top of a painful arc. He is like one of those perpetual motion goony birds: up and down, fast and faster. He feels a little nauseous.

John allows himself to relax. Dr. Sloan will succeed, or not succeed, in propelling him into the immediate future; he understands that he is trapped in time—a moment ago he watched gaped mouth as the Warrior Queen broke glass— in a second, or in several minutes, he will tumble onto the illicitly gained floor, or into the arms of the law—he isn't going anywhere just now: so he rocks, and waits.

Fiacre and the boy-savant Little Biggs, a refugee from Tisdale, Missouri, are at the bottom of an Endtimes stairwell leading to the Compound's Grand Hall, and are about to open the door to enter it. They are looking for John, and for the Warrior Queen Sloan, and do not know that John is nearby, trapped between that old time and the about to happen time and that he isn't able to move forward just yet.

Angel Cudrup, Little Billy Cudrup's replacement for the late, great Televangelism Superstar Donna Raye Cudrup, has awakened from her dead-a-away faint, and begins to shake the beam from her eye. "What happened?" she wonders out loud. "Who was that tacky man in my closet? Was there a tacky man in my closet?"

Wobbling, Angel gets to her feet and immediately begins to weep. Once, she had lived in a real place; now she lives in Withered Plum, Missouri, shackled in marriage to an old geezer who won't shut up about end times. He has wet lips and wears high heels; he hasn't 'known' her in months. Derelicts are popping out of closets now too, shouting scary stuff, and wearing really smelly T-Shirts about Jesus coming.

She wonders if she's having a reaction to all the anti-depressants she's taking; how long can you use Prozac and Xanax, Alprazolam and Benzodiazepine, Zoloft and Effexor, without hallucinating? Or, maybe she needs to up her dose; yes, that must be it: she intends to double down tonight.

As Angel stumbles back over to her dressing table, John continues to rock back and forth on the window sill. He is slightly amused at Dr. Sloan's increasingly frantic labors. But he is also becoming disoriented by her failed efforts to propel him into the future: he is there, then he is here; he rocks back and forth between now and then.

Finally, she stops. "A little help, Heartbreak?" she inquires. "Would it be too much to ask if you would please reach out and drag yourself forward a bit?"

211

"There a really terrifying afghan on the bed. It's full of cats driving Volkswagens and looking smug. I don't want to touch it."

Sloan has had enough. She takes her hands off his ass and crouches down against the wall beneath the window and crawls under John's dangling legs. She puts her shoulders and back tight against his legs and, like a collegiate fullback breaking toward the goal line, shoots straight up with Warrior Queen resolve. John tumbles through the window and into the future.

"Oh my word," he whispers hoarsely. "This is ghastly. The horror, the horror!"

"What?"

"There's a stack of Kenneth Copeland books on the nightstand! And they're paperbacks!"

Dr. Sloan clambered through the window. "You're such a snob, John," she said. "You live in a High Church Wonderland and look down on low churched slobs who don't share your elevated religious fantasy."

John picked himself up off the floor and moved away from the afghan on the bed. "Mission from God, not withstanding," he said. "I see we have a little missionary work to do with you."

Dr. Sloan ignored him and looked around the room. They were in an apartment, or condo of indiscriminate but new construction, that exuded the scent of impermanence. Perhaps that, she thought, was because the entirety of Endtimes's *raison d'etre* was the near term destruction of the Universe. One would certainly buy paperbacks under such a scenario.

"We need to blow this pop stand," Sloan said. "How do we get out?"

John pointed to the obvious door and began to shuffle toward it. Dr. Sloan attached herself to his arm and slipped around and in front of him. "Let us make haste, John," she said firmly. "I'll lead, if you don't mind."

John did mind, but he was eager to leave the frightening afghan and the paperback Copelands behind; he acquiesced and revved-up his shuffle to keep pace with Dr. Sloan's hurried pace. She crossed what appeared to be a living room and opened what was almost certainly a door leading out of the unit. She cautiously stuck her head out, and quickly yanked it back in, after slamming the door shut (in case you're keeping track of the order of things).

"Chet Chandler is running up and down the hall," she said breathlessly. "He's naked and being pursued by minions."

"Many minions? Mini Minions? Minor Minions? Or, are the minions full-blown Blackwater Consulting minions with automatic weapons and Slovenian accents?"

"Will you be serious?!"

"Sharon, I'm as serious as an Edith Wharton novel!"

"Hmmn. Serious indeed," she judged. "Alright, then. What do we do? We can't stay here?"

"I suppose we could go back out the window?"

"Are you kidding? And go through all that 'trapped between times' jazz again? Not on your Nellie!"

John edged around her and cracked the door open. He could hear rapid clomping and hammering of feet on carpet and shrieks—they had to be Chet's shrieks—but the sound was coming from a stairway at the end of a hallway of doors. The hallway itself was empty.

John opened the door and stepped briskly out into the hall—well, with a moderate lope—and motioned for Dr. Sloan to follow him. They turned left, away from the shrieks and clomping noise, and headed toward what they hoped was an egress to the Great Hall.

Eureka!

Standing in the Great Hall was Billy Cudrup himself. His hands were on his hips and he was looking toward the ceiling of the hall, shaking his head. Several people holding clipboards and wearing headphones milled around him; they looked anxious, and seemed to be trying to placate him.

"I'm not happy, people!" Cudrup said loudly. "We're on the air in 15 minutes and there is a crazy man running around. A naked man, in case you didn't notice."

Cudrup's voice was nasally and whiney and timbered with tight high notes that were curiously girlish and adolescent at the same time. He wore tight black jeans and a black turtle neck and, of course, boots with four or five inch heels. It struck John that, if Agnes de Mille were still living, if she was a man instead of a woman, if she somehow lived in Withered Plum, Missouri instead of New York City, and if she were a television evangelist instead of a dancer, she would look exactly like Billy Cudrup. And needless to say— but let me say it—vice versa.

"Fourteen minutes, people!" Cudrup shouted. "And where, for the Love of Sweet Jesus, is Angel!?"

"I'm here, darlin'," answered a weak voiced Angel as she entered the Great Hall from behind the stage and prepared to step onto it. "I'm all set."

"For God's sakes, what are you wearing," Cudrup said sourly. "And you haven't finished your hair! You look like a tramp!"

"I...there was a..." she stammered. "A man, a terrible man..."

A door to the left of the stage opened and Little Biggs stepped through it, followed by Fiacre. They both blinked into klieg lights that were suddenly turned on. Fiacre smiled.

"Hi Angel," he said amiably. "I'm afraid I gave you quite a start."

Angel stared, and then began screaming before crumpling to the floor in a weepy heap.

"Good heavens," John exclaimed, pointing across the hall. "It's Fiacre!"

"Oh, what now!" Cudrup screamed. "Ten minutes!"

Fiacre turned to Little Biggs. "This is going well. And look," he said, pointing at John.

"There's the dullard Heartbreak. And the Warrior Queen."

"Cool," Little Biggs said. "She's pretty tall."

Fiacre nodded. "It is the nature of Warrior Queens."

Chapter 37

Fiacre, and Sharon Sloan the Warrior Queen eye one another from opposite sides of the Great Hall. He is pleased at what he sees, and makes a note to congratulate John on his choice of *Deus Machina.* Dr. Sloan, on the other hand, is wary: she is unimpressed by Fiacre's attire and stature and thinks he resembles a bum she had to dodge near the parking lot of the college where she used to teach.

As he stares at Sloan, Fiacre is oblivious to the commotion surrounding the collapsed Angel Cudrup—the show's frantic director has to get her on her feet, and bubbly for the television cameras, in eight minutes. Sloan does not yet know Angel—although she will come to know her briefly—and remains fixed on the totality of Fiacre's tackiness.

"Is that what a saint of the Holy Roman Catholic Church looks like?" she sarcastically inquires of John. "I'd say he's been basting in alley wine for a while."

John shrugs. "No one knows what saints look like. When the Holy Ghost appears in the church garden his appearance runs the gamete from burning bush to Chicago Cubs fan. It is much the same with saints."

"Holy Toledo," Sloan mouthed quietly. "You weird me out when you talk like that. Holy Ghost. Why not say Hannibal Lector or Pecos Pete?"

"You despise me, don't you?"

"If I gave you any thought, I probably would," Dr. Sloan replied. "Especially now that I've been reduce to stealing dialogue from *Casablanca.*"

John nodded appreciatively. "I'm impressed though, that you got the Ugarte-Rick-Heartbreak-Sloan dichotomy so quickly. It's one of the things I love about you."

"As long as I'm Rick," she said. "Meanwhile, tell me why Fiacre is here. Isn't he supposed to be back in the garden, while I do the Fandangoing, and you're the wheelman?"

"I don't know. Maybe he'll critique you for future missions. Pastor Cudrup isn't the only counterfeit hell robber in town. It could be that Fiacre wants to set you loose on even bigger game. Maybe we'll fandango Benny Hinn next time."

Dr. Sloan glowered. "I'll *critique him*,' she said brusquely. "If I don't see some money out of this you'll both walk home."

The Warrior Queen presents something of a problem, Fiacre admits to himself. He had no doubt that she was capable of Fandangoing Billy Cudrup, whatever that meant, but he hoped that she could focus less on Cudrup's ill-gotten $6,000,000, and more on John's goal of Saving Normal Christianity—and not for God's sake, but her own.

Fiacre didn't care, and he knew that God didn't care—and wouldn't give a pig's whistle—about Billy's dough, or John's nobler goal. Neither did they care if Dr. Sloan succeeded; the whole money slash church thing was a human thing, and neither amounted to a hill of beans in the Mind of God, nor in the consciousness of a Time Traveler like Fiacre.

What God cares about is how Sloan plays the game. Both He and Fiacre want her to have fun playing it; they care about the story, and want the story to end happily. A few bumps along the way are expected— Billy Cudrup and Hiroshima are bumps—but it is the ending that matters.

Dan Krotz

Christianity is teleological and apocalyptic. It presents the lives of individuals alone, and of human kind collectively, as a linear story moving towards an End followed by timelessness: you die (so sorry!), get judged, and go to heaven, or at the very least, into The Book of Memory. Life is writing your page in The Book. What will we read on your page?

To the question 'Why did God make me?' we are taught that 'God made me to know him, to love him, to serve him in this world, and *to be happy* with him forever in the next world.' It doesn't take much of a leap to see that God designed humans to be Time Travelers.

Of course, the concepts and images of travel to (and from!) the next world haven't resonated with thoughtful people for a while. The idea of Time Travel and simultaneous recumbent *and* forward movement between planes and spaces is regarded with skepticism and embarrassment when eternity, that mystical place, is considered a destination. Fiacre believes this is because most Christians are afraid of becoming what they are intended to become—Time Traveling Mystics—because they'll have to give up all their stuff if they do. It is easier to dismiss the place.

Nearly every legitimate 20th Century theologian—at least the ones Fiacre met—ignored the idea of survival and time travel after death. Bultman, Barth, Bonhoeffer, horny old Tillich, even the Jesuit Karl Rahner, considered the concept of a heavenly world of light where the traveler receives a heavenly vesture, to be not only incomprehensible, but irrational. They reached that conclusion, not because they were competent theologians, but because they were incompetent mathematicians. Faith is a zero sum game, but it is a Boolean game that cannot be played by the incurious, or by those fearful of going beyond the saying that God is not the fact of things existing, but the basis of all things seen and unseen when, in fact, God is simultaneously the fact and the basis, making the logic of God a lattice work of an infinite number of dimensions. Zero is just the starting point. And still...

. . . Rahner wrote, "The soul by surrendering its bodily structure in death becomes open towards the universe and, in some way, a co-determining factor of the universe in the latter's character as the ground of the personal life of other spiritual corporeal beings," thereby accomplishing the nearly impossible: turning gold into lead.

Fiacre knew that that was so much metaphysical canoodling, a mere preference for self-abuse over the sweaty fun of a more anthropomorphic love affair. It was no wonder that crap artists like Billy Cudrup and his Television Evangelist peers flourished.

Up on the stage, Angel was helped to her feet, and onto a blue velvet settee center stage. A young stagehand was patting her on the shoulder, while another young person administered smelling salts. Angel's head snapped back when the ammonia capsule broke under her nose.

"Oh goodness," she whined, confusedly looking around the set. "I saw that terrible man again. He was in…"

"Just how many pills did you take this morning?" the stagehand asked her. "Are you going to be able to do the show?"

"Five minutes!" Billy Cudrup yelled. "Everybody on the set! We're on the air in five minutes! Do I have to do everything myself!?"

Fiacre and Little Biggs started moving along the wall toward the doorway in which Sloan and

Heartbreak took refuge. Fiacre was out of place among the audience of elderly fundamentalists and television production staffs near the stage, but the Endtime's security force was off somewhere chasing the naked Chet Chandler, so he was, at least for now, unmolested. True, Fiacre earned a few hard stares from the church ladies he passed, but they were unarmed and not disposed to interfere with his progress along the wall. There were about to...

"...Organ Boy!" screamed Cudrup. "We're on the air in three minutes..."

...when Pastor Cudrup spied Little Biggs scurrying along the wall with what looked like a wino. "Get me cued up, you moron! We're on the air in two and half minutes!"

Little Biggs looked at Fiacre and shrugged. "I guess I better go," he said. "Can I still leave after the show?"

Fiacre nodded and smiled. "Sure you can. Why don't you start Pastor Cudrup off with your favorite tune? I'm sure he'll be surprised. Then, I'll help you bust out of here."

Little Biggs grinned shyly. "Will you introduce me to the Warrior Queen? She looks interesting."

Fiacre nodded again and slipped past Little Biggs. "Yup, we'll do it. Now go get 'em."

John and Dr. Sloan left the safety of their doorway refuge and inched through the crowd toward Fiacre. Sloan was pleased to see that John was walking normally and had given up the serpentine subterfuge. She glanced approvingly in his direction and considered the possibility that he would behave well under pressure.

Billy Cudrup took his place on the television set and took his place in the host's chair. He looked at Angel and shook his head. Donna Raye had been a nightmare to work with, and she had her own drug problems for sure. But looking at the spaced out, disheveled Angel as she wobbled on the velvet settee, made Billy miss Donna Raye's risible stream of consciousness regarding everything from why a Rhino might make the perfect birthday gift for Sandra Z. Windermere's husband Raymond, who wrote in from Tulsa asking for advice about what to get a hard to please husband, to how Jesus was simply waiting to be asked to supply a winning lottery ticket number, so why in heaven's name didn't you ask?

Even before Billy had been released from prison for tax fraud, he knew he needed a wife, at least a new television wife, to regain the abundant audience he'd had when he and Donna Raye had been at the height of their *The Lord Loves You* television ministry. Without a photogenic helpmate by his side, the majority of his audience, 50 year old or older lower income Caucasian women married to or widowed or abandoned by unreliable blue collar Appalachian American men, might suppose he was a player, or gay, or afraid of commitment, and could not then, authentically relate to the sufferings endemic to the state of holy matrimony.

The fact that the majority of Television Holy Men (yes, add 'em up and they are a majority) *were* married but also happened to be players or gay or afraid of commitment, added an element of suspense and drama to Christian Broadcasting that is a terrific boost to ratings; everyone *knows* that it is only a matter of time before Billy or Jimmy or Joel or Billy James gets his zipper caught on some errant lip.

And oh[!], how the audience suffered along with Donna Raye, along with poor Betty Jean Hargis, along with sweet abused Frances Swaggart, and along with Tammy Faye Bakker, as one by one their husbands—so like the rats they were married to—cheated and swindled and fell into the laps of painted whores, some of them even Catholic. It was fantastic TV!

Billy knew that Angel was necessary to his success because he, like all of his evangelical preacher-brothers, needed the possibility of a sacrificed lamb for his audience to worry about. This audience, these armies of aggrieved, menopausal and post-menopausal women knew it was only a matter of time before Donna Raye, Tammy Faye, Frances, Betty Jean *et al*, would be humiliated, sullied, and betrayed—just as they were. How could they not tune in?

But would people care when—not if—Billy betrayed Angel? She lacked the sort of presence that Donna Raye had exuded. Where Donna Raye had appeared vulnerable, Angel was merely abstracted. Where Donna Raye convinced you that she and Jesus personally discussed what she would wear on that afternoon's program, no one really believed that Angel was in close communion with the Lord, especially about her clothes.

Neither Jesus, nor the *LLY* television audience, could be found culpable for the fashion crimes Angel committed daily, even with the advice of a Wardrobe mistress who was a holdover from Donna Raye's days.

"Angel wants to dress like glam band whore," complained the wardrobe mistress. "Donna Raye wore organdy and ruffles and stiletto heels with spaghetti lacing. This one," she said dismissively, "dresses like she really believes that the world is going to end. And her make-up? Forget about it. At least Donna Raye wasn't afraid of eye-liner."

As Billy looks Angel over, now just 15 seconds from air time, he wonders what he can do with her. Yes, he can cheat on her, beat on her, lure her into liaisons involving small boys and large poodles—these are all fantastic sub plotting opportunities and sheer fire ratings boosters—but he can't do the one thing she has been talking about: divorce her. Every old bat in every financed mobile home in America would dump him, just as fast as their unreliable, rotten, cheating, first, second, and third husbands had dropped them. He was stuck with her. Unless…

…The *LLY* director shouted "Places!" and began the countdown to air: "ten, nine, eight…"

Little Biggs waited for his cue. He was excited about the piece he was going to play, and felt a pleasant tremor of nervousness that he was ignoring Pastor Cudrup's Old Time Favorite in favor of a little hog killin' music. *Toccata!*

Chapter 38

Mrs. Heartbreak and Clara Jane are in Clara Jane's Winnebago, proceeding at a high rate of speed northward to Withered Plum, Missouri, and the very place Clara Jane passed through not sixty minutes ago. They are being followed by the radio personality Eddie Keever who, in overhearing the conversation between Mrs. Heartbreak and Clara Jane, has smelled a story he hopes to break tonight on his broadcast.

Young Keever—not so young really except by John's accounting, which we can dismiss out of hand—was responsible for culture east of the Kings River; he found it, no doubt, a thankless and hard job of work.

Berryville's various rodeos, swap meets, canning contests, high school basketball games, Electric Cooperative Soirees, tire sales, and Public Service Proctology Drives was thin gruel indeed when compared with Eureka Springs' Art Walks, Diversity Weekends, Gay Pride Parades, City Council slash Performance Art meetings, UFO Conferences, and Lumberjacks in Women's Dresses Support Groups. Easy it was for Richard Schoe, the Eureka Springs DJ, to make something of the news, but for Eddie Keever, it was not "something" he had to make, but miracles.

Thus, when he overheard Mrs. Heartbreak tell Clara Jane Smith Staley—the woman who had previously lived in the Keever's house—that John was on a Mission from God that involved the scandalous Pastor Billy Cudrup and his timeshare business Endtimes Ministries, Eddie's ears perked up, and his keen nose for news caused even more body parts to go on high alert. When Clara Jane had virtually wrestled Mrs.

Heartbreak into the Winnebago, shouting loudly, "We've got to stop him!" he hopped into his stylish forest green Ford Ranger pickup—okay, into his pickup truck—and began trailing them.

"This is Eddie Keever of CHIK News," he said, speaking into his MP3 recording device, "hot on the trail of local resident and semi-famous folk artist the Fabulous Mrs. Heartbreak. She is, as we speak, proceeding at a high rate of speed to interrupt or foil, according to an unnamed source, a Mission from God.

"Mrs. Heartbreak, well known to Berryvillians as a frequent Advisor to God, and by her husband, the dullard John Heartbreak, as the Voice of God, is not known for derailing Missions from God. What could be the cause of this new and unexpected *Deus Interruptus? Is it possible that Mrs. Heartbreak has gone over to the Dark Side?*

"Traveling with Mrs. Heartbreak is the former Clara Jane Smith, who most Berryvillians will recall is the founder of the Iowa Welcome Center located on the Town Square. Clara Jane, as you may remember, was a member of Berryville's First Methodist Church when Skip French was pastor at there, and lived on Pritchard Street before marrying former FBI Agent Orin Staley and moving to Forrest City Iowa where she and her husband opened a Winnebago dealership upon his retirement from the FBI.

"Incidentally, Mrs. Heartbreak and Clara Jane are traveling in a Winnebago. Not the Mini-Winnie, but the great big honking one.

"According to our unnamed source—that would be me overhearing their plans—they are traveling to Endtimes Ministries in Withered Plum to wreck some kind of plan that involves John Heartbreak and the Reverend Billy Cudrup. As you may recall, Billy

Cudrup served time in a Federal Big House for fraud, mail fraud, tax evasion, zipper trouble, and or having the good or bad taste, or the good or bad luck depending on your point of view, of having married Donna Raye Cudrup, now deceased."

Eddie put the recorder down and focused on the road as the Winnebago slowed to accommodate a series of sharp curves, and inclines and hilly declines, each of them wet and steaming with slick oil. Yes, it is possible to see the prior sentence as containing significant sexual content but, honestly, we're talking Ozark roadways so let's just say that he put the recorder down, put both hands on the wheel, and slowed the green Ford Ranger to avoid crashing and burning in a side gully. Safety first!

He hoped he wasn't on a fool's errand. Yet, something about the stricken look on Clara Jane's face and the confusion on Mrs. Heartbreak's, caused him to believe that he was on to a real story for once. What exactly was this 'mission from God' and why had Clara Jane suddenly reappeared in Berryville? Inquiring minds would want to know. Wouldn't they?

Eddie knew little about Clara Jane except that she had lived in his house just before he moved into it, and that she had opened the Iowa Welcome Center with John Heartbreak as a reluctant and unhappy partner.

Although the Iowa Welcome Center had been good for adjacent businesses like the Ozark Café, not everyone in Berryville liked having so many Iowans in town. They were so different from Arkansans and, frankly, were a rude people, where as the Native Arkansan is a friendly and helpful soul.

There were other differences as well: Iowans had money and Arkansans did not; they could read and Arkansans couldn't; they were Lutherans or Catholics and belonged to churches named Immanuel or St. Chester's, instead of churches named Elmer's Church of the Redeeming Unsullied and Perfectly Holy Underpants, or the First and Last Right Thought Revealed Primitive Anabaptist Ark of Latter Day True Believers. And then there was the whole corn subsidy business…but don't get me started on that. (If you read the first book about John Heartbreak then you know how incredibly boring the topic of corn subsidies can be.)

Anyway…

Eddie could tell that the reunion between the two women had been sweet, but it had also been brief. He didn't know that Clara Jane largely attributed her decision to be born again as a Christian to Mrs. Heartbreak's good example, while Mrs. Heartbreak, in turn, felt that her own Christian faith was strengthened and validated by Clara Jane's coming to Christ.

That grand and sweet mutuality was made possible and fostered by the two women's shared commitment to Social Order Theory, an optimistic belief that operation of the Universe can be made orderly and predictable as long as others will allow them to lead and manage. Clara Jane had organized and improved the world by arranging serially and voluminously the timely deaths of bad apples and the chronically rude, while Mrs. Heartbreak more prosaically organized and improved her husband John. That was all the evidence they needed that Social Order Theory was more, much more than mere theory.

In many respects Mrs. Heartbreak has had the more difficult job; one that Clara Jane herself would agree was far less rewarding and far more complex than her own human resource management obligations. What, after all, is the defenestration, shooting, knifing, bombing, garroting, fricasseeing, strangling, smothering, clubbing, gutting, or beheading of another compared to spending an entire evening listening to John describe why Louisa May Alcott is America's most under-rated writer—particularly when John believes that Louisa May is taking part in the conversation?

But as the poet Winfield Townley Scott had written, "They loved each other because their ailments are the same," so it was with Mrs. Heartbreak and Clara Jane. Though their reunion had been brief, so attuned were they to each other's psyches that Mrs. Heartbreak knew instantly that Clara Jane's marriage to ex-FBI Agent Orin Staley was in trouble, and Clara Jane knew that Mrs. Heartbreak was vexed (again!) by whatever fool's errand John was momentarily about.

It was only when Mrs. Heartbreak began to relate the somewhat abbreviated and admittedly confused story that John "was on a mission from God" to "fandango" the Reverend Billy Cudrup, that Clara Jane became concerned and, frankly anxious that now, now of all times, a time when she needed rest and comfort from her good friend Mrs. Heartbreak, she might in fact be at cross purposes with Mrs. Heartbreak's husband; cross purposes so deeply etched if one can imagine a purpose and a cross being etched at all, that she, Clara Jane, might have to kill the dullard John Heartbreak. Such circumstance might well dull the sheen of friendship between the two women, an outcome that Clara Jane would regret.

And why should, would—we know that she could— Clara Jane kill poor John, a man she had previously worked with and for, under odd surely, but ultimately (for her) satisfying purposes?

Because, minutes before leaving Forrest City, Iowa and on toward her destination in Berryville, Sincerely Dewayne Wayne Darby, her pastor at the Church of God with Signs Following had said to her:

"Trust no one, Clara Jane. The world may end while you wind your way to Arkansas—"we know not the hour!"—and the path you follow between me and that sin infested hellhole named Berryville, is strewn with the Handmaidens of Balaam, the Henchmen of Lucifer, and Satan's own spawn. Beware, I say to you!"

Clara Jane had shaken her head. "Pastor Dewayne Wayne, John is a harmless old duffer. And it was really Mrs. Heartbreak who brought me to Christ. I think I can trust them."

"If they are not among the elect, Clara Jane, they cannot be trusted. Not ultimately, not totally. And what you've told me about this Heartbreak character is troubling. You say he speaks to the Holy Spirit, but that he also speaks to dead writers, some of them atheists! That is hardly the description of someone who you call harmless."

"I *have* heard him speak to Sinclair Lewis and Jack London," she said, nodding dubiously. "I guess they were not believers."

"But worse, Clara Jane, much worse," he thundered, "he not only speaks to dead writers, he reads them too! He's one of them book reading, foreign language spouting intellectuals! No, I wouldn't trust him for a minute."

"Are you telling me to forget about going back to Berryville? I really feel like I need a break."

"No, Clara Jane," Pastor Sincerely DeWayne Wayne Darby replied. "It is possible that this Mrs. Heartbreak you speak of is trustworthy—although I have my doubts. Otherwise, why would she have spent years

229

with that sin laden vessel of decrepitude she calls husband?

"Just be careful, is all I'm saying. Trust no one, except the Lord. And possibly, now that I think of him, Pastor Billy Cudrup."

"Pastor Cudrup?"

"Yes. An old friend who has a ministry called Endtimes, in Withered Plum, Missouri. Just north of Berryville, so he'll be close at hand if you need a spiritual confidant.

"Billy and I met while we were—well, while we were between ministries, so to speak," Pastor Darby continued. "Billy has started over in Withered Plum and has a perfect understanding of *Revelations* and its meaning for you, for me, and for the few elected souls who are to meet our Savior."

Before leaving Forrest City, Clara Jane had promised Pastor Sincerely Dewayne Wayne Darby that she would look Billy Cudrup up when she got to Arkansas, and to seek guidance from Pastor Cudrup should she need it.

Thus, when Mrs. Heartbreak had informed her that John was on his way to fandango Billy Cudrup, and was traveling with a woman she said John called "the Warrior Queen Sloan," Clara Jane's well-developed sense of impending chaos had begun ticking like a Geiger counter. After all, John had, all alone among 5,000 Berryvillians, instantly known her to be a serial killer; if he could pick her out of such a crowd, on what basis had he picked Sloan?

Mrs. Heartbreak was not used to being hustled about—if anyone hustled anyone it was usually she— but then Clara Jane's look of consternation and panic had moved Mrs. Heartbreak to, for once, set aside her usual mode of operation and to hop to. In this case, to hop into, Clara Jane's Winnebago. Neither she, nor Clara Jane, had observed the Ace Reporter Keever's surveillance of their conversation.

And so it came to pass, as readers of the Book of Mormon will recognize as a transitional and habitual phrase that she, Clara Jane, and Eddie Keever sped headlong through the rolling Ozark hills toward Withered Plum, Missouri.

Eddie picked up the MP3 recorder as the Winnebago hit a short stretch of flat spot in the road. "We are nearing the entrance of Endtimes Ministries," he said in a hushed tone. "What will we discover here? Will Mrs. Heartbreak prevail in upsetting Billy Cudrup's Ecclesiastical Applecart? What role does the dullard John Heartbreak have to play here? What, pray tell, is this Mission from God? And who, friends, is "the Warrior Queen Sloan?

"Don't touch that dial!"

Chapter 39

It will not surprise you to learn that when Little Biggs sat down to play the introduction to the *Billy Cudrup Show* he fired up that most famous of organ works, Johann Sebastian Bach's *Toccata and Fugue in D Minor*. What will surprise you is that Bach probably didn't write it, and if he did, he wrote it for the violin in, oh say, about 1740.

Who (ever) wrote it was responsible for writing John's favorite single piece of music. Thus, when Little Biggs began to play, John grasped the Warrior Queen's arm excitedly and broke into a wide grin. It was the last piece of music he expected to hear on something as prosaically perverse as the *Billy Cudrup Show* and, by Billy Cudrup's dumbstruck reaction to it, it was the last piece he had expected to hear as well.

Little Biggs started with the typical north German free opening, that single voice flourish in the upper ranges of the keyboard, doubling the octave before spiraling downward toward the bottom where a diminished 7th chord appeared to resolve itself into a D major chord, taken obviously from the parallel major mode. John couldn't wait for the four voice fugue and hoped that the organist—who he intended to heartily pat on the back—would attempt the 16th note approach with the implied pedal.

Fiacre watched the expression on John's face change from his usual, slightly sleepy expression to one highlighted by delight, with amusement. Leave it to John Heartbreak to love music most folks couldn't stand.

Fiacre liked the *Toccata* well enough, even if it was a tad hoity toity for his taste. Still, he had appreciated

Deep Purple's version in *Highway Star*, and Keith Emerson's upside down take on it when he was with Emerson, Lake, and Palmer, was pretty good.

What was just *killing* Fiacre right now, though, was the look on Billy Cudrup's face, and the way his mouth opened and closed like a beached basses'. That, and the way his skin mottled into dark purple red blotches under his make-up. God, thought Fiacre, that is *so* funny.

The audience, comprised mostly of old (old, old) people, looked bewildered and shocked. Why, they wondered, was Pastor Cudrup playing that ghostly music? It sounded like...well, like music to kill hogs by. Was Cudrup telling them that the end, THE END which he so confidently predicted was nigh, was actually NOW? They began twisting in their seats, glancing first at the boy playing the horror show, then back over to Billy, where he was sitting, pole axed, on the stage. His wrinkled face resembled a soft, over-ripe plum that became even more pronounced as a string of drool rolled from the corner of his mouth. It hung off the end of his chin in a long dangle.

"Maude," said an elderly man sitting close to the stage with his wife. "I think we need to get out of here. It's end times for sure and we need to call the kids." He got up and, tugging at his wife's arm, began to shuffle toward the studio's exit. A pair of duffer couples creaked their necks to watch Maud and her companion leave; they looked anxiously around and began to tremble.

Fiacre couldn't remember when he'd had a better time. When God sent him to Berryville, he had to admit that he'd felt a bit out of his depth. He was a gardener after all, and while the First Christian Church certainly had a garden, and John Heartbreak was certainly its principal gardener, there was no connection that he could see to the whole 'Saving Normal Christianity' agenda that he aimed to fill. But so far, things seem to be going well. Don't you think so?

Fiacre glanced up at a television monitor and laughed. Billy's television audience was catching the whole drama as it happened, right down to the dying bass routine and the gob of spit dripping off Billy's chin. The program's Director didn't know where to place his camera shots. At the far back of the studio a cadre of security guards was wrestling with some naked guy wearing bunny slippers; the studio audience sat in stupefied fear, gobbling nitro tablets, or quaking like a forest of aspens. When in doubt, as he was now, he took the path of least resistance and followed Billy's habitual advice: "you can't keep the camera on me enough, got it?"

Angel Cudrup seemed transfixed by the music and shook her head to clear it. She attempted to stand, but gave up at half-mast and dumped herself back onto the velvet couch. She turned toward Billy for a directional cue, and then brought a tight little fist to her lips: Billy's face was the maroon hue of a beautiful 1954 Ford Victoria that her father owned at the time of her birth. Angel hadn't thought about that car in years and, for no reason at all, she was suddenly filled with a feeling of well-being and happiness. Billy croaked and croaked. She smiled.

The Director saw the smile, the oddly beatific smile on Angel's face, and quickly cued the #3 camera to focus on her. How curious, he thought, that the drug addled Angel should be the one island of calm amid what was an increasingly chaotic set. He attracted Angel's attention and mimed a smiley face, pointing at his teeth. Angel nodded and flashed her teeth as Little

Biggs moved into the final entry of the fugal melody where the composition resolves into a held B major chord.

She continued smiling, and began nodding in time to the music as Little Biggs played the coda section, much like the *Toccata* itself, before falling into a series of chords and arpeggios that progress, step, step, step, to other paired chords, each a little lower than the one preceding. Almost casually, she looked over at the apoplectic Billy, pointed at him, and giggled. "How about that, folks?" she laughed. "Billy's speechless!"

Fiacre turned his gaze away from Angel and searched for John. There he was, still smiling and still as loopy looking as ever. The Warrior Queen, standing next to John, was neither smiling nor loopy looking. She has an intense, fierce expression on her face, and was pointing her finger directly at Fiacre with her right hand and shaking the fist of the left.

"Where's my money!?" she mouthed.

"Hmmn," Fiacre said to himself. Dr. Sloan certainly looked the part of a Warrior Queen—tall, strong, angry—and, my goodness, why was her wrath directed at him rather than, say, the croaking Cudrup, or the dullard Heartbreak? What had Fiacre, poor Saintly Gardener that he was, ever done to her? Had he not already died and been dead and gone to heaven he might feel quite afraid of her. As it was, he still felt a shrill tremor of desire to flee.

As Fiacre assessed the Warrior Queen's potential for violence on his person, Mrs. Heartbreak and Clara Jane entered the Endtimes compound and pulled the Winnebago into the parking lot. During the drive, Clara Jane had informed Clara Jane about the unsatisfactory state of her marriage to Agent Staley, and of the important role that Pastor Sincerely Dewayne Wayne

Darby had played in transforming her from a devout, middle of the road Methodist into a new kind of Christian that Mrs. Heartbreak had no trouble at all identifying as lunatic. For the last ten miles of their trip she had only been able to say:

"But Clara Jane…"

…before Clara Jane interrupted her with increasingly delirious and vivid descriptions of THE END. Now, as Clara Jane switched off the key to the Winnebago, Mrs. Heartbreak sat mute—yes, birds fell from the sky, and NORAD informed Pentagon brass of strange and peculiar changes in natural and electronically sourced air and atmospheric waves that could not be identified, but appeared to be derived from a location in Northern Arkansas or Southern Missouri—and saddened by the change in her friend. Clara Jane, once so rational and clear headed, was now crazier than a bedbug.

Eddie Keever pulled into an empty spot two vehicles over from the Winnebago, and shut his truck off. He picked up the MP3 recorder and said:

"Mrs. Heartbreak and the former Clara Jane Smith are leaving the Winnebago and heading over to the front entrance of Endtimes Ministries. For some reason Mrs. Heartbreak isn't speaking and birds are falling from the sky…lots of birds…holy cow! … actually. What can the meaning of this unnatural event be?

"The two women are now at the entrance into the Endtimes TV studio. *Oops*, as Clara Jane opened the door, several people—old geezers—strike that!—Senior Citizens and God bless them!—are hurriedly leaving the building. They look scared. Actually, they look terrified.

"Oh my gosh! A large hairy man wearing only bunny slippers has stormed through the door!

Semi-Faithful: More Coffee with John Heartbreak

"Friends, we aren't in Berryville anymore!"

Chapter 40

It is interesting to see the differences in how the Warrior Queen Sloan and the Radio Personality Eddie Keever perceive and experience the grand happenings at Endtimes just now. Keever is filled with excitement, albeit hidden behind the professional's obligation to merely report and not participate in the on-going zeitgeist. Dr. Sloan, on the other hand, is quaking with dismay and anxiety as she observes Pastor Billy Cudrup rise and then weave and stumble in an apparent apoplectic fit.

She is anxious that Cudrup not croak before she is able to fandango on the top of his little head. True, and in the fashion of academics everywhere, she would have no trouble kicking him while down, but she is also an artist and knows that the artful, satisfying canvas must synthesize the purity of classicism and frankness of impressionism with an edge of modernism and the brute nihilism of abstraction.

Her vision of the fandango has involved a sword and armor; she leads a band of angels through a crowd of fierce invalids, looking ever so like the blade wielding Jeanne d'Arc (classicism). The studio's lights will bounce off the silver plate of her armor, strobing and shimmying, ricocheting if you will, bouncing on, off, the chromed domes of retirees in the audience (impressionism) while the breath of the accompanying angels turns to beads of fire (modernism) as they congregate on Billy Cudrup's hood in preparation for dance. Then, she herself morphs; the Maid of Orleans into Kahn, Genghis, as the wheeling arc of her blade crashes (abstraction) into a piñata that, bursting and shredding, rains down currency bearing the likeness of Salmon P. Chase ($10,000), Woodrow Wilson ($100,000) and James Madison ($5,000); she will use the Grover Cleveland's ($1,000) to tip the angels.

But no, not if Billy is grimly ripped before she reaches him, if she cannot land on him before Bach lands on him first; how sad, how humiliating really, if Billy's reformation is death by *Toccata* and not remittance by fandango. Dr. Sloan surveys the television studio and sees that, if she leaps up onto the nearest table, she can hop from that table to the next table—and then to the next—blazing across the distance with 10 or so well timed hops until she lands on the stage and to within a foot or so of Cudrup himself. Just as she begins to crouch, as she feels adrenalin and iron surge into her calves, as her feet prepare to trigger a sharp high shot into the air, a hand pops under her nose and waves some sort of hand held device.

"Dr. Sloan, Eddie Keever and CHIK Radio here! I have it on good authority—that would be the fabulous Mrs. Heartbreak from Berryville, Arkansas—that you are here on a Mission from God. What might that mission be, and how is that you were chosen to be the vehicle to launch it?"

"Hello, Eddie," John interrupted. He stepped out from behind Sloan the Warrior Queen and gazed, perplexed into Keever's face. "What in the world are you doing here?"

"Not now, John," Eddie said firmly. For once the Gods of Media were favoring him with what looked like a hot story. The last thing he needed was to waste precious air time on the dullest man in Arkansas. He turned back to the Warrior Queen and repeated his question.

Sloan was stunned. There was a certain vigilante character to her proposed venture, a venture not sanctioned by law enforcement and one most certainly unacceptable to Endtimes Security Force. Had the Endtimes force not been otherwise engaged in high pursuit of the bunny skippered Chet, it would be she rather than Billy who was fandangoed, hog-tied, and abused. Keever's now insistent demand for media coverage voided her chance of anonymity from the law and the benevolent happenstance of the security force's distraction. She sputtered and pushed his hand away.

Sloan vaulted onto the nearest table top and prepared to launch herself toward the stage. As she planted her feet for take-off she was momentarily unbalanced by a backward tilt. Young Keever had hopped up on the table to stand beside her and, once again, shoved the recorder under her nose.

John stood, befuddled, amazed. What he saw was a scene from a painting by Botero; two imposing people, each abstracted by distinctly opposed means and ends. The only thing odder was his awareness that the author is transcribing these events in the manner of Edith Wharton, she of the funny hat and very large butt.

Yet, it was all John's fault: it was he—wasn't it!—he who had brought Botero up and screwed any chance of your having a consistent 8th grade reading level to muscle through, all because of his Baroque inspired segues. Edith Wharton indeed! What next? Proust?

No! (Excuse me. I don't know what happened.) Now then:

Dr. Sloan and Keever gazed determinedly into one another's eyes. They ignored John's gape mouthed stare, and were unaware of Mrs. Heartbreak's and Clara Jane's sharp elbowing through the increasingly anxious television audience. John fails to see them as well, which is truly a shame, since Clara Jane has begun to swing a nun chuck in an increasingly violent circle that will momentarily smack his head.

"I'm not going away without an interview," Eddie says flatly. "Are you, or are you not, the Warrior Queen, and are you, or are you not, here on a Mission from God?"

Sloan is undecided. Billy has begun to weave back and forth and stagger. His color is pure puce: his goose is nearly cooked; five seconds and his pop up button will signal all done. Yet Keever was clearly not going to abandon his appointed round.

She thought about cold cocking him—a swift Warrior Queen hook to the nose—but reconsidered the wisdom of getting on the wrong side of the 4th Estate, especially in these early days. If it happened that she was arrested she would need a friendly media contact and, oddly enough, Keever was her sole reference point among local Guardians of the 1st Amendment. Meanwhile, John brushed away an annoying whizzing sound next to his right ear.

"Okay, Keever," she irritably said. "Yes, I'm the Warrior Queen. And no, I'm not here on a Mission from God. I'm on a Mission from an even scarier deity, the IRS. And that man," she continued, pointing at Fiacre, "can answer all your questions. He started this fine mess!"

Eddie looked in the direction Sloan pointed. Surely she hadn't meant the wino in the '*Jesus is coming! Look busy!*' T-shirt? Fiacre saw Eddie's glance and smiled and waved. He turned both forefingers inward and pointed at himself, as if to say "Guilty!"

Billy Cudrup collapsed on the stage. Does an unobserved Cudrup make a sound when it falls? Perhaps not in a forest, autumnal or otherwise, and perhaps not even in a television studio when all eyes are suddenly fixed on a duo of Boteroesque fandangoers. And why was that woman swinging a Bruce Lee-like instrument of death?

Dr. Sloan sensed, rather than heard, Cudrup fall and instinctually turned away from Keever. She began leaping from table to table, scattering elderly Christians and glassware without regard for the inevitable breakage. John leaned forward to catch the falling newscaster who was unbalanced from his table top perch by the charging Warrior Queen's departure.

John's charitable act thus and summarily allowed him to miss the first swing of Clara Jane's nun chuck; it whizzed harmlessly through the air until it collided with the forehead of Mrs. Hanna Schygulla—the vinegary spinster Primitive Baptist from Toad Suck, Arkansas and not the sumptuous German Actress of the same name—knocking her right into the arms of Jesus, and Praise God brothers and sisters!

In the mean time:

"Billy Cudrup, you scoundrel," yelled Dr. Sloan, as she reached the stage. "Where's my money?!"

Angel Cudrup got up, and stood between Sloan and the camera. She smiled brightly.

"Howdy alls ya'alls. Welcome to the *Angel Cudrup Show*!

Chapter 41

Fiacre is still enjoying himself immensely. Watching Sloan catapult from table to table—she can do it!—was more fun than watching the Battle of Hastings, which, all disambiguation aside, was ten guys throwing rocks at one another. And anyway, the Norwegian King, Harald Hardrada, was out of the running by then too—so who cares who won a mostly trivial battle? Fiacre was, however transcendent a figure, before and ever after transcendence, an Irishman and habituated to loath the English. Bede was the only exception.

But—back to Dr. Sloan, and with apologies for this utterly banal Battle of Hastings segue. (Yet, who am I to manage the mind and ruminations of a time traveling saint? Apology retracted. Just get on with it. Saints will do what saints will do.)

Yet again: Sloan:

Watching Sloan catapult from table to table to the stage at the front of the audience was more fun than…than Fiacre had had in a long time. He would be having even more fun if he hadn't just now— FINALLY—remembered why he was at Endtimes: Dorothy Day's note.

Do you remember? Fiacre had been commanded by Dorothy Day to give John a note, a note which John in turn is supposed to give to the now apoplectic Billy Cudrup.

"Sometime," Dorothy [had] said, handing Fiacre a slip of paper…"sometime early in the next century, you will go to Arkansas, also like New York City a part of the United States of America—though you'll find that hard to believe when you get there.

"Once there, you will direct a man named Heartbreak, and a Warrior Queen named Sloan, to Fandango the apostate named Cudrup. He is selling indulgences. Make sure you give them this note so that they can give it to Cudrup.

"Cudrup's receipt of the note will be his last chance for redemption. If he rejects its message, the Warrior Queen and her companion will initiate Operation Fandango."

"Dorothy, I have two questions," Fiacre recalled asking. "First, who is the Cudrup person? Second, what is a Fandango?"

"Cudrup is a counterfeit hell robber; he pretends to save people from the fires of hell. As to the exact nature of a Fandango...well, I don't exactly know what that is. I am sure," she [had] concluded, "that it is a spectacular thing to observe."

And so, Fiacre had gone to where Dorothy had predicted he would go—to Berryville, Arkansas, where he had, in fact, met John in the garden. And now, he was within spitting distance of a very purple Billy Cudrup, in Endtimes, Missouri. Yes, he had forgotten to give the list to John, but he would do so now. He reached into the right hand pocket of his Bermuda shorts, grasped the note, a list really, and pulled it out. He quickly scanned it (for your edification).

10 Rules for Getting into Heaven

1. *Think about God all the time. It gets easier with practice.*
2. *Listen when God speaks to you. PS: If God talks to you about someone else's sinfulness, it isn't God who is talking.*

3. *God respects manual labor. He especially expects at least a little of it every week from federal employees, priests, pastors, and intellectuals of every stripe.*

4. *Guilt is a sign of good mental and spiritual health. Deal with it.*

5. *God does not belong to your church. If you get mad at your church and start a new one, God won't join your new church either. You might as well stay where you are.*

6. The Book of Revelations *is an important book. It is also* The Book of Scoundrels. *Watch out for people and preachers who spend too much (of your) time there.*

7. *Unless they are holding a gun, everyone you meet gets a fresh start. Every time you meet them.*

8. *Pray for a peaceful death every day. If you go with a clear conscience you have lived well.*

9. *Read holy books. There are a lot of them, including some novels.*

10. *The devil is a spectacular failure. People and preachers who spend all of their time talking about the devil worship a false god and are behaving scandalously. They should worry more about what God is up to and less about what the devil is up to.*

Fiacre had nodded. He had agreed to deliver the list. But how? Sloan has leapt from teetering table to teetering table, having escaped the attentions of radio journalist Edward Keever. Free at last from the media, she is frantic that Cudrup might escape the delivery of her righteous and fuming indignation. How to interrupt the imminent fandango in time to deliver Dorothy's instructions to Cudrup?

The fandango's complicating "meanwhile," is Keever pointing at Fiacre with disbelief. Is Fiacre, Keever wonders, the root cause of this demented ruckus? John, narrowly ducking Clara Jane Smith's swinging nun chuck—while Sloan table hopped—has said so, but Keever is disinclined to accept John's word. I mean, would you be so inclined, knowing what you know about John?

Little Biggs has finished the *Toccata*. Angel Cudrup beams in his direction and claps her hands in delight. "Little Biggs! You Sweetheart!" she chortles into the mic. "That was mighty fine! What do you all call such a thang?"

Little Biggs is startled. To be called 'sweetheart' was an unexpected bequest. He glanced in Fiacre's direction for guidance. No help there; Fiacre is smiling at Eddie Keever and pointing to himself, as if to say,"yes, it's me!"

Angel looks down at Billy, who is kicking his heels against the stage floor, and grasping at his wattled neck. Billy's platform shoes make a dim, hollow *thump thump thump thump* noise as they bang on the floor. "Hold it down, Billy, honey," she says. "I want folks to say howdy to Little Biggs."

She turns away from Billy and gestures to Little Biggs. "Come up here, Sweetheart, and take a bow." Only when Little Biggs begins a tentative, apprehensive approach to the stage does Angel become aware that her audience is crawling, clawing, its way toward the exits: wheel chairs bump and grind into one another, aluminum walkers clank and shimmy, canes flail. "Folks! Folks!" Angel calls out. "Where are you going? The show's just starting!"

Donnie Duane Wayne Tuttle, Pastor Emeritus from the First and Last Word Fellowship of the Ever Loving Lord and Beaming Redeemer in Mountain Home, Arkansas, turned away from the exit long enough to shake his cane at Angel, and yell, "Stuff it, sister!" We know End Times when we see it!"

"I WANT MY MONEY!" Sloan bellows again. Little Biggs takes a bow. Billy bounces up and down on his back. Clara Jane whirls a nun chuck. Eddie Keever whispers into a microphone. Mrs. Heartbreak taps John on the shoulder. He turns to her, smiles.

"You've got a lot of explaining to do, John," she says. She is not smiling.

"STOP!"

Fiacre has stopped time. Well. Not stopped it. He has slowed it down. A lot. Sloan bel... Billy bou...Clara Jane whi.. Eddie whis... Mrs. Heartbreak ta... John tur...ned. All the geezers, including Pastor Donnie Duane Wayne, are frozen in hasty mid-step.

You are frowning. Or sniffing. You disagree that time can be slowed down. You are in the ballpark, disagreement-wise, science-wise. But otherwise-wise, you are quite wrong. While time is immutable, it is manageable and imaginable in any way. Any shape. Any form. Do you think I'm kidding? Take a look at how we think about time, imagine time, manage time:

A good time was had by all, a moment in time, a race against time, a stitch in time saves nine, ahead of one's time, all in good time, all the time, an idea whose time has come, as time goes by, at a time like this, at the present time, at the same time, at this moment/point/particular point in time, be ahead of one's time, be behind the times, beat someone's time, better luck next time, bide one's time, big time, closing time, daylight saving time, do hard time, do something in jig time, doing time, don't waste your time, double time, every time it rains it rains pennies from heaven, every time you turn around, fall on hard times, father time, fight against time, for a limited time only, for old time's sake, for the first time, for the time being, from time immemorial, from time to time, frozen in time, full-time job, get me to the church on time, get time off for good behavior, get time to catch one's breath, give someone a hard time, good-time Charlie, half past kissing time, time to kiss again, hard times, hardly have time to breath, have a hard/rough time of it, have a whale of a time, have the time of one's life, have time on one's hands, have time to burn, hit the big time, hot time in the old town tonight, if you do the crime you must do the time, in due time, in good time, in less than no time at all, in no time flat, in one's spare time, in the course of time, in the nick of time, it seemed a good idea at the time, it was the best of times, it's about time, just a matter of time, keep up with the times, kill time, last of the big time spenders, legend in one's time, life and times of..., live on borrowed time, long time no see, make good time, make up for lost time, mark time, neither the time or the place, never is a very long time, nick of time, no time like the present, no time to lose, now is the time for all good men to come to the aid of the party, once in a lifetime, once upon a time, one day at a time, one more time, only a matter of time, only time will tell, out of time, part-time job, pass the time of day, passing time, peace in our time, pressed for time, puts on his pants one leg at a time, prime time, quality time, race against time, real time, right on time, run out of time, same time next year, sands of time, second time around, sign of the times, since the dawn of time, someone doesn't know what time it is, stands the test of time, summertime and the living is easy, surviving the test of time, take one's (own sweet) time, tea time, that time of the month, the march of time, the sands of time, the second time around, the time is right, the time is ripe for something, the time of your life, the times they are a'changin', there's a first time for everything, there's a time and a place for everything, third time is a charm/lucky, third time loser, time after time, time and tide wait for no man, time and time again, time bomb, time flies (when you're having fun), time heals all wounds, time-honored tradition, time is a great healer, time is money, time is on one's side, time is running out, time is up, time marches on, time of the year, time off for good behavior, time on one's hands, time out, time passes slowly, time stands still, time stood still, time to kill, time to party, time travel, time will tell, time wounds all heels, troubled times, try it one more time, trying times, turn back time, two-time someone, until the end of time, wasting time, when the time is right, where does the time go, while away the time, with time to spare, wouldn't give someone the time of day, (and my favorite) you're a long time dead...

...See? You're simply wrong to sniff, to frown. We can do whatever we want with time. So: we agree that it is possible for Fiacre to SLOW time down to such a degree, that the blink of an eye becomes a drive across Kansas (see the corn see the corn see the corn see the corn see the corn see...), the passing of your rich spinster aunt, a dentist drilling, any page written by Ayn Rand. *Etcetera.*

Fiacre puts his hands on his hips and surveys the muddle and jumble around him. He walks over to Clara Jane and gently dislodges the nun chuck from her small hand and carries it to a conveniently located trash can.

"We can't have John *non compost demented*," he says to himself, and drops the weapon into the bin. As he walks back toward Clara Jane he perceives the most basic and primitive commencement of a scowl forming on her plain but otherwise pleasant and frozen in time features. He leans into her shoulder and whispers in her ear.

"My dear," he says. "I am sorry to tell you that you are the victim of a rather comic and ordinary hoax perpetrated by that remorselessly silly ecclesiastical fraud, Pastor Sincerely Dwayne Wayne Darby. He, like the apostate Cudrup, now prone and dying on the stage up there"—Fiacre points—"is a counterfeit hell robber and has no authority to speak for the Boss."*

"Let me be clear, dear," he continues. "End times is real, certainly, but it is not a single event. It happens every day, every minute. You, above all people, should know that.

"When you ran Chuckles Lachine through a wood chipper near that cabin outside Traverse City, Michigan, it was end times for sure, but only for Chuckles. When you garroted Stevie Canada from the backseat of his Lincoln Town Car just after he got behind the wheel—1:06 AM on Tuesday, July 19th, 2005—it was end times. But just for Stevie."

"As you are well aware, I am able to provide another 32 examples of how you facilitated end times. I am not judging you," Fiacre said. "I am simply providing information about the nature and character of End Times as a category of fraud. Yes, end times is real. It happens one soul at a time. If anyone tells you differently, especially Pastor Sincerely Wayne Darby, they are either lying, or so grossly ignorant as to be

---

*Fiacre is, in this case, referencing God and not Mrs. Heartbreak. Just so you know.

guilty of clerical malpractice. Thus, I command you, by the power invested in me by the One True and Almighty God, and by a Brain with enough commonsense to come out of the rain, to shun, ridicule, and walk away from any and all End Times Provocateurs that you may encounter, now and in the future."

Fiacre looked up at the studio lights and laughed. "God," he said. "That felt good." Then he turned back to Clara Jane. "Now listen up."

"John Heartbreak is not a fraud, and while silly, is not remorseless. He has great affection for you, and he and the Warrior Queen Sloan"—he pointed at the glowering figure standing over Billy Cudrup's body— "are on a Mission from God. You are not to interfere with them.

"Instead, the moment I release time—and you— from its current manifestation, you will turn around, get into your Winnebago, and drive back to Forrest City, Iowa. When you arrive, you will take your husband, Agent Staley, by the hand, lead him to the kitchen table, and haul his ashes from there to Kalamazoo, and back again. Repeat, every hour, on the hour."

Fiacre paused. "I would be more directive," he said, "but the author of this book permits no sex, violence, or strong language. Still, I'm sure you get my drift.

"On Sunday next, you will return to the First Methodist Church in Forest City, and thereafter attend regularly, and with appreciation. I understand that the hymns sung are dreadful, countrified, and a step below tunes sung at the County Fair by barber shop quartets, but you will get over it. There is nothing I can do about the state of your church's theology. It is a product of the Protestant Reformation, otherwise referred to as

Dan Krotz

"Amateur Hour" by Those in The Know, but you will get over that too. Enjoy your Church Family.

"As a final point, I know that Mother Staley gets up your nose. Especially when Agent Staley defers to her, rather than to you, his wife. May I suggest that you and Agent Staley purchase Mom a ticket on the September 7th voyage of the Caribbean Cruise Line, which leaves Miami for St. Thomas at high noon that very day. I understand that the ship will encounter... well, never mind. Just buy Mom a ticket." Fiacre spun Clara Jane around and shoved her—through time—toward the exit.

"Go in peace, Child," he shouts after her. "Enjoy your life! We'll see each other again before you know it!"

252

Chapter 42

As Clara Jane departs Endtimes—think of her slipping along a worm hole through time—Fiacre turns back toward the stage and unhurriedly maneuvers through the crowd of fleeing geezers, now frozen like the concrete deer ornaments and Little Black Sambo jockeys that littered the yards of their manufactured homes. He leans into each one as he passes by, whispering into gnarly ears. "Sit down, Honey bunch. Rest a while, Sugar. You won't want to miss what's next!"

The Endtimes stage is 40 inches higher than the floor. Fiacre has to pull an audience table up next to it, and then a chair next to the table, to facilitate his getting up on the stage. He was even more impressed by Sloan's rather dazzling footwork as he clambered up on to the chair, then the table and finally, with a grunt on to stage. Slightly out of breath, he paused and took in the sights:

Angel was center stage, smiling fixedly through an anti-depressant haze at the departing audience. Cudrup was, of course, flat on his back in mid gasp, like a beached bass; Sloan stood over Cudrup, one foot drawn back to kick him where it might hurt, her fist cocked and aimed to fire.

"This *is* too good to miss," Fiacre said. He stepped over to Sloan and started to search through her pockets until he found her cell phone. He put his cheek next to hers and smiled broadly. "Say cheese, Dr. Sloan," he said, snapping a selfie. He laughed and put the phone back into her pocket. "What do you want to bet that that one won't make it onto Facebook?

"Okee doakee. Time to get down to business."

253

Fiacre bent over and grabbed Billy by the collar. He dragged him out from under Sloan's cocked foot and fist, and propped him up into a sitting position against a chair, as a prelude to hoisting him up into the chair. Once he got Billy settled, he reached into his back pocket and pulled out a pint of wine, took a drink, and then put the bottle into Billy's hand. "There!" he exclaimed. "Don't you look disgusting! You drunken degenerate!"

He sat down next to Billy. Now what, he thought?

Dorothy Day's instructions had been clear. He was to give her note to John and the Warrior Queen. They were to give it to Cudrup. Cudrup would read it, see the error of his ways, repent, and make the End Times boo-boo go away.

But Billy was unavailable. Yes, he was alive, but how alive? Was he the victim of a stroke? Heart attack? Massive indigestion? Was he now brain dead—how could one tell really? Given the colossal, the monumental scope of his fabrications and mendacity, the utter and unqualified moral slobber of what popped out of his brain as it operated *a priori*—how was it possible to know if such a brain worked, or didn't work?

It was possible for Fiacre to back time up a bit, back to the hour before Pastor Cudrup keeled over, and to arrange for Sloan and Heartbreak to intervene then. But that would cause them all to run up against the Grandfather Principle, and all the moral resistances and riddles that such an error imposed.

Perhaps, Fiacre thought, he could get away with backing things up just a smidge, to the moment that Cudrup had keeled. This would allow, perhaps assure— if it involved a time traveler's nudge—that an ambulance was called in time to get Cudrup medical attention. Then, the Warrior Queen and Heartbreak could visit an introspective and penitent Cudrup in the hospital, softened up, so to speak, and present Dorothy's demands bedside.

But Fiacre knew that would require at least one extra chapter to this book, and disrupt what is an admittedly wretched, but obviously available if not obviously literary climax. Fiacre, for all his faults, knew he shouldn't do that to the poor chump writing this, or to you, the reader who has, against all odds, managed to hang on so long.

Well beyond the complex storytelling predicaments facing us, is the obvious dilemma of Dr. Sloan. "What can I do," pondered Fiacre, "to get the Warrior Queen off the IRS agenda, and on to the task of Saving Normal Christianity?" In his centuries of experience dealing with God's children, Fiacre had found men to be relatively easy to deal with. But women?

From birth to age 15, almost anything could be resolved for the male animal with the offer of a cheeseburger. From 15, on to about age 50, one had to alternate the offers of cheeseburgers with sex; it was merely a matter of timing. After 50, when men finally entered adulthood, things became more complicated, but were still and usually resolvable.

Women and girls were another matter. They were kinder, smarter, far more generous, and with far greater abilities to see and access the spiritual dimensions of a thing. Suppose, if you will, a woman reads a poem. A line from the poem is *"My kite is blue, my kite is red, my kite is pomegranate! My kite cuts wind!"*

"Yes, a woman will cry out! Yes, what a lovely poem! How deeply it resonates with my inner child! Yes!"

A man will laugh his ass off. "Cuts wind! Get it!"

Fiacre understands how patently sexist, offensive really, the preceding five paragraphs are. Worse, it is extraneous from what is fundamentally required now, which is to move the plot along and solve real problems, as opposed to wasting time (time!) and space (space!) by representing Fiacre as the usual sitcom male who, also fundamentally, is unable to comprehend the innate seriousness of human beings of both genders. Time considered (wasting away!), let us clarify that Fiacre is fully evolved. Though a 7th century male, he has only once left a toilet seat up since its invention, he has fully participated in decisions centered on the purchase of linens, and he accepts the mindboggling reality that there are gay Australians. Hear it now: Fiacre is up to the task at hand.

So, what to do about Sloan? And by extension, Dorothy Day? Here are two women, one who presents a task (a problem to solve), another who seeks justice … and $6,000,000 … (on behalf of "the people," of course). Fiacre scratches his head. This helps very little. He leans over and scratches Billy's head. He knows this won't help either, but it was fun to do. He ponders, he thinks, considers, supposes, imagines, contemplates, deliberates, reasons, and concludes that time waits for no man. He leaps to his feet and hops over to Angel. He leads her to the program host's chair, the one where Billy usually sat.

Sloan is a more problematic move. She is eighteen inches taller than Fiacre and is standing on one leg; Fiacre is not sure how to move her without them both tumbling over. Her hands are also clenched into fists, and she is poised to kick Billy, who is no longer within kicking distance. It is possible that, as he moves her, they will both tumble, and a mighty Warrior Queen fist will smash into his noggin.

After a brief assessment of the geometry of the matter, Fiacre slips in under Sloan's torso and fists and clutches her towards him in a fireman's carry. He stands upright, and then staggers under her weight, to a chair next to Angel's. Fiacre leans sideways and rolls Sloan into the chair. No fists flail. No animals were harmed in the writing of this paragraph. Sloan's eyes bore into Fiacre's.

Although time appears to have stopped, it has, as you know, not stopped. Time always moves, must move and is moving, into the future. But very very slowly. The second hand on the stage clock, to the right where Little Biggs heads off and over to the organ, has ticked off three seconds since Fiacre yelled **STOP!** And…. there! It ticked off a fourth second. Angel's brain, however, is just now receiving the sound of "S" in Fiacre's shout. That's what Dr. Sloan, and Mrs. Heartbreak, and the fleeing audience, are hearing too. That's where their brains are, back at "S".

John did not hear the "S", or much else, because he is deaf. He won't know that Clara Jane tried to murder him with a nun chuck, or that she had even been at Endtimes and was thus the cause and source of Mrs. Heartbreak's presence. John will only know that Mrs. Heartbreak is here, next to him. When normal time resumes—in about six minutes—John will finish the smile he began when everyone else was hearing "S", and tell Mrs. Heartbreak how glad he is to see her.

When John speaks to Mrs. Heartbreak—when normal time resumes—everything that has happened since Fiacre yelled **STOP!** (his conversation with Clara Jane, her exit from Endtimes, his slow and amiable walk through the panicked crowd, his labored appearance on the stage, and his dragging of Billy's body from floor to chair) will flash through their fully

257

operational brains, but so quickly it will make no more impression than the subliminal messages spliced into movies suggesting the purchase of a Coca-Cola.

Fiacre's leap and hop toward Angel will be part of the flash messaging. She will subliminally recall getting stuffed into *The Lord Loves You* television ministry host's chair, the chair where Billy usually sat, and how the diminutive wino-man in the *"Look busy! Jesus is coming!"* T-shirt, had then taken the oddly posed, fiercely scowling woman from her place Stage Left, and plopped her into Angel's usual chair, next to the host's chair where Angel now sat.

Fiacre stepped back from the now seated Sloan and Angel Cudrup and assessed the tableau. He was tempted to arrange Dr. Sloan's face into a smile, but realized, just in time, that Sloan would never forget or forgive, however minimally subliminal the act, his laying of hands on her person. He satisfied himself by turning Angel's head in Dr. Sloan's direction and amping up Angel's smile. He shrugged. It would have to be good enough.

All that remained was the problem of John Heartbreak. (As you may recall, John was identified as Problem Two in Chapter One). Fiacre looked across the *LLY* studio and saw the dawning smile John would fully bestow on Mrs. Heartbreak when normal time resumed. It would be a shame, Fiacre knew, to cheat them out of so loving a moment.

Fiacre made a command decision. Dorothy would have to be satisfied by the delivery of the note, not to Billy Cudrup by John, but by Fiacre himself to Angel Cudrup. He put Dorothy's note into Angel's hand. It would be she who would accept the task of Saving Normal Christianity, or suffer the consequences for refusing. He shouts **"Start!"**

Chapter 43

Angel has loved the *Toccata,* and she has fallen head over heels for Little Biggs. Somehow, Bach has broken through the chemical haze she's lived in since the early days of her marriage to Billy Cudrup, and she believes, rightly, that Little Biggs has been the delivery system. She doesn't know who the woman sitting beside her is, but she isn't worried about it. She feels confident and alive, and has in an oddly roundabout way, simply assumed that she can handle anything, including the sputtering, emblazoned woman sitting in her old 'Look at Billy Adoringly' chair. Angel casts Dr. Sloan a friendly nod, then turns and speaks out loudly to the audience.

"Folks! Folks! Ya'll come on back. What you've been hearing is another way that God speaks to the Anointed! You are Anointed, are you not? Yes! You are Anointed!" Angel steps away from the host's chair and moves to the center of the stage. She claps her hands, and looks at Little Biggs. "Work with me, darlin'," she mouths.

"You are Anointed," she shouts, tapping her foot and nodding her head. Little Biggs picks up on it, tootles a little Blues riff in time to the nods, the taps. The geezers have turned around; they look at her. She beckons with both hands, drawing them to her bosom, smiling a smile as big and sweet as any their old Ma had ever smiled.

"Come back, Sweethearts." She exclaimed. "You are Anointed! Come on back and sit you down! You are Anointed!"

Fiacre stands behind the *LLY's* program director, Larry Laverentz. Fiacre has given Laverentz the heads-up; summarily, that Angel is the new Billy. "Go with it," Fiacre had commanded when he'd set time free.

Laverentz is a grizzled veteran of TV evangelism and knows how and when to go with the moment. Nothing happening on the stage is new to him: he has captured Joel Osteen's sweat and Jimmy Swaggert's tears, and made of them rivers that flooded living rooms across America. Nothing Angel does fazes him; he goes with the flow, intersperses shots of Little Biggs' dancing keyboard with close-ups of Angel's beaming smile, and wide angle views of the geezers coming back, and sinking into the Great Hall's chairs. When she can see that they are all settled, Angel nods to them, and toward Little Biggs.

"Give Little Biggs a hand folks," she says. "He knows how to scare the Devil out of folks, wouldn't you agree!" She begins clapping her hands and, one by one, the audience stands and joins in. Little Biggs bows his head shyly, then takes an awkward bow. He smiles toward Angel and she blows him a kiss. "Later, darlin'," she whispers.

Chapter 44

Laverentz shouts, "Places, everybody!" and begins a five count down. "Five, four, three, two… " and jabs a forefinger at Little Biggs when he says "one!" Little Biggs hammers out a *Beat me Daddy Eight to the Bar* slide across the organ's keyboard instead of the usual *Old Rugged Cross* program entrance. Laverentz shoots Little Biggs a startled look, then shrugs. "What the heck," he thinks. "I've worked with Benny Hinn. I can't be surprised."

If Angel is surprised by Little Biggs' musical choice, she gives no indication of it. She beams a smile across the audience and nods welcome. "I'm so glad you could join me and Jesus today," she says, "along with our special guest…" she casts a bewildered smile in Dr. Sloan's direction … "who needs no introduction! Praise Jesus, and welcome to *The Lord Loves You*, sweetheart!"

Dr. Sloan has been on television before. In her relative youth she had been a member of the Dallas Walking Dead, a televised women's roller derby team. She held the Jammer spot and played under the handle "Zombie Wombat". During the lost years in Germany, she had also been a frequent guest on the weekly talk show, *Die Welt ist zum Kotzen*, a program devoted to explaining why the glass is always half empty. Sloan was particularly appreciated by chronically depressed members of the audience for her empathically stated views that the glass was not just half empty, but empty entirely.

Still, she was unprepared for the moment. The last thing she was conscious of was standing over a choking

Billy Cudrup, eagerly prepared to tell him that his glass was empty. But now, here she sat, across from a woman she confidently adjudged a Bimbo, and one who had called her "sweetheart" no less, in front of a pile of old geezers and God knew how many viewers across the *LLY* television audience. What if her disciples in Dallas saw it? Or, God forbid, her old depressive fan club from *Die Welt ist zum Kotzen*? On the air or no, Sloan was about to pop Angel in the kisser when the subliminal last few minutes scrolled across her eyelids in a cognitive burst: Fiacre stood behind the Program Director, smiled encouragingly, and nodded. He poked his forefingers on either side of his mouth and pushed his lips into a smile.

"Smile, *sweetheart*," he mouthed. Sloan shot Fiacre a furious and bruising glance and shouted, "I WANT MY MONEY! You deadbeats owe me $6,000,000!"

Angel pushed back in her chair, startled and speechless. Little Biggs cued up *In-A-Gadda-Da-Vida*. It wasn't every day he got to play Iron Butterfly. "Okay," the Program Director said quietly. "This is interesting." He turned around and braced Fiacre. "Do you know the broad who wants the money?"

"In a manner of speaking," Fiacre answered. "May I suggest, however, that you call her 'Dr. Sloan' if you happen to meet her. 'Warrior Queen' will also suffice. 'Broad' may rankle a bit. You won't want to do that."

Laverentz nodded. "Got yah. Who are you?"

"I am Fiacre, Saint of the Roman Catholic Church, Patron of Gardeners, Time Traveler, and Emissary of God."

"Uh huh." Laverentz nodded again. He'd directed shows for Creflo Dollar and Apollo Quiboloy. Fiacre didn't have a thing on those boys. "She isn't dangerous, is she?"

"Well, Sloan's an academic," Fiacre answered. "There is no argument too small to wage, no libel too great to hurl, no bridge too far, if it means damaging, depreciating, or destroying a colleague. But in terms of actual blood, or physical harm, probably not."

Little Biggs was winding up *In-A-Gadda-Di-Vida* and looked at Angel for guidance. Should he go on? He was ready to play Limp BizKit's *Counterfeit* if she gave the sign. But Angel shook her head, and pushed her palms down: "Wait," she was saying. Composing herself, she turned back to Sloan.

"Darlin', whatever do you mean?" Angel asked sorrowfully, but calmly. It was possible that Sloan was a developmentally disabled serial killer who had wandered on to the show by accident. Angel needed to keep her wits about her, and her guard up. "What money are you talking about?"

"I am talking about the $6,000,000 your husband, Billy Cudrup and his ex- and now deceased wife Donna Raye Cudrup owe to the taxpayers of the United States of America and, by extension, to me. I am, by the way," Sloan paused dramatically, "Dr. Sharon Sloan, a real doctor, and not some sawbones with a medical degree.

"You do know about the money Billy owes, don't you?" Sloan queried (querulously).

Angel looked up toward the audience. How were the geezers taking it? Fine, from the looks of them; their rheumy eyes were riveted on the stage. Laverentz was nodding his head too, and smiling. He knew that after sex, money was something everyone was interested in. Neither the studio audience, or the couch potato at home, wanted to miss what would happen next. Angel followed Laverentz's lead. She could give folks what they wanted. Her eyes welled up with manufactured tears. She began to weep.

Dan Krotz

"Hey," Sloan said nervously. "Hey. Don't do that." Her vision of Fandango involved turning Billy into a piñata, one that would rain currency down on lucky celebrants. It definitely did not include a TV airhead-cry baby in a size 4 dress. Sloan glanced at the audience. Were they on her side? It was too early to tell, although one old guy (David Chilcote from Mamule, Missouri, whose church home was the First After Everything Else Probability Tabernacle of the Toned and Atoned of Mamule) was shaking his cane at her. "Hey," Sloan said again. She hated feeling so tentative. She was a woman of action, not a sidekick. "Stop crying, okay? Cut it out."

Angel ignored Sloan and looked into the camera for a close-up. Tears rolled down her face; mascara ran like the bulls in Pamplona. "Oh Honey," she said, into the camera. "You don't know the trouble I've seen."

She looked upwards, toward heaven. Laverentz cued the lighting guy to lower the studio lights and spotlight Angel's tear drenched face. "Lord, dearest Lord, come rescue me," Angel moaned. "Oh Lord Jesus, look at that!"

The audience—and camera—followed Angel's outstretched arm and pointing finger to the unconscious Billy, slumping in the chair where Fiacre had dumped him. The wine bottle was still nestled in his hand; his lips burbled around small choking sounds and grunts emanating from behind the wetness off his mouth. Sloan's head swiveled back and forth, from Billy's to Angel's face; Laverentz cut rapidly from Angel to Billy to Sloan, and back again. Little Biggs dug into Nox Arcana's *Melancholia*. Angel's weeping turned to wailing. "What a pro!" thought Laverentz.

"The fearful, and unbelieving, and the abominable," Angel shouted, *"and murderers, and whoremongers,*

and sorcerers, and idolaters, and all liars—and you, Billy!—*shall have their part in the lake which burneth with fire and brimstone! It is the second death."*

"Amen, sister! Amen!" Shouts erupted from the audience. "You tell it! Say it!"

"Crap," Fiacre muttered. Angel was slumming in *Revelations*. He was okay with her throwing Billy in with the usual crowd, but why do it with such a cheap trick? Hadn't Dorothy specifically warned against it?

Angel whirled past Sloan over to Billy and jammed a finger under his nose. *"And the great dragon was cast out,"* she shouted into his face. *"And that old serpent, called the Devil, and Satan, which deceiveth the whole world, he was cast out into the earth, and his angels were cast out with him!*

"And you, Billy, you drunken monster, you who have drugged me and held me captive and *used* me—that's right, sisters!" Angel shouted over her shoulder into the audience—"in unspeakable ways, I cast you out too!

Angel slumped and bowed her head. She turned away from Billy and pointed toward Sloan before facing the audience. "And our poor sister here, Dr...Dr Sloan, is it? And here is our poor sister, Dr. Sloan, who was also deceived by Billy, who has been left impoverished and filled with pain, and is now homeless and bankrupt and hungry, all because of Billy. For all we know, *Billy may have used her too!"*

Angel turned to face Sloan. "Did Billy *use you too, Honey?"* she whinnied. "Did he *lay his hands on you*?"

Sloan stood up and smiled. She punched Angel in the nose, and knocked her flat on her back. Then she walked to center stage.

"Welcome to *Dr. Sharon Sloan's Saving Normal Christianity Hour*" she said.

"We'll be back right after these messages from our sponsors.

Chapter 45

During the commercial break Little Biggs cued up Rob Zombie's *Return of the Phantom Stranger*. He was starting to enjoy himself. Not so the audience. They had been freaked out, been drawn back in, and were now freaked out again. They had been won over by Angel and had bit hook, link, and sinker ... (Go ahead, sniff at "hook, line, and sinker." Make up a less hackneyed phrase. Note, however, that such literary elitism can only delay our discovery of how Sloan intends to save normal Christianity. Will she, like Nee, profess to be led by inner leadings? Will she justify this subjective means of revelation by saying that the ways of God are not known by external means, but by "internal registrations?" Will she, also like Nee, subscribe to a type of Pentecostal theology and speaking in tongues? Nee himself, mind you, did not regard tongues as unbiblical, but he never spoke in tongues himself. Friends of Sloan, on the other hand (again, another hackneyed phrase), are often convinced that she is speaking in tongues; God only knew what might fly out of her mouth.) ... into her sad summary of sadistic Satanic Billy, and how he had *used her*, if you know what I mean, (and you do) for his own selfish satisfaction.

Not only had the studio audience succumbed to Angel's lamentations, but viewers from all across America had been phoning in, texting in, and more to the point, *pledging* in from the moment Angel tucked her finger under Billy's comatose chin and begun wailing. Larry Laverentz, the Program Director, was finally flummoxed: he had seen it all, yet knew that he was seeing it all again, and in spades. "Huzzah," he said quietly, but loud enough for Fiacre to hear him.

"Huzzah, indeed," Fiacre said in answer. "I believe the Warrior Queen has begun Fandango."

"Fandango? Is that what's she doing?"

"Yeah. She's on a mission from God." Fiacre cocked his head to the back of the studio. "See the fat guy standing next to the dishy redhead? That's John Heartbreak. He's with Sloan."

"Is he gonna get up on stage?" Laverentz asked.

Fiacre laughed. "Good heavens no. He's the dullest man in Arkansas. You wouldn't want him anywhere near a camera."

Laverentz made a wry face. "Well, he'd fit in. I mean, look at these people."

Fiacre turned around and gazed at the audience. They were either sitting in stunned silence, or whispering back and forth across their tables. Most of the faces were drawn in fear, but also in anticipation. They had been eyewitnesses to a tolerable accident and couldn't, wouldn't leave, until they had a body count.

"By the way," Fiacre said to Laverentz, "You're doing a commendable job, if you don't mind my saying so. For a bald fat man you don't sweat much, and you're certainly keeping up with what appears to be substantial proof for Chaos Theory."

"I get by. Although I'm not sure what's going to happen next." Laverentz laughed. "I suppose I'll be out of a job after today. I may have to go to work for Pete and Lizzie Popoff. I won't like that much."

"Oh no, no," Fiacre protested. "You're needed here. Sloan needs you. And together, you'll have a grand success."

"Success? How do you know that? More Chaos Theory?"

"I visited you next month," Fiacre said. "You're all doing fine. Dr. Sloan is an unlikely but rather effective

Television Evangelist, and Heartbreak and you are an effective team."

"Ah, I'd forgotten," Laverentz said. "You're a time traveler. Glad to hear that all will be well. But you haven't actually endorsed old Heartbreak up to now. Frankly," he said, pointing at John, who was smiling vacantly across the room, "he looks a bit dim."

Fiacre laughed. "No, not that Heartbreak. The other Heartbreak. The Fabulous Mrs. Heartbreak. She's the dishy redhead next to him." He paused, then said, "You've caught a bit of a break there, if you don't mind my saying so."

"She's certainly a step up. And anyway, I don't care who I work for as long as they pay me. 'Paris is worth a mass', so to speak."

Fiacre nodded. "Good," he said. "Now, I suppose you'll want to get on with the show? What do you propose happens next?"

Laverentz raised an eyebrow and spoke. "We should call 911 and get Billy hauled away, on camera. Lights, action, the whole bit. As they load him on the stretcher, Sloan will pray over him ..."

Fiacre broke out in laughter. "Riiiight," he said. "Sloan praying. Let me alert CNN."

"... and we'll get an ice pack for Angel. Maybe Organ Boy can play a little exit hymn as she's led off the stage."

"Sounds like a plan," Fiacre agreed. Then he frowned, remembering, and put a hand on Laverentz's shoulder. "I'm going to need a second," he said.

Laverentz watched Fiacre move hurriedly toward the stage and then, laboriously, clamber onto the stage. Fiacre bent over Angel's cold cocked frame and pulled what looked like a sheet of folded paper from her twitching hand. Laverentz could hear Angel groaning, and the buzz of chatter between Fiacre and Sloan as he handed her the paper. Laverentz turned an overhead mic on so he could overhear them.

"Not on your life, Wine Boy," Sloan snarled. "I'm going to save Normal Christianity by making it pay. I don't need a list of rules!"

"You certainly have a choice, Dr. Sloan," Fiacre said pleasantly. "May I suggest, however, that the choice you're making is a rather bad one and will ultimately involve locusts, boils, the wrath of, and etc."

She snorted. "You know that's BS. If it was remotely true, Donald Trump would be covered with warts. He wouldn't be able to get a date with himself."

"There is that," Fiacre admitted. "Consider then, the consequences, metaphorically. Do the right thing, dear. You really don't want to be another Billy Cudrup, do you?"

Sloan glanced down at Dorothy's list, wagged her head to and fro, considering, weighing. "Can I edit this? I've got several ideas. Actually, I wouldn't mind running the Universe for a while. As a matter of fact …"

"… I'm sure you do, Dr. Sloan," Fiacre interrupted. "And I have no doubt you'd make a cracker jack despot. But the list was composed by God, and handed down to an estimable woman who knocks on the door of canonization. Perhaps we ought not …"

Sloan wants to argue, but she and Fiacre hear Laverentz shout, "Places, everybody!" and begin a five count down again. "Five, four, three, two …" and jabs a forefinger at Little Biggs when he says "one!" Little Biggs tootles a little *Master the Tempest is Raging*. Fiacre ceases arguing with Sloan, but wags his finger at her. "Do the right thing," he whispers. She huffs, and turns to the camera.

"Welcome back to *Dr. Sharon Sloan's Saving Normal Christianity Hour*," Sloan says gruffly, frowning. Fiacre, crouched near the edge of the stage mimes a smile. Sloan complies half-heartedly. The result is a bit ghastly, but Rome, as Fiacre well knew, had not been built in a day. Mrs. Heartbreak, and the reliable, unflappable Laverentz would help, he was confident, with the on-going construction of Sloan's television persona.

Sloan looks directly into the camera, and then glances at a nearby monitor. She frowns again, then stops herself mid avalanche, and smiles brightly (well, brighter).

"As soon as we get Tammy Wynette here off the stage," she says to the geezers, "and while the Medics haul Billy away, I'm going to pass along a message to you that I am told, on good authority, comes from 'You Know Who.'

"This is the Straight Dope, people! Listen up! I've got a little list…"

Chapter 46

John Heartbreak stooped to pick up the skeletal remains of a human hand. He has been digging potatoes in the church garden when, along with a few spuds, the hand appears. It was entirely intact, each of the four fingers and the thumb present and accounted for, and connected to eight little bones that made up the palm of the hand. These eight bones are also attached to each other, and then to a radius and to an ulna that shot up about four inches, until truncating at a couple of deep chop marks. John gives the hand a little shake. It made a pleasing flamingo-castanet like sound.

John is naturally curious about how the hand has gotten into a hill of potatoes in his church's garden. His immediate assumption is that Dr. Sharon Sloan has dispatched Billy Cudrup—who has been missing for some time—and has buried the old cheat among John's spuds.

Despite Sloan's rather unexpected success as a Televangelist, due undoubtedly to Mrs. Heartbreak's wholly expected managerial competence as Executive Producer of the *Dr. Sharon Sloan's Saving Normal Christianity Hour*, Sloan had been acting peculiarly of late, and had in fact been exhibiting some violent ideation specific toward Billy who still owed the IRS, and by extension, Sloan, $6,000,000. It was possible that she had done it, mathematically speaking, probability-wise.

'Naturally curious' might strike you as an understatement for what you'd feel if you had discovered human remains in your garden. But John Heartbreak thought about things differently than most people do. There was nothing he could do about the dead hand, or with it, for that matter, since he was not musically inclined, and there was no opportunity, anyway, for flamingo dancing in Berryville, Arkansas. Consequently, John's thoughts shifted almost immediately to the condition of the soul of the dearly (perhaps) departed, and the condition of the soul of the one who had departed him.

If Sloan was ruled out, then Pastor Hopwood English was a possible candidate. Not as the owner of the hand because John had seen him just this past Sunday when Hopwood preached in the church adjacent to the garden, but as the perpetrator of the chop and drop. This wasn't as grand a stretch as it might seem.

Prior to entering the ministry, Hopwood was an up and coming Las Vegas magician, slated by all accounts, for the big time—maybe even the 10 O'clock show at Caesar's—when a trick involving sawing a volunteer in half went tragically wrong. It hadn't helped that the volunteer was a county commissioner. Hopwood was promptly arrested for manslaughter and, only after excruciating legal expense and a career ending trial, was he able to get on with his life.

"Getting on" entailed ordination, turning his back on the material world, assumption of holy practices, and keeping his nose clean. But how clean was his nose? How real was the assumption of these holy practices? Perhaps we can only assume such assumption?

Whatever we assume, we know that Pastor English is the only person in Berryville with both a history of dismemberment, and the skills to do it. Yes, sawing the county commissioner was ruled an accident. But was it? Was it possible that Hopwood English was, by day, a somewhat jovial vicar, but by night a serial killer?

"Hello, Hopwood!" John said to himself. He gives the wrist a little shake. It clicks and clacks nicely.

Notwithstanding the distraction of a new found object, John feels a bit of annoyance. He recognizes how equivocal 'a bit of annoyance' is as an expression of being. Why modify a perfectly fine, stand-alone noun, you may ask? Is he annoyed, or not?

Yet, why *should* John, simply to satisfy the preferences of snooty lit-elites, be one thing, or another? No one can force him to be unequivocal. If he wants to waver, then by God, he will waver!

The source of John's annoyance is the Authorial I of the present book. This book, the one in hand. Throughout the course of its writing, John, along with Sloan, Keever, Laverentz, and the Fabulous Mrs. Heartbreak, have requested and demanded editorial conferences, along with weekend retreats at expensive resorts, to argue for and against certain authorial strategies, ploys, and what they perceive to be errors in judgment. They are at it again. And why not?

After all, isn't John as real as memory? You have a memory of Huckleberry Finn, don't you? Of Hedda Gabler? Aren't they real to you? Why shouldn't John have a say-so in the book?

And isn't Sloan real out of the book, as well as in the book? Isn't Mrs. Heartbreak fabulous on the page, as well as off it? Isn't the book itself proof that existence trumped time, and that space itself—on the page, off the page, perhaps on another undiscovered page entirely—was proof of time's malleability?

Eddie Keever is among the most vociferous of critics. "Dude," he exclaimed, "You've left me stranded at End Times with a dead microphone in hand, and no ground breaking story! How about I win a Pulitzer, and become famous as an investigative reporter!"

Angel Cudrup also complains. "You've left me cold cocked, and flat on my back," she whines. "How pathetic!"

"Fiacre's happy," the Authorial I says. "Right?"

"Right as rain," Fiacre says. "I am a barely known medieval saint who pops up once in a blue moon as a concrete lump in suburban gardens. I've loved being in this book! Finally, a bit of vindication!

"And you, Heartbreak," Fiacre says with a jab. "What a putz you are! If it wasn't for the Authorial I, you'd be sitting on your back porch, pissing and moaning about the lack of a lawn care ethic among Southern rednecks. Get over it."

The Authorial I sighs. "Let me apologize, John," I say. "But please look at it from my point of view—all of you—look at it as literature. You, John, you've chosen to be 'a bit annoyed.' My preference is to write more active, less cluttered sentences. I want to write declarative stuff: 'John was enraged.' 'John was despondent'. But I can't. And it's your fault.

"The fact is, John, that you *are* equivocal. Say you've just won the lottery, and someone asks how you feel? What does John say in real life? He says, 'Not too bad." Say that your mother has died, and your dog's been hit by a car. Someone asks, 'how do you feel?' What does John say? He says, "Not too good.

"I'm sorry, Heartbreak," I continue, "But you haven't given me a lot to work with. I know that you are a faithful man, on every level. But if I left you to your own resources, and gave you the editorial control you ask for, you would say, 'Well. I guess I'm faithful. Maybe. Well, I'm semi-faithful, at least.'"

John is *quite* annoyed. "Well," he exclaims. "Semi-Faithful? Well! Well. Maybe. Maybe not … God, you're a know it all."

"Let me make it up to you all," I say. "Eddie, I have indeed left you in the lurch. How about this:

"You leave End Times with John Heartbreak. Not only do you miss what could have been a career making story, but you have to give the dullest man in Arkansas a ride back to Berryville because his wife needs the van. She will drive Dr. Sloan home after the show. For some reason—perhaps she was called by God—Mrs. Heartbreak has forced herself onto the stage and taken charge. You know what she's like, right? I mean, you've seen her in action.

"Filled with depression, you go to the Rowdy Beaver in Eureka Springs, after dropping John off. It is Karaoke Night, and you sing an Elvis Presley medley that includes *Can't Help Falling in Love.* Julie, the waitress, hears you, and falls deeply in love. You do too! You run away together to Western Nebraska, and hire on with Clear Channel Radio. You become King of the High Plains Air Waves, and live happily ever after. Is this good?"

Eddie agrees.

"I'm glad," I tell him. "Because it is what *is*, in the book, and out of the book. The happy part is not yet written. But it can be.

"Angel," I continue, "I know that I left you in an embarrassing predicament. Let me make it all better.

Little Biggs leads you off the stage, and ministers to you. He mends the cruel wound that Dr. Sloan ..."

"Hey!" Sloan protests.

"... that Dr. Sloan was responsible for. But you recover.

"And there is more good news. Little Biggs has fallen for you, a 'woman of a certain age.' Fallen hard. And you, as we know, have fallen for him—with a little help from Bach. He leads you away from End Times, and the two of you form an '80s glam band that becomes a hit in Branson. You, Angel, lip sync Peter Frampton tunes, and Little Biggs plays Led Zeppelin songs. Each night, you haul one another's ashes in a manner not unlike the hauling of ashes that Clara Jane and Agent Staley haul back in Forrest City, Iowa, yet hauled in your own unique and special ways. What do you say?" I ask "Are you good with that?"

Angel smiles. Nods. I smile and nod back. She looks great in her Frampton wig. Way better than Frampton does, actually.

"As for you, John," I say, *"I have been faithful to thee, Heartbreak, in my fashion.'* Semi-Faithful, so to speak. Let's call us even, and end the book, shall we?"

John agrees, but he looks at me and shakes the boney hand he's just plucked from the garden. It does indeed make a pleasing, flamingo-castanet like sound.

"How do you explain this?" he says. "And why drag in Pastor Hopwood? What's he doing in the book?"

Never mind. That's for space in another time.

www.ingramcontent.com/pod-product-compliance
Lightning Source LLC
Chambersburg PA
CBHW060546180626
46817CB00002B/747